I0525935

Henry

The Collectors

by

Nathaniel Nielsen Burbury

First Leaf Publishing

Copyright © 2025 by Nathaniel Nielsen Burbury and First Leaf Publishing

All rights reserved.

No part of this book may be reproduced in any form or by any electronic or mechanical means, including information storage and retrieval systems, without written permission from the author, except for the use of brief quotations in a book review.

No AI was used in the creation of this book.

ISBN (ebook): 979-8-9932674-0-1

ISBN (paperback): 979-8-9932674-1-8

Foreword

On March 13th, 2017, I sat down in a small pub in Reykjavík, Iceland. It's since been replaced by a new and improved gastropub, but at the time, it was a perfect, dark dive named Koffin Bar. I put on a song called "Broken Bones" by KALEO and began writing what would eventually become the story contained in these pages. I listened to "Broken Bones" on repeat for countless hours while writing and editing to keep myself in the state of mind I was in when I started it. I recommend giving it a listen while you read the first chapter or so.

Chapter One

Henry was alone on a porch, cigarette in hand, coffee beside. It was October first, and as he sat taking in the crisp morning air, he was blissfully unaware that it would be one hell of a month.

A messy job had kept him up late. A barking dog had gotten him up early. Now it was time to get paid.

I hate this part.

He took the last drag of his cigarette and flicked it into the air, then grabbed his Colt .45 off the table, dropped a heavy, silver coin down in its place, and stepped off the porch of the cafe, pushing his black hair straight back on his head as he put on a well-worn cowboy hat. He had just started walking down the path towards the gate when he heard a gasp come from the cafe.

Henry turned to see the young lady who had served him looking down at the coin he had left on the table.

She looked at him and smiled, her eyes betraying her shock.

Henry smiled good-naturedly and tipped his hat. *That never gets old.*

The sun peeked up from between two monolithic buildings and was warm against his face. Though it was the first of October, summer still hadn't yielded to fall. He rolled up his shirtsleeves, revealing a tattoo on his left forearm—a serpent coiled around the hilt of a dagger, flourished by roses. The Collector's mark.

He walked up to Bentley, a regal stallion, patted his strong brown neck, and scratched at the white star between his eyes. Bentley greeted him with a snort and a stamp.

"Eh, what's that, old boy? You want to get laid tonight? No? Oh, don't be coy, you dirty dog. First, we need to get our money." Henry swung himself into the saddle and began down the street.

The city had always made him uneasy. He rode through the shadow of the remains of a massive black tower. Vines crept along the sides of it, and small trees grew off some of the dilapidated balconies. He wondered how tall the tower had been before the Crash and wondered if today would be the day it fell entirely. It made Henry uncomfortable, almost claustrophobic. He preferred small towns and large forests, but there was more work for a Collector in the cities.

Henry and Bentley made their way to the house of their most recent Asker. The Asker's name was Blake. "Just Blake," the man had insisted when asked about his last name. *Obviously, his first time Asking.*

Henry patted Bentley's neck as he spoke. "This should be a pretty good haul today, old boy."

Bentley snorted.

"Well, what do you mean, 'what if he doesn't pay?' He'll pay! Askers always pay. One way or another."

Bentley jerked his head.

"I know, old boy, I know. I'm sure it won't come to that."

Bentley didn't respond.

"You know the game, as ugly as it is. Effective, not fair. 'Ours not to reason why.'" He rubbed his left forearm. "I am but the sea that catches those who fly too close to the sun…I am nothing but a consequence."

Bentley maintained his silence at Henry's pragmatic observation.

"Oh, don't be like that, old boy. I'll pay the priest a visit if it makes you feel better." They walked on for a few blocks. "You're too soft for this line of work, old boy. Too soft."

Henry hummed softly to himself, some half-forgotten, lilting tune from his childhood in Ireland. It made him feel vaguely sad, but it soothed Bentley, so it was worth it.

After thirty more minutes of riding, they approached Just Blake's house on Braxton Street. It was a nice part of town, quiet and calm. Henry stopped in front of the house, appraising the green lawn and aging fence. It was in a long row of post-Crash-built homes. Each was fairly well taken care of and served as housing to people who were well off, yet not so well off enough as to buy land and become barons.

"I'll only be a quick thirty, old boy," he said, looping Bentley's reins through a ring on the fence. He pushed, and the steel gate swung open, the rust on the hinges screaming in momentary protest. All was quiet as he approached the door. He glanced back over his shoulder at the perfectly groomed lawn. If only he had time to take his boots off and stand on the soft, trimmed grass.

He knocked twice and waited. After a moment, he heard some movement, then the door opened. Not slowly as most doors in the city did; it swung right open to reveal a little girl, maybe nine years of age. She wore a light blue dress with red flowers and had brown hair pulled back into a neat ponytail. Henry loosened his grip on the razor in his jacket pocket.

"Hi," said the girl. "My name's Iris."

Henry removed his hat. "Well, good morning, madam. Is your husband home?"

"I don't have a husband!" giggled Iris. "I'm only six and a half."

"Really?" Henry played along. "Well, is this not your house then?"

"It's my papa's house," she said, stretching her arms wide to gesture all around her, not hesitant in the slightest to be speaking to a stranger.

"Is your papa home?"

"Iris!" A voice burst out before Iris could answer.

Henry raised his eyes to see Just Blake standing at the top of the staircase, his face taut with a smile that was anything but friendly. He took a sharp breath through his nose and managed to unclench his hands. "Iris dear, why don't you run along to your room? Your new friend and I have some business to discuss."

Iris, seeming not to notice the tightness in her father's voice, gave Henry a curtsy.

Henry gave a short bow. "M'lady."

Iris scurried off down a corridor, taking all the joy in the room with her.

Just Blake gave Henry a dark look before jerking his head slightly. "Come on then." He turned and entered a door at the top of the staircase.

Henry walked slowly up the stairs, taking in all the woodwork and cleanliness of the place. He stepped into the room Just Blake had entered and sat in the leather wingback opposite the man's desk.

"Ten grand." Just Blake nodded solemnly and opened one of his desk drawers. "I have it right here for you." He placed one hundred gold coins on the desk in four neat stacks. "Please take it and leave."

Henry made no move to reach for the coins. Instead, he stood and walked over to the bookshelves that lined the walls of the study and began examining the titles absently. "There were eleven men."

"I beg your pardon?" snapped Just Blake, his eyes narrowing.

"There were eleven men," Henry said, staring cold at Just Blake for just a moment before returning his eyes to the books. "The Asked had ten bodyguards, and they had souls too. Souls all cost the same. Especially when they've got guns in their hands."

Just Blake squirmed in his seat.

"You don't seem surprised," said Henry, allowing a measured tinge of irritation to seep into his voice.

Just Blake kept his eyes down, fixed on the open drawer full of money. "The best I can do is seventy."

"Seventy," said Henry, taking a pause for drama. "Seventy could work. I usually value an Asker's fingers at ten thousand a pop. Would you prefer I take them all from the same hand, or should I spread out the damage a bit?"

Just Blake looked up abruptly. "You wouldn't."

Henry raised an eyebrow. "I just killed eight men with my shaving razor."

Just Blake flushed white. "Have you no soul?"

"I know a priest."

Just Blake rubbed his face hard with both hands. "One hundred and ten grand," he muttered.

Henry watched him peripherally as he pretended to examine a title on the shelf in front of him.

Just Blake's shoulders slumped, and he pulled a key from his desk drawer.

Henry allowed himself a smile as he saw the fight go out of Just Blake's eyes. Negotiations were typically a smooth and speedy process for Henry, as he was six-foot-five and carried a gun. In his less sober moments, he liked to think it was his charisma that got the job done, but in the cold light of day, he knew better. Other Collectors who were shorter or looked to be slightly built had a harder time of it. But not Henry. Not that it mattered in the end. All Collectors either got what they asked for or took it off the corpse of whoever refused them.

Just Blake looked at him and sighed. "Wait here."

There was something in his tone that made Henry's hands go cold.

The man stood and quickly left, giving Henry a moment to take in the room. It was beautiful. The bookshelves occupied three of the walls from floor to ceiling, and the fourth was mostly a large window with a cushioned bench seat. The floor was dark hardwood, the furniture all either leather or green velvet, and the ceiling was shiny, pressed tin. His palm drifted down to the handle of his revolver, polished to a sheen from years of constant use.

Henry noticed a book on the shelf, its foiled gold title emblazoned on the spine. It was at the end of a row, held in place by a marble bookend in the shape of a fish. The book was one he had heard of but never had the privilege of reading: *The Odyssey* by Homer. The sight of it evoked something forgotten in Henry. It made him feel off balance. He wanted to steal it off the shelf, but he had nothing to hide it in, so he forced his eyes away from it.

Just Blake re-entered the room, closing the door behind him. He carried a small, black leather bag and returned to the desk. He produced a heavy gold bar from the bag and placed it on the table next to the stack of coins for Henry to examine.

"There's no lead in the center of that bar, I give you my word. Not that it means a lot to a man like you."

"Says the Asker," retorted Henry.

Just Blake flinched at the comment but remained quiet. Funny how these men always thought they were morally superior to those they paid to do their dirty work.

"There's one more thing," said Henry, breaking an awkward silence. "That book on the shelf by Homer. How much for it?"

"I inherited it," said Just Blake matter-of-factly.

"No, how much to buy it?" pressed Henry, an almost desperate tone infecting his voice.

Just Blake looked up from the bag on his desk. "Consider it part of the deal, friend."

Henry looked down. For some reason, he didn't feel like looking at Blake right then. "Thank you." He turned to take the book off the shelf when he heard a sound. The floor creaked as Just Blake shifted his weight. Henry kept his cool. He slowly reached for the book, but at the last moment, his hand drifted to the marble bookend.

In a fluid motion, he snatched it from the shelf and leaped to one side as he spun, bookend in hand, and threw it as hard as he could at Just Blake, who had a small pistol raised.

A shot broke just before the bookend thumped hard into Just Blake's gut, doubling him over. The bullet missed Henry and tore into the bookshelf.

Henry took one bounding step and vaulted over the desk, crashing knee first into Just Blake, sprawling him on the floor. With his left hand, Henry smashed Just Blake's gun hand against the floor, pinning it there, and with his right, he drew his revolver. Just Blake tried to struggle but Henry hit him hard on the nose, bouncing his head off the floor, then he shoved the barrel of his .45 into Just Blake's open mouth, chipping more than one tooth as he did. Just Blake froze at the taste of cold steel.

Henry's thumb cocked the hammer into place, and he

took a breath to steel himself when he heard the door open and glanced over.

Iris stood there, eyes wide, clutching a toy bunny.

He looked down at Just Blake's pleading eyes and then back at the man's terrified daughter.

"Release the gun," Henry said.

Just Blake's hand went limp, letting the pistol rest on the floor. Henry snatched it up as he stood and backed towards the shelf. He slid his own revolver back into its holster but kept Just Blake's gun trained on its owner. He took the Homer book off the shelf and walked back over to the desk, putting it, the gold bar, and the gold coins into the bag.

Just Blake started to get up, but Henry pointed his little pistol at him again. "Stay down," he said just above a whisper.

Just Blake complied.

Henry dumped all the rounds out of Just Blake's pistol, letting them clatter to the floor, then he tossed the empty gun onto a small couch. He tipped his hat to Iris as he left the room and made his way down the stairs to the front door.

"Mr. Henry?" said a soft, familiar voice as he stepped out of the door.

"Yes?" said Henry, turning to face a scared Iris.

"Is my papa...a bad man?"

Henry knelt to face her. "Is he bad to you?"

"No! He's so nice to me. He always reads to me at night, and he always takes me to the country to see my grandma."

"If he's a good papa, then he's a good man, m'lady. We just had a misunderstanding."

Iris considered this for a moment. "Are you a bad man?"

Henry's breath rattled as he inhaled. "Yes."

Iris looked down, sad and confused. "You were good to me," she offered but did not smile as she waved goodbye and closed the door.

Henry crossed the beautiful lawn, mounted Bentley, and gently placed the book and package of money into a saddle bag.

Bentley snorted.

"I'd rather not talk about it, old boy." They started down the street. "What do you say? Up for another job again so soon? No? Well, I can't say I'm surprised. If it was up to you, we'd be retired by now. You really need to improve your work ethic, old boy. But I guess we can take an afternoon off."

Chapter Two

They rode on in silence for much of the day with no particular destination, past many taverns and inns and rows of relatively well-kept houses. A bookstore caught Henry's eye, but he only slowed for a moment to glimpse the titles they had in the display window. There were a few pre-Crash classics, a smattering of titles on cooking and gardening, an almanac, and one entitled *Method of Memories: How Priests Saved Literature*. Henry chuckled; he had no great love for priests of any flavor. *But credit where credit is due, I suppose.*

It was a rather nice day for riding. The leaves were turning, and Henry knew that in a few short months, everything would be cold and frozen, and riding would no longer be a pleasure. He and Bentley stopped for food at a little hotel and later found a bank where Henry exchanged the bulk of his gold for diamonds. They took up less space in his saddlebags, lightened Bentley's load, and could always be exchanged back to gold in any decent-sized town or village.

For the most part, Henry enjoyed being alone with his thoughts. Sometimes, they caught a snag on an unexpected

memory and spiraled wildly. But in general, he could maintain the helm of his imagination. He let his mind wander and
wonder about the city as it used to be, or may have been, and
he mused about what it may one day become again, but both
were so far ahead or behind, and he was in the present, the
dusty, dangerous present. But dust never bothered him, and
he was dangerous, too.

Eventually, they came across a tavern. After a day of
aimless meandering, Henry began to feel the old restlessness
rising in him. He hitched Bentley by the road and patted his
shoulder. It was a dark but clean establishment. The record
player spun softly in the corner, the needle clicking across the
surface of the coil, a magic Henry never could truly wrap his
mind around. The barman stood polishing glasses diligently.
He was a stout man, balding with a mustache, goatee, and
strong hairy arms, and there was only one patron sitting at the
bar with a nearly full pint.

"What can I do for ya, son?" the barman asked gruffly.

"Help me ease the passing of the day," replied Henry,
clicking down a heavy silver coin on the bar top.

The barman picked up a proper pint glass and filled it
with a golden ale. He set it down in front of Henry, along with
an uncorked bottle of whiskey and an empty shot glass.

"More where that came from," said the barman, tapping
the side of his nose.

Henry nodded respectfully and took a sip.

The barman flipped his polishing rag over one shoulder
and leaned against the bar. "Where you from, son?"

"All over, and far from here before that," replied Henry,
pouring himself a whiskey and chasing it with nearly half his
pint. "Bring a second glass if you want," said Henry as he
examined the bottle.

"I mean no offense, but I only drink with friends," said the bartender casually.

"None taken."

"If you're offering..." said the other patron.

At a nod from Henry, the barman set down another glass. Henry filled it and his own and slid the glass to the man sitting a few stools away.

"To life," said the man.

"To life," said Henry, then they drank.

Henry caught the eye of the barman and motioned him over. He rolled up his left sleeve past his elbow, revealing the tattoo on his arm. The barman's demeanor changed. He tensed visibly.

The other patron stood up. "I think it's time I got a move on. Good to see you, Gerald. Thanks for the drink, stranger." He put a coin on the counter and left, trying not to look like he was in a hurry.

"I'm between Asks," said Henry, setting the barman at ease.

The bartender smiled a tense smile and set another shot glass on the counter. "Any Collector is a friend of mine."

Henry filled the glasses and held his up. The barman did the same.

"Henry," said Henry.

"Gerald."

They nodded to each other, clinked the glasses together, tapped them once on the counter, and threw them back. Henry chased it with the rest of his beer, and Gerald fetched him another.

"Are you looking for work?" the bartender said as he set the glass down on the counter.

"Truthfully, I'm looking for some goddamn peace and

quiet, but it's hard to find when all the noise is on the inside. So I guess another job will have to do."

Gerald nodded. "Most of the Collectors I know have the same problem, and the ones that don't are the ones that really scare me."

"The reptiles give the rest of us a bad name," said Henry

"Indeed, indeed," said Gerald. "Well, as it happens, there's plenty of work to be had in the city. There's an old merchant on the corner of Founders and Market Streets that is Asking for the soul of a young man who he swears seduced his even younger wife. That would be an easy one. The Asked is a bright-eyed lad who wouldn't see a bullet coming if it was tossed to him underhand."

"Young love barely seems like a cause for my services," said Henry, taking a sip.

"There's a banker on 9th and Aberly who had most of his finest jewelry snatched from him. Swears it was a chap who works down near the port. He would be a tougher Ask but..." Gerald paused and looked Henry up and down. "I don't think he'd stand much of a chance."

Henry shrugged. "I don't much like bankers. I always have a sneaking suspicion that I'm going after the wrong man whenever I work for one. Any other jobs around?"

"Well..." Gerald started polishing a glass nervously. "There's a baron. He's at Thirteen Wall Street, but I don't know anything about the Asked. The baron himself is a dangerous fellow. Connections out west, land upstate, and one of the finest compounds in the city. It takes more than gold to get what he has."

"A baron. They certainly make for interesting jobs."

"Word of advice? Be cautious of that man. I know he's turned down several other Collectors. I think he might be looking for one of those reptiles we mentioned earlier. You should just go see the banker."

"I'll take that under advisement," said Henry. There was more of an edge in his tone than he had meant to express.

Gerald chuckled nervously as Henry poured out two more shots as a peace offering.

"You have a family, Gerald?"

The barman looked like he was going to say something, but then he stopped; there was a faraway look in his eyes that Henry knew all too well.

"Once," said Gerald. "You?"

"Once," replied Henry.

They picked up their glasses and nodded to each other. The glasses clinked, tapped, and were thrown back.

"Thank you much," said Henry as he stood, finishing his pint in three large swills.

"Let me make some change for you," said Gerald, picking up the heavy silver coin, but Henry waved him off.

"The whiskey was very fine, and I appreciate the information."

"And that's why any Collector is a friend of mine," said Gerald, tapping the side of his nose with a twinkle in his eye.

Henry nodded to the man with an easy smile. Then he rolled down his sleeve, put on his hat, and returned outside to Bentley.

"We've got options, old boy." Henry unlooped the reins from the fence and swung into the saddle. "There's a young man who's guilty of love, a hard thief who's accused of stealing, or some unnamed, unknown, unlucky bastard who pissed off a very powerful man, who I'm sure has plenty of coin he's willing to part with."

They rode to the center of the city and found a large pond surrounded by a thick stand of trees. It was the only part of the city that Henry truly liked. He slipped out of the saddle and unbridled Bentley so that he could drink freely from the water and nibble on the little tufts of grass. Henry sat with his back against a fine tree, looking over the surface of the pond. An occasional fish jumped, and he wished he had a pole about him. He mulled over the three options in his mind for a while. By the time the sun began to set, he had almost convinced himself that he hadn't already made up his mind.

They headed out of the park toward Wall Street. The city seemed more alive now that the sun had gone down. Much of it was abandoned. A few sections, however, were still very much inhabited, and at night, those parts of the city bristled with energy. Brass bands and string bands cranked out music on the sidewalks and in small bars and taverns; it was lively, and the streets were filled with people. Most of them were drunk, and the rest were about to be.

Henry didn't have time to stop, though at the sight of all the ladies, he wanted to.

They rode on. After several blocks, the crowds began to thin out. A few more blocks, and there were only a handful of unsavory-looking characters scattered here and there. A few blocks after that, the streets were empty again, but there were still lights in the windows that Henry passed.

On the ride there, he second-guessed himself a few times, knowing that he could just take the easy Ask. Bentley seemed to think the easy Ask was the better option.

"You may be right, but if I do, I'll just be right back where I am now by this time tomorrow, only with a little more blood on my hands and a little more gold in the saddlebag. Where's your sense of adventure, old boy?"

Thirteen Wall Street was a large, well-built compound. Henry tied Bentley next to the gate, made his way up the side-walk to the door, and knocked.

The door opened, only a little at first, and Henry found a pair of eyes glaring at him above the bolted chain. "State your business."

Henry pulled up his left sleeve and presented the tattoo.

The door closed momentarily as the chain was undone, then slowly opened again. A sturdy man of about thirty-five stepped aside, letting Henry enter.

Henry moved by the man into the house.

"This way," said the man gruffly. He led Henry through a dimly lit entryway, then a rather grand corridor, and then out back to a courtyard, the sight of which took Henry aback.

The courtyard was spectacular. Green grass, thick and lush, was cut short, and four stone paths led from four entrances to a stone circle in the middle of it. Lanterns were lit along the walls, and lights flickered in lampposts that illuminated either side of each path. In the center of the large circle were several semicircular stone benches. A well-dressed man with gray hair and a strong body sat on one of the benches. He looked at Henry with hawkish eyes as he approached.

"And who is our guest, Preston?" the man asked the doorman without taking his eyes off Henry.

"Another Collector, sir," replied Preston in an emotionless tone.

The gray-haired man nodded and stood, extending a hand to Henry. "My name is Charles Bickford Lipton, but my friends just call me Buck."

Henry shook Lipton's hand and gave him a nod. "It's a pleasure to meet you, Lipton. My name's Henry."

Lipton's expression changed upon hearing Henry's name. "Henry, you say. Your reputation precedes you."

"Collectors all have the same reputation," Henry lied.

"Oh, don't be modest. Please sit." Lipton gestured toward one of the benches as he spoke.

They both took a seat, and another servant entered the courtyard from one of the other doors, carrying a tray with two glasses and a bottle. He walked with purpose and set the tray on the bench between them before returning the way he came.

"That will be all," said Lipton, smiling with too many teeth. Preston nodded and took his leave.

Lipton turned back to Henry and picked up the bottle. "Have you ever had Scotch?" asked Lipton as he poured two generous servings.

"I usually just stick to the local stuff," replied Henry, accepting the glass as Lipton handed it to him. He took a sip. As much as he wanted to not be impressed by it, he had never experienced so many subtle flavors in a single drink.

"You like it. Have as much as you want." He slid the bottle towards Henry.

Henry nodded, taking another sip. "Why am I here?"

"Right to business," replied Lipton.

Henry nodded with an easy smile. "Right you are."

Lipton took a deep breath. "Well, Henry, I've got the Ask of a lifetime for you. You'll never have to work again."

Henry puffed out of his nose in what might have been a chuckle. "What if I like working?"

"You don't strike me as that type of Collector. Even so, I never said you wouldn't be able to, but after this job, you might be inclined to take a short retirement." Lipton pecked a taste from his whiskey glass.

Henry savored another sip. "We'll see. What's the job?"

"Have you ever been out west?"

"I spent some time in Seattle when I was young. Almost died coming back over the northern Rockies."

"Well, you'd be traveling in style this time. I've used the Cross several times now. I assume you didn't go by train when you went the first time."

"Horse," said Henry, taking another sip. "What's the job?"

"Well, I won't lie to you. It's a big undertaking. Almost as big as the reward."

Henry said nothing.

"I want you to kill Clarke Fairchild."

A smile loosened Henry's face, and after a moment, he laughed aloud. "If you want, I can storm the pearly gates and kill God and all his angels when I'm done."

Lipton did not laugh.

Henry's smile began to fade. "Forgive me, I believe I must have misheard you. I thought you said Fairchild."

Lipton beamed. "Indeed, I did."

Henry's smile left him, and he began to wonder if he'd prematurely taken this man's sanity for granted. He took a deep breath and asked once more for clarification. "You're asking me to travel across the continent to Collect one of the most powerful people in the Americas?"

"Yes," Lipton nodded, now smiling with not enough teeth. "Their baronage, if you could even call it that, more like an empire, is going through some...restructuring, and I see an opportunity to expand my own. For too long, the West has lived under their mismanagement. It will benefit everyone except Clarke."

"You want me to kill a Fairchild? They're a dynasty. Their generals control more land than most barons do," said Henry in a tone somewhere between disbelief and anger.

"It's true. They have been very powerful for a very long time. But that time is at an end," said Lipton confidently.

"According to you," scoffed Henry. "Their wealth is immeasurable! They have whole armies at their command.

And even if I do kill this Clarke, the rest of them will have me in hand before I could even reach a saddle."

"Yes...well, that won't be an issue, as I want you to Collect all of them."

Henry's stomach tightened into a knot, a sensation he hadn't experienced in quite some time. "All of them?"

"'All' does not necessarily mean 'many.' If there is one rat in a cage, and you drown it, you have effectively drowned all the rats in that cage."

"What happened to all the other rats?"

"And here I thought I was the Asker."

Henry did his best to not bristle at having his question dismissed. "If you're going to take the land by force, why even have me kill the Fairchild?"

It was Lipton's turn to bristle, his cold eyes made a chill run down Henry's spine. He spoke slow and clear. "Who said I was taking it by force?" There was no perceptible hostility in his tone, and his face was in the shape of a smile. *But that look in his eyes.*

"Find another rat killer," said Henry cold and flat.

"But I haven't even told you how you'd be compensated," said Lipton.

"It doesn't matter. You're out of your mind, and there's other work for me on this side of the Rockies." Henry stood and went to drain his glass.

"A million dollars," said Lipton.

The glass stopped halfway to Henry's lips.

"And a patch of land with a nice stream running through it."

For the time it took him to take a sip and lower his glass again, Henry pictured himself sitting by a stream catching trout that he would take back to the cabin and fry up for himself and...

He shook his head. "How many Collectors have already turned you down or died attempting this?"

Lipton chuckled. "No Collectors have attempted to kill Clarke yet."

Henry drained his glass. "Thanks for the Scotch. If you're done, I'll be leaving now."

"There's no need to rush away so soon, Henry," said Lipton, standing up. "Stay for the evening."

"I usually prefer to sleep under the stars," he lied.

"You only say that because you have never slept under my roof," said Lipton with a broad gesture.

Henry again exercised his power of silence.

"If you stay, I will have your clothes washed and mended, your horse groomed."

"He's not my horse."

Lipton gave an amused smile. "Nevertheless, I'll have him groomed and your saddlebags filled, assuming the saddle is yours. I also have a luxurious bath in one of my guest rooms, and my chef is legendary."

Henry was quite hungry.

"Just stay for the night," Lipton continued. "The Cross leaves tomorrow morning at eight on the dot. It'll give you some time to reconsider your decision. And if you don't change your mind, you'll at least get a good meal out of it, along with something to laugh about with your friends." He said the last with that toothy smile that did not quite reach his eyes.

Henry considered this. He knew rich men could never take no for an answer, but he was stubborn too. *A bath does sound nice.* "If you insist," he said at last.

With a gesture from Lipton, Preston strode into the courtyard. "Should I take you to your room, or would you like to fetch anything from your saddlebags?"

"I'd like a moment with Bentley before you stable him."

Preston nodded and led Henry back through the entryway to the front door, opening it for him but not following him outside.

Bentley snorted and stamped indignantly as Henry approached.

"Sorry, old boy. That took longer than expected."

Bentley nuzzled his snout into Henry's sternum as Henry patted his neck and scratched behind his ears.

"I need to talk to you about that meeting, Bentley, and I need your honest opinion. Don't spare my feelings. Tell me what you think."

He proceeded to explain the whole situation to Bentley, who agreed wholeheartedly with Henry's decision to decline, but did also very much like the sound of a nice patch with a stream running through it.

"He's going to give us the royal treatment tonight, old boy. Tomorrow we can get out of the city and start traveling down the coast. I don't want to be here when the snow comes. There's plenty of patches with streams this side of the Rockies."

Bentley wanted to leave immediately, but Henry had already made up his mind. The Scotch was very good, after all.

Chapter Three

An hour later, Henry was submerged in a massive bathtub as his clothes were washed, mended, and pressed by the seemingly invisible army of servants keeping the compound as spotless as it was quiet. Dinner had been marvelous; duck with a rich, red wine sauce, roasted carrots, mashed potatoes, and an assortment of leafy greens. He had declined dessert. Henry could only assume that Bentley was receiving the same lordly treatment that he was, though as nice as the hot water felt, he did wish he could talk to Bentley.

He heard the door open, and he turned to see a young woman enter behind him. She had fair skin and long, reddish-blonde hair that fell voluptuously over her shoulders. Her delicate hands nervously began to work on the front buttons of her dress.

"Excuse me, ma'am."

She stopped and faced him. Her green eyes stared out guardedly. She looked terrified.

"I wish you wouldn't do that. Not just yet, at least."

"What do you want me to do?" she asked, mustering her most sultry voice.

Henry wasn't convinced. "For starters, I'd like you to re-button your dress, love."

"Mister Lipton insisted, sir."

"Allow me." Henry stood, dried himself quickly, and slipped into the linen shirt, boxers, and trousers that had previously been laid out for him. She watched him pensively. He stepped towards her slowly but steadily, and as if he were untangling a wild animal from a net, he buttoned up her dress.

She looked confused.

"Can I pour you a drink?" asked Henry, walking to the liquor cart in the corner of the room.

"I like wine," said the young woman apprehensively.

"But nothing too dry?" inquired Henry with a smile.

She replied with a tentative smile of her own.

He poured two glasses and sat on a small couch, motioning for her to join him. She looked amused and cautiously curious, then sat down beside him but hesitated to take the glass he held out.

"Should I...send for a man?"

Henry chuckled. "That's not my bent."

"Lipton insisted that..."

Henry held up a hand to stop her. "You have my leave to tell your employer anything you like about your visit to me tonight."

Her shoulders relaxed, and she accepted the glass that Henry had handed her.

"Thank you."

"My pleasure."

"I..." she started but trailed off. "No one's ever offered me the wine before."

"You should keep better company."

"I'm not the one who chooses my company."

"All we have are our choices. You shouldn't let those be robbed of you."

She gave him a smile that was almost sympathetic. "Things are rarely so simple."

"Well, as a start, just for tonight, your choices are your own."

"In that case," she pondered for a moment, "in that case, I choose to drink some wine."

"Here's to choices," said Henry.

They clinked glasses and took a sip.

Henry waited for a moment. "The gold chain around your neck," he said softly. "It has two rings on it. One would make you a widow. Two makes you an orphan."

She leaned forward slightly. "I choose not to regale you with the tragic tale of my life." She smiled at him deviously before leaning back and taking another sip. "What about you? Are you an orphan?"

"Once," said Henry. "But that was long ago. Now I'm just a Collector."

"I couldn't help but notice you have a chain of your own. But yours only has one ring."

Henry opened his mouth to speak, but his breath seemed hollow, and no words came. He noticed the slightest tremor in his hand.

"I'm sorry," she said quickly, her hand drifting to his forearm, steadying his tremor. "How about we choose silence for a while?"

He smiled and nodded, then they sat quietly sipping wine. Her hand rested on his arm for a moment to keep the tremor away.

After about half a glass, Henry began to grow quite

sleepy. He vaguely remembered that this was why he rarely drank wine. He found that his eyes began to close on their own accord. She stood, taking his hand and guiding him to his feet. They looked at the bed. It was enormous.

"I'm expected to stay the night," she said.

"Which side do you choose?" asked Henry through a yawn.

"The one farthest from the door."

Henry nodded and crawled between the covers, discarding his clothes except for his boxers. He lay on his side, facing the door and her. She turned off the lamp before undressing down to a silk slip. Even in the dark, he could see her form. She crept into the cold sheets and pressed herself up against his back, sliding one arm under his head and the other around his chest. She was warm, and the comfort of it made him all the sleepier.

"My name's Scarlet, by the way," she whispered, her breath hot against his ear.

"I'm Henry." He began to think about the other Scarlet he had known but banished her from his mind.

She squeezed him a little, and a moment later, he was asleep.

He dreamt that he was alone on a porch, and it was warm, yet the only light was from the stars and the candle inside. He turned to go inside, but the door had no handle, and the windows were locked. He left the porch to pick up a rock from the yard to smash out one of the windows. When he turned back to the house, rock in hand, the house was gone. Then, something hit him from behind, and he lurched up out of bed, panting. Light had filled the room; by the angle of it, he guessed it was about 7:30. He felt the back of his head, but the pain had disappeared with the dream.

Scarlet jolted awake next to him and checked the time.

"Oh no!" she said, then leaped from the bed and grabbed his pants. "I was supposed to wake you. I even meant to give you a little head start!"

"Head start?"

"Please don't hurt me. Lipton said you would probably be angry." She held his pants close to her chest.

Henry wondered if she was even doing it consciously.

"I'm not going to hurt you," Henry said, standing and taking the pants. "Why would I be angry?"

"Your horse." She handed him his shirt.

"He's not my horse," Henry said, doing the buttons.

"Well, whoever's horse it is, he's on the Cross," she said, then all but braced for a blow.

"The Cross?" said Henry in a moment of disbelief.

"Lipton said it was the only way. I'm sorry. I had no involvement in it. They didn't hurt him, he's safe and sound. I—"

"My boots!" commanded Henry, snatching his belt and strapping it on as fast as he could.

She fetched his boots, and he nearly jumped into them. He tied one while she tied the other, and she finished first. She handed him his hat and jacket as he dashed out the door. He ran through the corridors and down the stairs. Out into the street, he ran with a fury. He passed a large clock that read 7:59. He wasn't going to make it.

He turned abruptly down a side street and kept running at a dead sprint for three times longer than he felt he could have. His lungs ached and his chest and legs throbbed, but he reached the little stone overpass just as the first train car passed beneath it. Taking only an instant to catch his breath and pick his car, he climbed over the railing, cursed himself, god, and everything, then jumped.

He landed on the roof of a train car and began to slide, but he found a lucky toehold on a protruding metal bolt and kicked off it as best he could towards the following car. The patio car. He slid off the roof, pushing himself away from it as he fell attempting to clear the gap between the moving cars. He did, but it was at the expense of a vacant table, which crumpled beneath him in splinters.

He stood up, brushed himself off and tipped his hat to an amused steward who held a manifest as he tried to catch his breath.

The steward looked at the manifest, and then up at Henry. "Mr. Henry, I presume? Mr. Lipton gave no last name."

"For the love of God, just call me Henry and take me to the stable car."

"Yes, of course," said the steward. "Lipton mentioned that you would want to check on your horse."

"He's not my horse," said Henry, hands on his knees, pulling in breaths as fast and deep as he could manage without throwing up.

"This way, please."

The steward led Henry through several cars to the back of the train, where he found Bentley tethered, fed, and groomed as well as Henry could have done himself. Bentley rested his forehead on Henry's chest, and Henry hugged his muzzle.

"Lipton mentioned that he left some supplies and a note in the saddlebags," said the steward. "You'll find your cabin in car seven. That's three back from where we are now." Then he nodded and took his leave.

"Goddamn, I thought I lost you, old boy," said Henry, patting Bentley's neck.

Bentley was happy to see him.

Henry checked his saddlebags. In addition to what he had

put in there himself, he found a Bowie knife with a small note attached to it that read:

> You'll need a good blade where you're going —
> Preston

And another note, in a different hand that read:

> One million dollars, Henry, and a 100-acre patch
> with a nice stream running through it. Just think
> about it and enjoy the ride. My contact will meet you
> upon your arrival. — Charles B. Lipton

Henry was so relieved to have made it to Bentley that he barely had room for anger. Barely. He made his way to his cabin. There was a small bed and a comfortable chair. The car before was a bar car, and the car after was the patio car. Once he had settled in, the steward brought him a tray of crackers and an assortment of cheeses, jams, jellies, and smoked meats as well as coffee and a small glass of dark liqueur.

"Lipton insisted that we provide you with the very best experience the Cross has to offer." The steward then bowed and backed away.

Henry had to admit that it was all excellent, and the chair was comfortable, and the hum and rattle of the train was more relaxing when you were on the inside of it than when it was thundering by you on the tracks.

The buildings swept by the window faster and faster as the train slowly gained momentum, racing towards the edge of the city. Then it began to rain. Then the rain began to assault the windows of the train in torrents. Henry found the chaos of the storm comforting. It reminded him of his almost-forgotten homeland, Ireland. He had loved the rain as a boy.

The train moved out of the city, beyond the reach of civilization, but still very much in the middle of the storm.

Chapter Four

They got from New York to Sacramento on the morning of the third day. After a couple days of relaxation and good food at regular intervals, he had made up his mind to at least hear out Lipton's man in Sacramento, if for no other reason than to get a lay of the land before commencing a great wandering for the winter.

The haze was the first thing Henry noticed when he stepped off the train. At first, he thought it was a heavy morning fog, but they were not by water, and the smell of it was oppressive. A stench, somewhere between burnt sugar and raw sewage, carried in a thick, smoky haze that permeated the air and reduced visibility to only a few hundred yards.

It made Henry cough at first and gasp for air, but there was no clean air to be had. The haze could not be escaped. As he moved to the stable car to collect Bentley, his legs felt very heavy, and his head very light. His stomach was turning, caught between the gravity of the two.

All of the other passengers had coaches waiting for them, and within a few minutes, they had been ferried away. The air was cool, yet it seemed sticky with the humid smoke of the haze. Henry could feel it covering his skin and his lungs with its putrid, sickly-sweet stench. They took in their surroundings, waiting for the guide that Lipton had promised.

Across from the train platform, a man's nude body hung by the neck from a post. The dead man had an emblem burned into his chest, a symbol Henry didn't recognize. He didn't have to strain his sight to notice that the next corner up had a hanging body of its own. The next one too. The last flies of the year buzzed around the men's eye sockets. No one walking down the street even seemed to notice them hanging there.

They waited for another forty-five minutes. Passersby began staring at the pair of them, and even with his weapons and array of skills, Henry began to grow unsettled. Not to mention that he felt far from sober. His mind felt like a sludge of raw emotion sloshing about in his half-empty skull. He had a painless headache. Throbbing nothingness spread through his entire body, and he was both sleepy and frantically alert all at once. He tried to set his eyes on the farthest points in the limited visibility of the haze to keep his stomach from turning, but he could only see about three blocks in any direction.

"That seasickness thing. That's all in your head." He vaguely remembered a sailor saying that to him as he puked over the side of a ship as a child.

When was that? Was it even me?

Eventually he felt so claustrophobic and smothered by the air itself that he couldn't bear to sit in it a moment longer.

"I don't know where this guide is, but I need to get out of this smoke," he said to Bentley.

The horse seemed uneasy, but Henry was tired of waiting.

"I guess we better just go on then, old boy."

As they rode down the street, Henry began to grow

increasingly appalled at all the bodies hanging from the posts, and the fact that no one else even seemed to notice them as they moved around caught in the same half-alive intoxication that Henry found himself trapped in.

Most of the buildings were factories for processing poppy and coca. Some of them processed tobacco and cannabis, indicated by rough signs nailed to the crude walls. The rest of the city consisted of slums and housing for factory workers. The streets were filled with the thrumming sound of various man and steam-powered machines from the factories. There was a din of defeated voices ruminating from the sidewalks and old rows that people somehow managed to live in. There was no singing. The smells were acrid, and the sights were worse. Henry did not want to linger in this place.

Bentley convinced Henry that they should buy a map, or else they would inevitably get lost in the hopeless entanglement of roads without ever finding their way out. Henry reluctantly agreed. He'd tried asking a few people where the nearest general store was, but they either ignored him or gave him confused looks before they shuffled away wordlessly. After what seemed an immeasurable period of time, they happened upon a small general store.

"I'll be right back, old boy. Surely this place has a map out of this infernal shit hole."

Bentley was too ill to be optimistic.

He hopped off Bentley's back, his legs turning to rubber as soon as his feet hit the ground. He broke his fall with his hands. It was not pleasant, but it was better than landing on his face. He stood up shakily and pulled the sharp pebbles out of his now bleeding palms. Steadying himself on Bentley, he regained his balance. He hadn't tried walking since exiting the train. The haze was affecting him more than he had realized. The shock of the fall made him feel like crying and killing in a fit of rage, and remorse all at once. He held onto Bentley as his drug-addled mind slowly spun away from him, and then back in a whirling, unstoppable arc. He could barely keep from vomiting.

Once he regained his bearings, he looped Bentley's reins on the ring of the hitching post outside the store and approached the door.

People had noticed his fall, but no one seemed to care. A few stared a little bit longer than the others: a child, a tattered-looking bum, and a tall, dark figure.

Taking off his hat, Henry pushed back his hair, placed it back on his head, and entered the nearly empty store. As he approached the counter, the elderly attendant took no notice of him at all.

"Could you point me in the direction of a map out of the city, sir?"

The old man, with an annoyed look on his face, finally looked up from his book. "Sorry, what?"

Henry repeated his question.

"Why would you need a map out of the city?"

"I need to find my way out of it."

"You and everyone else," said the attendant dismissively before returning to his book.

"I need to get out of here."

"Walk north."

Henry was losing his patience but felt too sick to threaten the attendant.

"Please, man. I've never been to this place. The haze is killing my horse. I just need directions out of the city."

The attendant paused for a moment, then lowered his book...and his voice.

"I'm sorry, stranger. Thorpe and his watchers intentionally make it difficult to get out of the city. They can't have their slaves finding a better life elsewhere. Your only hope is to find a guide. Someone who's made it out before. Those are few and far between. The ones who make it out rarely ever come back."

Henry felt all the hope in his body drain out the soles of his boots.

"Why can't people just pick a direction and walk 'til they're out of the city? Is there a wall around it?"

"The Haze."

"What do you mean?"

"If you think the haze is bad here, in the middle of the city, you should see it in the outer ring. It's so strong that if you try to walk through it, you'll either die or go crazy and then die. Over half the opium that the factories produce is used to make the haze. It's more effective than a wall. You have the original Mr. Thorpe to thank for that."

Henry leaned forward, resting his elbows on the counter, and ran his fingers through his hair. "He sounds like a bastard," he muttered under his breath.

"You mentioned you have a horse?"

"Yeah," sighed Henry.

"Then you might be able to make it through the gauntlet."

Henry lifted his face.

"The gauntlet," said the attendant with the slightest breath of enthusiasm, "is a two-mile stretch leading out of the city. It's the most direct way. It's how all the barons leave once they've off-boarded the Cross. They pile into an airtight coach, then the horses charge at full speed through the gauntlet before it can kill them. But the driver has to recognize you as a baron to gain passage. You can also board with a baron who vouches for you, but you don't look like someone who rubs shoulders with barons or baronesses."

"Not shoulders," replied Henry, recalling a vague

memory of a dark-haired baroness with green eyes. Then the vision turned on him, and he burped.

The attendant gave him a quizzical look but moved on dismissively. "Let me jot down some directions for you, but fair warning—people will kill you and steal your horse to try the gauntlet themselves. It was a smart move to have those men hold it for you while you came in."

"What?"

"The men. The ones who led away your horse."

Henry snapped his head around to look through the plate glass pane in the door.

Bentley was gone.

Time seemed to slow as Henry frantically snatched the single-sheet map from the attendant's hand and sprinted out of the store. His balance was not what it should have been, and he tripped over the threshold and scraped his knee as he stumbled back to his feet.

"Bentley!"

But there was no Bentley.

He ran into the street, hoping that maybe, just maybe, he would glimpse Bentley still being led away.

But there was no Bentley.

He felt like he was going to be sick, and his legs failed him. Dropping to his knees, he leaned forward, his palms on the dusty street. His vision went foggy, and he felt something wet land on the back of his hand.

A tear.

Only she could make him cry, or so he thought. Apparently, her horse could, too.

Chapter Five

Today's the day. At least that's what the letter had said. The Minister had a ball of nervous anticipation in his gut. He muttered a few half-conscious prayers under his breath, then peered through the crystal-clear lenses of his mask at the approaching train.

Within a few minutes of its arrival, all the passengers had been carried away by the air-filtered coaches. All except for one, a tall man with his sleeves pulled down to his wrists. The Minister watched the Collector for a moment. There was something visceral about the man. Something that the Minister could not articulate; something that made his guts churn. Something familiar.

The letter had instructed him to greet the Collector as soon as he arrived, and the Minister was about to go introduce himself, but he heard a ruckus from down the lane to his left in front of one of the factories. For a split second, he almost ignored it but decided to at least see what it was all about. As he walked, he knew he should turn around, the letter had been very specific, but when he saw what was happening, he couldn't bring himself to walk away. *I'll have to catch up with the Collector after.*

There was a perimeter of bystanders around three Watchers attempting to subdue a man probably sixteen years of age. Though he was younger than the Watchers and significantly smaller, it appeared that he knew how to handle himself, or so the Minister gathered by the bloodied condition of one of the Watchers' faces.

By the time the Minister had broken through the crowd of onlookers, two of the Watchers had managed to hold the young man while the third began beating him. At the sight of the Minister, he held his punches.

"What seems to be the issue, Watcher?" asked the Minister coolly.

The Watcher who had been doing the beating turned on the Minister aggressively, but upon seeing his mask and his appearance, he subdued himself slightly. "This whelp was trying to leave his shift early."

"How does that warrant a beating?" asked the Minister taking a casual step forward.

"He belongs to Thorpe," growled the Watcher.

"As far as I know, Thorpe controls all the food and factories in the city, but he has no claim on its inhabitants."

The Watcher laughed. "Sure, that might technically be true of most of these meat machines," he said, sweeping his hands over the crowd, "but this particularly unlucky bastard was sold to us by his father. So, unless you feel like paying us ten thousand dollars, he is going to finish his work."

"I will be paying no such fee, Watcher," the Minister said, "though the boy will be coming with me. I'm sure your employer will understand if he is absent for one afternoon. In fact, I don't see how they would ever find out."

"Fuck off, God boy. Walk away while you still can."

The Minister looked at the boy; dirty, scared, hopeless. *Walk away.* The Minister's shoulders relaxed. "The boy is coming with me," he said in spite of his better judgement.

"You and what army? There are three of us, God boy. Don't suppose you learned to scrap at the parish?"

"Not at the parish," replied the Minister, sliding his hands into his pockets.

"You've got some minerals," snarled the Watcher.

"It would be easier if you stood down and let the boy leave. There would be no harm in it."

"I think not, Minister. I've got a better idea. I break your fucking legs and let you watch as I beat some work ethic into this piece of shit." The Watcher spat out his words as if they were bitter to the taste.

"I cordially invite you to try," said the Minister, widening his stance.

The Watcher drew a billy club from his belt, as did the two others, letting the young man fall limply to the ground. Then they charged the Minister.

Forgive me, Father.

The first Watcher swung downward ferociously. The Minister leaned to the side, avoiding the blow. Spinning, he landed a hard elbow strike to the back of the Watcher's head. The steel reinforcements in his coat ensured the Watcher's unconsciousness. Then he quickly parried left, striking right, then parried right, striking left, leaving the other two Watchers bloodied and unconscious.

The Minister tried to not think about the inevitable consequences of what he had just done. It would take him a while to find the Collector again, but this was more urgent.

He returned both of his brass knuckles to his pockets and walked over to the awestruck young man and helped him up.

"Come with me."

They turned and began walking away. The crowd dispersed, and the Watchers did not stir as the Minister stepped over them.

"What's your name, boy?"

"Todd."

"It's a pleasure to meet you, Todd. Most people just refer to me as the Minister."

"The Minister," repeated Todd, looking like he was trying to remember why that meant something to him.

"Yes. I'm going to ask that you don't speak openly or frivolously about what happened today. I generally try to keep a low profile."

"Sure," said the young man, seeming somewhat dazed.

"Do you have any family?" said the Minister as they waited for a mule cart of raw coca to pass through the street.

"My ma."

"Once you've gotten cleaned up, bring her to the location that I'm bringing you to now. Do it in a hurry and don't be seen. Can you manage that?" said the Minister, walking with an impressive gait from one alley to the next, checking for Watchers in the street as he crossed.

"Sure." Todd had to jog every couple of steps to keep stride with the Minister.

"And another thing. Have you ever had a steak dinner?"

Todd was taken aback at the question. "No."

The Minister smiled and clapped him on the shoulder. "Well, I can promise you, tonight won't be the last time you do."

"I don't understand," said Todd with a tinge of apprehension.

"Do you want to leave Sacramento?"

"Of course," replied Todd in a desperate tone. "But...I'm an owned man."

"The Watcher said your father sold you?" They walked briskly around a deep, oily puddle that spread nearly the length of an alley.

"Yeah. Ma doesn't talk about it much. Apparently, he didn't care enough to take her with him when he left."

"I'm sorry to hear that. But they let her raise you instead of taking you to the children's house?"

"I guess they thought it would be cheaper if Ma paid for my grub and my cot instead of them."

"I'm getting you both out of this city tonight. You're not an owned man. Such a thing doesn't exist."

"If you say so," said Todd.

They walked for a while, and Todd seemed just as comfortable with not talking as the Minister. He appreciated that.

"Here we are."

They stepped inside the compound, a long, low building with narrow alleys on either side. It was built pre-Crash, as was apparent by the strange sort of cement that was used at the time, having the appearance something between glass and stone. It was not a pretty building, but it was sturdy, functional, and well kept.

"Good afternoon, Minister," said a cheerful voice upon their entrance.

"Hello, Charise."

Charise was petite and well-formed. Her round face held two large, blue eyes and a warm smile.

The Minister said, "Charise, would you mind taking my new friend, Todd, to the kitchen? Have the cook prepare him the best we have on hand."

"I can do that, Minister," said Charise, her eyes sparkling at Todd.

"Feel free to give him the grand tour after he's eaten," said the Minister with a smile as the two youths escorted each other out of the room with the awkward fluidity of those their age.

Another voice spoke. "Sir, do you have a moment?"

"Yes, what is it?"

A man stepped fully into the room, his hands dirty from hard work. He had a gruff, matter-of-fact voice to match his stout, wild boar appearance.

"It's about the new tunnel, sir. There was a collapse in the fourth and final quadrant last night. No one was hurt, but it will delay us at least seven weeks."

"That's too long," said the Minister, shaking his head.

"We're already working 'round the clock."

"Take more men from other projects. See who's willing to come in from the ranch. Even a month is too long. We can't use the other tunnel for a while. We were almost discovered yesterday evening."

"I'll do my best sir," replied the man with a nod.

"I know."

"Oh, another thing, sir," said the man, turning back in the doorway. "Dembe arrived an hour ago. He said he had to speak with you urgently."

The Minister sighed. The longer he left the Collector alone in the city, the harder it would be to track him down again later. "Where is he?"

"I sent him to the Althing Tower."

"Good, thank you. I heard a rumor that the cook is preparing steak. Why don't you offer your assistance in judging its quality?" the Minister said.

A broad smile crossed the man's face. "As you say, Minister."

Chapter Six

It took about twenty minutes to reach the tower, and the Minister's mind raced the whole way there. Dembe never came into the city if he could help it. The last week had been even more hectic than usual, thanks to the letter that had arrived on the previous Cross. A letter that detailed the plans of a coupe to unseat the Fairchilds, something between an offer and a threat. The offer was generous, but the Minister, like any man, did not like to be threatened.

He turned a corner and could see the tower rising black into the haze. There was only one Althing Tower in the city, though the Althing had several other towers like it up and down the West Coast. They shared a common builder in the peak of the previous civilization; seemingly indestructible, they remained bastions to a time lost. The top five floors were safely above the haze, and despite the animalistic city that surrounded them, the towers themselves were sacred ground, making it a safe haven for any powerful or connected person passing through the city. They were controlled by the Order of the Althing, and no one, not even the Fairchilds, dared to overstep the Order of the Althing.

The Minister breathed a little easier once the Althing guards nodded to him and unlocked the heavy doors that blocked out the savagery of Sacramento. He felt the pressures of the day begin to fade as the doors locked again behind him.

Another Althing guard was in the grand lobby, drinking coffee and preparing for his shift.

"Good day, Minister," said the guard in a thick Icelandic accent. "Did the Watchers give you any trouble today?"

"A bit."

"Savages," said the guard, his words heavy with contempt.

The Minister made no reply and pulled off his mask as he entered the elevator.

Dembe had made himself quite at home in the tower. He had made an entire pot of coffee and cooked approximately all the bacon in the kitchen. He greeted the Minister with a smile and a bear hug.

"Ah, little brother. You look very well. Have something to drink!"

Dembe was one of the largest men the Minister had ever known, standing about six feet, seven inches, looking like he'd been carved out of polished stone. He was also the Minister's oldest friend. He had known Dembe longer than he had known God, and they had saved each other's lives more times than either cared to remember.

"Thank you, brother. How are our new friends doing?" His voice was more relaxed now that he was talking with Dembe.

"Better than they ever have previously," said Dembe as he handed the Minister a cup of coffee. "You should've seen the look on the youngest one's face at breakfast this morning. I don't think he knew so much food could exist in the same place at the same time."

"Good," said the Minister, sitting down in a large chair.

"Yes, but I did not come to talk about food." Dembe's ebony face hardened as he spoke the words. He leaned forward and set down his mug. "Two people came today. A soldier, and then an hour later, a woman. Beautiful like a blade. She asked for you, and when I said you were gone, she said she was returning to Chico and would wait for you there at the Hotel Madison. She must be the one Lipton mentioned in his letter. I like her though. She's got fire," he added with a smile.

"I saw the Collector arrive on the Cross this morning," said the Minister.

The two friends sat in silence for a moment.

"It's just a gut feeling, but I don't think we can trust Lipton," said Dembe.

"I agree, but we don't have much of a choice." The Minister paused, not wanting to say what he had to say next. "I knocked out three Watchers today."

Dembe closed his eyes and drew a deep breath in through his nose. "Little brother."

"I know," said the Minister, hanging his head.

"Why?"

"They were beating a boy."

"They beat boys every day," said Dembe, his jaw clenching.

"I know. But it gets worse," said the Minister, grimacing slightly.

"How?" asked Dembe, not trying to hide his disapproval.

"The boy was owned. We need to get him out of the city as soon as possible. And his mother. They'll kill him for what I did."

"They might kill *you* for what you did. After last time? Anyone but you, little brother. Anyone but you can go around doing the brunt work. You're a fucking baron." Dembe spoke passionately, but there was no malice in his tone. "I'm sorry." He took a breath. "I know you were just following your spirit, but if Thorpe is motivated enough, he could use this to get the Fairchilds to approve direct action against the ranch."

"Which is why we need Lipton to succeed," said the Minister.

"But who knows Lipton's full plans? He may scrub us away as soon as he's in power. We at least need a backup plan."

"I don't disagree, but I have no viable ideas."

"I'll go to the Vault," said Dembe, his voice low.

The Minister shot him a look. "You know the cost of their help. We both do. I can't be a Collector again, Dembe, and I won't let you go back either."

Dembe gave an apprehensive shrug.

"I'll talk to the Althing, too. If they were to help, they would require the ranch as payment, but at least the people there would be safe."

The two friends looked at each other, both knowing the other's thoughts.

"Let's hope this Henry fellow is as good as Lipton says he is," said the Minister.

"Indeed," replied Dembe. "And if all fails?"

"If all fails...then we fight if we need to. Die if we need to."

"Eli."

The Minister winced at the sound of his real name. "Yes?"

"Do you have our old gear?"

"Yes." Eli's face darkened. "It's in sublevel B. I never thought that I would ever have to return to that room."

"Show me."

Eli donned his coat and reached under the coffee table, feeling around for a moment. Then he felt it; a cold, small key held in place on the underside of the table by a leather strap and two cold nails. He pocketed the key.

"This way," he said to Dembe.

They took the elevator to the lobby and then took the stairs to the second of several sub-levels. Eli lit a grease lamp and proceeded to the end of the dark and eerily cold corridor.

"This will be it," he said as he fit the key to a locked steel door. The hinges moaned their protest as Eli pushed the door open. He placed the lamp in a contraption of mirrors, and the room was illuminated.

On a stand in the corner hung a coat identical to the one the Minister wore, only much, much bigger. Dembe strode over to it and slipped it on.

"There never were tailors like those at the Vault," he said with a reluctant smile.

"Yes, the craftsmanship of the Vault truly is unparalleled..." Eli trailed off, remembering the mystery behind some of the tools and weapons gifted to Collectors by the Vault or passed down by their teachers. There were many mysteries surrounding the Collectors.

Then they both stepped over to the wall opposite, which contained a small arsenal of blades, pistols, and poisons. They armed themselves. Dembe took a mask like the one the Minister had put on that morning. Eli took another one and hung it on his belt. Finally, they each grabbed a long, coiled whip with a weighted handle. There were more to these tools than met the eye.

"Little brother."

"Yes, Dembe?"

"That .45. Are you sure you want to bring it?"

"Quite sure. Don't worry. I intend to keep my oath. It's just that no one else needs to know that."

Dembe chuckled. "There is one thing I will not permit."

"Do tell!" said the Minister with an air of playfulness in his voice.

"The poisons. Give me all the lethal ones."

"Fair enough." Eli handed them over.

They were all in an assortment of steel vials that fit perfectly into the bullet slots on the cross straps they wore on their chests. Dembe held them in his hand for a moment and looked at them. Then he replaced all the non-lethal poisons in his belt with the lethal ones and slid each non-lethal vial into the Minister's cross straps.

"Dembe..." Eli started.

Dembe cut him off. "In these next few weeks, you might be Eli more than you are the Minister, but you must not forget yourself. You are a symbol of peace and hope to those we save and serve. Don't lose sight of that. I am no symbol. I must reach Seattle unnoticed. Over the next few weeks, I will have no use for non-lethal poisons, little brother."

Eli knew that Dembe was right. Neither the Fairchilds nor Lipton could know that he was appealing to the Vault or the Althing, and there were a lot of men on the road between Sacramento and Seattle. There could be no sign that they were stepping outside the lines of their instructions.

"I'll find the Collector. You should get the boy and his mother out now and head north immediately," said the Minister.

"I can do that."

"Don't take the time to bring them all the way to the ranch. Take Charise with you. She can guide them once you're out of the city."

Dembe nodded, then the two old friends embraced and parted ways.

It had been some time since the Minister last had to track a man, but the skills soon returned to him. A man riding a horse was almost unheard of within the city, and it took only an hour or so to find him. It was near a small store. The man looked very different than he had earlier that morning, obviously not at all used to the haze.

The Minister leaned against the building across the street from the store and watched. The horse walked slowly to the hitching post and stopped. The man tried to dismount quickly, but it seemed his legs could not bear their own weight. He fell hard to the ground. "Henry," muttered the Minister, reminding himself of the man's name. The man stood up and staggered into the store.

The Minister watched him. He almost felt pity mixed in with his distaste for the Collector. Henry entered the store. *God, I do not trust this man.*

There was nothing for a moment, save the discouragement growing in the pit of his belly. It began to overwhelm him, as the discouragement grew into despair and spread from his belly to his mind. Then, in the stillest place in his being, he heard it. A voice so familiar it could have almost been his own thoughts, but so strong he knew it could not have been.

Trust me.

Then peace. *Okay.* Despair and the memory of it lifted. "Okay," he said again, out loud this time.

Just then, two unsavory-looking characters crossed the street, untied Henry's horse, and led it away. The Minister recognized the men. They were Watchers assigned to a small processing complex in Sector 7. He saw his opportunity. Now all he had to do was wait.

He knew that the Watchers would take the horse back to the complex and sell it to some desperate sap the next day. Only, instead of handing over the horse, they would receive payment for it, then shoot the buyer in the face. The process would be repeated until someone else stole the horse from them and started their own dark extortion.

The Minister never was sure why people fell for the trick. It was not an uncommon racket. *Hope is blinding to those who have never known it, and desperation never made men wise.*

The two men and the horse were out of sight now. A few more minutes had elapsed, but the Minister was nothing if not a patient man. Then, Henry burst out of the store and ran to the street, yelling something the Minister could not make out.

Henry had a maddened and delirious look about him, then he collapsed in the street. The Minister approached. As he drew near, he could hear Henry sniffling quietly.

He stood a few feet away in utter surprise. *Why is this man crying?* He felt a pang of sympathy in the pit of his stomach. *Well, this is unexpected.* He walked over to Henry and stood behind him.

Chapter Seven

The tear on the back of Henry's hand was soon joined by another, then another. He did not know what to do. How was he supposed to get out of the city without a horse? How was he going to survive without Bentley? He was all Henry had left to remember her by.

Henry felt someone behind him. The tears stopped. An icy stillness filled Henry. He listened and saw. A man in black. His hand clenched the razor in his coat pocket. He waited to feel the motion of an attack, but it did not come.

"It's been a while since we've had a Collector in the city." The voice was deep, imposing, and muffled.

He turned and looked up at the tall black figure behind him. A mask covered the face. Henry never did trust masks. He stood up quickly and faced the figure. His head spun from the haze, but he held his body steady.

"Who are you?" Henry asked.

"I'm here to get you out of the city. We need to keep a low profile."

"You're late," said Henry.

"I know who has your horse."

"If you're lying, I'll kill you." Henry spoke the truth.

The figure repeated, calm as ever, "We really should leave now, but if you want, we can get your horse and then leave."

Henry did not want to trust the man, but he was desperate.

"I'm not leaving without Bentley."

"This way. But first, put this on." The man held out a mask identical to his own. "It will clean the air you breathe. It may take a few hours for the effects of the haze to wear off, but it will help you clear your head."

Henry stared intensely at the dark eyes behind the mask.

"Put it on," the man commanded, holding the mask closer to Henry's face.

Henry snatched it out of the man's hands and slid it over his head. It was actually quite comfortable despite limiting his range of vision.

"Show me," he repeated.

"We'll need to be careful. There will be—"

"Show me. Now." The words were ice in Henry's mouth.

The man nodded, turned, and began moving down the street. Henry followed. They walked quickly for about fifteen minutes before the man slowed to a stop. "There will most likely be at least eight of them," the man said, "so our best bet is to wait until it's dark and sneak in then. If we draw attention to ourselves, your whole mission will be jeopardized."

"I never agreed to any fucking mission," said Henry. "Is it this building?"

"Yes. We need to wait until tonight."

Henry slowly walked up to the warehouse and touched it. He closed his eyes and reached into his mind. A memory flooded back.

"Listen and know," his teacher spoke firmly.

He had been practicing since his last birthday but had

barely been able to make any progress since then, and that was ten months ago.

"All things move. Existence is motion. Movement is sound. Though not all sounds you can hear, some you must feel. Some you must see. All matter sings, all you must do is listen." Rust spoke the words as if he had said them many times. "Now, how many men are in the bar, and what are they doing?"

Henry felt their motion. Their life. Their heartbeats.

"There are eleven of them, only two have guns," Henry said, his eyes still closed. "They're small. They aren't expecting company. And they've already started drinking."

"So, you're one of *those* Collectors then," said the man in black.

Henry glanced at the whip on the figure's belt. "As if you're not."

The razor flashed out of Henry's pocket, only a fraction of a second after he had unhooked his .45. He noticed the man in black grab the handle of his whip.

"Wait!" commanded the man.

"No," said Henry. He charged the door and kicked it in with the fury of a god. Eleven heads turned and faced him from the poker table.

Henry began firing, and six heads successively turned to mist and mangled flesh. One man stood frozen in shock, while the remaining four charged.

The .45 was back in the holster. The razor switched to his right hand.

One throat opened, then another. One man flew backward, a muddy footprint on his chest. Then another throat. The man stood up off the floor and barreled towards Henry, who sidestepped as gracefully as if he was dancing and opened the final throat as it passed him. The last man looked in shock at his dead and dying companions, then at the two figures in front of him. He dropped the bottle he had been holding like a club and ran as fast as he could through a side exit and down an alley. Henry wiped off the razor and returned it to his pocket. *Bentley's in the next room.*

"What have you done?" shouted the dark figure. "We need to move, now!"

Henry ignored him and walked out of the small office into the main space of the warehouse, filled with boxes and barrels. Bentley was there. Henry rested his head on Bentley's muzzle.

"You old bastard. You had me worried. I can't believe you'd walk off with someone who wasn't me." He rubbed Bentley's forehead "What do you mean, you put up a fight? They were all still intact when I found them, so it must not have been that much of a fight." Henry turned to the man, now standing in the doorway. "Thank you."

"You don't know what you've done," said the man. "Follow me if you want to live. Now."

Henry nodded and followed, leading Bentley behind him.

He had to walk quickly to keep up. They walked for nearly thirty minutes, not talking. Henry was still nauseated and disoriented from the haze, but the mask was helping. Eventually, they reached a building, and the man guided Henry to the back, leading him into a stable of sorts.

"You can leave your horse here while we go inside and talk."

Henry shook his head. "He's been stolen twice in the last five days. If it's all the same to you, we can talk here."

"If you insist."

"What's your name?" asked Henry.

"You can call me the Minister," said the man formally.

"Fuck off. I asked what your name was, not your job title."

The Minister's silence filled the room. Henry's eyes drifted to the whip coiled and hung on the Minister's belt.

"It's been a long time since I've seen one of those," Henry said. "The craftsmanship of the Vault is unparalleled."

"Truly," said the Minister.

"Well, Minister, my name is Henry. A pleasure," he said, extending his hand.

"If you say so," said the Minister, reluctantly shaking it. "Here's the thing. I already know who you are and why you are here. I'm here to ensure it gets done."

"Lipton sent you?" asked Henry.

"In a sense, yes."

"Hmm." Henry reloaded his revolver.

"What?"

"I never agreed to Lipton's Ask. I'm only here because he stole Bentley and put him on the Cross."

"Well, you're here now. Thanks to your recklessness, Thorpe and his Watchers will be looking for you, and I'm your only way out of the city."

Henry considered his options. "Not if I get right back on the Cross."

"And return to New York? Lipton would kill you as soon as you arrived."

Henry knew that was probably true. A million dollars and a nice patch of land did appeal to him, but he hated feeling pressured into decisions. *And that bastard stole Bentley.*

"You can get me out of the city?" he asked.

"I'm the only one that can get you out of the city," said the Minister.

They stood in an uncomfortable silence for a few moments.

"Let's move inside. I give you my word your horse is safe here," the Minister continued.

"He's not my horse."

"Then whose horse is it?"

"What's your name?" asked Henry.

They stood in silence for a moment.

"I'm parched," said Henry, breaking the stalemate.

"There's water inside."

Henry nodded and followed the Minister. He drank two glasses of cool, clean water but it did not seem to sate him. Nausea gripped him by his core, and his head pounded and spun so intensely that he put a hand on the counter to keep himself steady.

"Withdrawals," said the Minister. "You won't be right until this time tomorrow."

"How do people live in this?" asked Henry, observing that the Minister still wore his mask.

"Miserably," said the Minister.

Henry did not have time to comment. A stout man burst into the kitchen, red-faced.

"Minister, the Watchers are here," he said, voice frayed around the edges.

Henry followed the Minister and the man into the front room of the building, where there were a handful of hard-looking men awaiting orders from the Minister. They stayed back from the windows, but Henry could see a small crowd of uniformed men gathered outside. With them was the man that Henry let escape when he rescued Bentley.

At their front was a different man in a mask who was projecting in an official tone. Something about "violating agreements" and "we know you're in there" and other posse nonsense.

"If you want to live, do as I say," the Minister said to Henry.

Henry nodded.

"Mask on. Follow me."

"We'll make sure they don't notice you leave," said the red-faced man.

"Thank you. Be safe and avoid violence if possible. We don't want to give them any more reason to move on the ranch than we already have," commanded the Minister, then he headed back to the stable.

It took only a moment for the Minister to saddle his horse, then Henry and Bentley followed him out of a back alley away from the building. When they were about a block away, the sound of gunfire erupted from behind them. They heeled their mounts and moved as quickly as the city streets would allow. The movement made Henry sick; it was all he could do to keep the water down. His vision was blurred by his headache and obstructed by his mask, and he left it mostly to Bentley to stay on the Minister's tail. They rode hard for a while before reaching a derelict building. He helped drag sheet metal out of the way of an opening and saw a large tunnel leading down into the earth. They mounted again and went down into the darkness.

The Minister lit an oil lamp and removed his mask, Henry still couldn't get a good look at his face in that light. "The air is clean down here," the Minister said.

All Henry could see was the shadow of the horse and rider in front of him, and a bit of the reinforced walls they passed through. The withdrawals were getting worse. He felt himself slipping in and out of consciousness, and then he knew no more.

Chapter Eight

The sunlight passing softly through Henry's windows beckoned him to consciousness. It must've been nearly ten. He didn't get up at first, just laid in the massive, clean bed taking in the room and trying to remember how he had gotten there. The previous day was foggy in his mind. After a few minutes, he turned his attention to his present surroundings. The floors were light hardwood, the curtains white, as was the nightstand. It was peaceful. Eventually, he sat up and pulled on his trousers.

The door creaked as he pushed it open, and he stepped into the corridor. He was standing at the top of a staircase in an old but well-kept farmhouse. He could hear faint conversation and laughter coming from somewhere below him.

Walking down the stairs, the familiar smell of bacon and onions greeted him, and he began to realize how hungry and thirsty he was. The kitchen was easy to find. Two women and one man were sitting around a table, sharing a pot of coffee and what seemed to be a lively conversation.

"You must be our guest!" said the most motherly-looking lady in the group. She was rotund with short hair and had the sort of smile that made it difficult not to trust her. "Did you sleep well?"

"Yes, ma'am, like a baby."

"Oh good, good. Come sit down. You must be famished."

"I certainly wouldn't turn down a meal," said Henry as he took a seat.

"What's your name, dear?" asked the woman as she set down a steaming mug of coffee before him.

"Henry."

"Henry." She pondered the name for a moment and said it again quietly as if to commit it permanently to memory. "It's good to meet you, Henry. You can call me Martha. This is Harriet and Jack. Though, I don't suppose you'll be here long enough to have a need for our names."

"A pleasure just the same, ma'am." Henry spoke with an easy smile.

Harriet was thin, tall, and beautiful. She had curly brown hair that concealed her ears and two of the most striking blue eyes Henry had ever seen. They seemed to look directly into his soul. He looked away quickly as if to protect himself from her gaze.

Jack had dark hair, dark eyes, and a dark beard. If Henry had to guess how old he was, he would've said forty or so. Even so, it was impossible to guess the age of a hard man who'd led a life as violent as Jack obviously had. Though he bore no obvious physical scars, there was something in his eyes that Henry found all too familiar. Something in his jawline that made Henry pity any fist that had broken upon it.

Jack nodded, Harriet smiled, and Martha set a comically full plate of food in front of Henry. Pancakes, eggs, bacon, and sautéed onions, peppers, mushrooms, and tomatoes.

"There you are, love." She spoke kindly, and her words bubbled over with an invisible peace and joy.

"You're an angel," said Henry, and he meant it.

Martha smiled and ruffled Henry's hair as if she had raised him. The three carried on talking as Henry ate. He felt quite at ease. The next thirty minutes consisted of Martha regaling them with stories of her childhood. Henry, quite frankly, was too preoccupied with his breakfast to truly listen. After his third cup of coffee, he felt awake and alert enough to join the conversation.

"Where exactly are we?" he interjected appropriately into a lull in Martha's overblown stories.

"The Minister's ranch. We are slightly northwest of Sacramento."

"I see."

"The Minister said you may be able to help us."

"He did?"

Martha smiled and tilted her head. "He said you were here to..." She trailed off. "Well, why are you here, love?"

Henry had to think about it. "It's been an eventful couple of days. I've just been trying to stay alive and keep Bentley alive, and I somehow found myself here this morning."

"Staying alive can be difficult," Martha said. "What do you plan to do now?"

Henry couldn't help but answer honestly. "I haven't the slightest idea. It wouldn't be safe for me to return to New York. But I don't know the West all that well. Truthfully, I haven't been thinking ahead until just now."

"Well, there's no better place for lost souls than the ranch. It's the Minister's specialty."

"Right, of course," said Henry. "Where is he, anyway?"

"Oh, he's out tending to the horses."

"I see."

Martha stood and cleared his plate, only to replace it with another bearing a large wedge of apple pie.

"Where's my pie, Martha?" asked Jack, with a surprising amount of playful vitality in his voice.

"Don't pretend like you don't know where the pantry and plates are, you slothful degenerate!" Martha fired back with a grin and a wink.

"Such cruelty!" exclaimed Jack in a mockingly dramatic tone.

Martha gently, but firmly, smacked him upside the head as he stood to fetch his pie.

"So, what exactly is this place?" asked Henry after taking a bite.

"Did the Minister not tell you?" Martha sounded genuinely surprised.

"No, we haven't talked much."

"Oh. Well, this is his ministry."

"Come again?"

"His ministry," affirmed Harriet. She'd been mostly silent up until this point. For some reason, Henry expected her to have a frail voice. He was wrong. Though soft, her voice was strong, decisive, and even smokey.

"Do tell."

Harriet locked eyes with Henry. It made him uncomfortable. He felt like she saw and knew all there was to see and know about him.

"We rescue people from the city. Mostly children, but a few men and women as well. We sneak them out through tunnels."

"Aren't the barons over the city a little upset with you for stealing their factory equipment?" Henry immediately regretted his choice of words. Harriet seemed to notice his instant remorse, and all in an instant, he felt forgiven for his insensitivity. It was unusual. *She is something else.*

"Of course, Thorpe has been appealing to the Fairchilds

for years to allow him to wipe us out. So far, they haven't allowed it because it would create an immense amount of unease with the other small barons in the Fairchild's empire." Then a storm crossed her face. "Until now," she added.

"What changed?" asked Henry.

"Yesterday, the Minister..." She looked at Jack.

Jack spoke up. "Yesterday, the Minister beat several Watchers into the dirt with no legal basis to do so, and then a few hours later him and an associate killed several more watchers in cold blood. Word is spreading. It seems like that may have been the last straw."

Henry felt flutters in his chest. "The Minister didn't kill anyone. And I'd barely call myself his associate."

"That may be, love," said Martha. "But that's not what Thorpe is saying."

"What will you do?" asked Henry, finding himself caring for the plight of these good people more than he expected to.

"That depends entirely on what you do, Henry," said Harriet.

Fuck.

Henry took a sip of coffee and yearned for a cigarette.

Martha cleared her throat and changed the subject. "Once the children are here, we educate them, and they work for the farm. We keep track of how many days of work they put in. Once they turn sixteen, we give them all the money they earned while they were here. Then they can either head out into the world with money and valuable skills, or stay with us. We, of course, give them the best living situation we can manage while they're here growing up."

"I see. What exactly do they do while they're here?" Henry was eager to think about something other than the crisis he had caused.

"Whatever they choose to do. We have horses, cows,

sheep, goats, pigs, chickens and other fowl, and rabbits as well
as herding dogs. They can either work with the animals or the
crops. We grow nearly every grain, fruit, and vegetable that
can survive in this climate, which is quite a long list, especially
because of our greenhouses. If they don't want to work with
the animals or the crops, they can learn crafting: leather,
wood, metal, as well as glass and ceramics. The children can
learn anything they want. We even have an apothecary.
When they leave, they're educated, they have a craft, trade, or
skill that they have honed to mastery and enough money to
start a business in any city they want. They can also choose to
stay, which many of them do. We are always growing and
buying more land."

Henry had never heard of anything like this.

"Everyone just lives here in perfect harmony?"

"Oh, I don't believe there is such a thing," clucked
Martha. "But we've gotten good at resolving conflicts when
they arise."

"And the Minister, he started all of this?"

"No." Martha's eyes smiled as she spoke, as if remembering. "He saved it. This is an old place. It was here long before
the Crash as a monastery, and afterwards was a refuge for all
sorts of spiritual people. They learned from each other and
cultivated the land together. It was in disrepair when the
Minister found it. But he fell in love with the place and
bought it from the Fairchilds. He revitalized it and made it
what you see now."

"Interesting. And what did the Minister do before all this
heroism?"

"His history is no concern of mine. He's a very private
person."

Henry noticed that Martha looked away when he asked
about the Minister's past. There was a set to her jaw.

"So, he's hiding something?"

Martha's smile remained, though it tightened a bit. "You'll have to talk to the Minister if you want to learn anything about the Minister."

Henry nodded. "Breakfast was divine. Thank you, truly."

Martha beamed at him. "Of course. Harriet, dear, show our guest to the horse pasture. He should convene with the Minister. And I'm sure Henry would like to see his horse."

"I can do it," interjected Jack. There was the slightest air of hostility in his tone.

Finally, something familiar.

"It's fine," retorted Harriet. "It's this way. You'll be needing your boots."

"Oh, I um..." Henry looked around a bit embarrassed. "I actually don't know where I've left them."

"They're by the door," chuckled Harriet. "The same one you entered by last night."

"Right. Of course. I was rather...tired."

"Yes, I know." She smiled playfully. Her gaze somehow warmed him to his core.

Without any clear memory of arriving, Henry was embarrassed, unsure of what he'd done or said. But somehow, Harriet's smile made him not mind that much.

"This way," she said.

Henry pulled on his boots and followed her out the door. The ranch was rich with lush, plentiful beauty. It was mostly flat with a few rolling hills. There were quite a few people about, each doing their task, but they all seemed to blend together into a sort of white noise compared to Harriet walking beside him.

"Over that way are the orchards, and in that direction are the grain fields. All the gardens lay beyond that far rise. That area with the house is where most of the lodgings are. Ahead are the barns and storehouses and beyond those are the pastures."

"It's all so nice."

"Yes, and somehow peaceful. Even when it's not, it is."

"How long have you lived here? Did the Minister rescue you from the city?"

"No, not from the city, at least. I've been here for four years. I met the Minister and Dembe, who I'm sure you'll meet someday. I had run from my life back east looking for adventure. Instead, I found meaning."

"How so?" Henry looked at her as he spoke.

Harriet was silent for a minute, then peered into Henry's soul again before answering. "I grew up in a place called New Brunswick. My father had a successful lobster and fishing business. Mother was a very special lady. She comes from a very old family. You wouldn't believe the half of it if I told you." She spoke with clear, delicate words.

Henry felt that he would believe her, but she continued.

"My parents had everything—money, land, connections. But their most prized possession was, well, me."

"That doesn't sound so bad."

"It wasn't. Just empty. They gave me everything I ever wanted—money, clothes, parties, and luxuries of every kind. In return, I had to take it. Eventually, I couldn't take it anymore. I couldn't bear the thought of being a pet for the rest of my life, so I stole as much money as I could fit in one bag and came out west.

"For the first time, I felt scared and excited. Alive. I partied and explored for a while in Washington, then Oregon. After a time, I ran out of money. I found myself penniless, in Chico, and there I experienced something else for the first time. Hunger. Then desperation. I tried to get a job, but I had no skills or experience of any kind. All I had were my looks and my body.

"One night I decided to do what so many hungry and desperate women have done. Thankfully, the first man I approached was the Minister. He and Dembe bought me food, then told me that they had a different sort of job for me if I wanted it. They brought me here. Gave me a home and a life. This place gave me purpose."

"What do you do here?"

"I take care of the new children. The young ones." She smiled broadly. "I teach them to stop fighting. I help them choose what they want to do here. Sometimes I read them stories I've written to help them sleep. I help them resolve their arguments and listen to them when they're scared or angry. It seems simple, but it's so far from easy. I think that's why I like it."

They walked on for a moment. Henry couldn't help but be enamored by the sound of her voice.

"What made you approach him?" he said, breaking the silence.

"Who?"

"The Minister, that night in Chico. Why him out of everyone else in the city?"

"He looked the loneliest."

Henry pondered her words. "I suppose loneliness can be easy to spot sometimes."

She looked through him with those eyes and giggled a little. "Yes. Sometimes very easy."

They had reached the edge of the pasture. Then something strange and unexpected happened. She kissed him on the cheek. It was not done in romance, but comfort.

"Keep going. You'll find what you're looking for." She

pointed out across the expanse of land, and then she turned and began walking back to the house.

Henry kept walking in the direction in which she had pointed, passing a few trees here and there as he went, his cheek warm and slightly wet from her soft lips. He felt oddly at peace there. It felt like the forgotten memories and neglected parts of himself were thawing out in the bright October sun. It was almost uncomfortable, but not unpleasant.

When he reached the top of the next hill, he could see two figures atop another hill a little farther away. He smiled. Nothing like that had happened in years. Not since her. He continued walking towards the two figures ahead.

He assumed that they saw him, so he did not wave or act intentionally conspicuous. Henry found it very rude to sneak up on people unannounced unless he planned to kill them. Even then, everyone deserves a fighting chance.

There was a slight breeze that day. Henry couldn't help but notice all the fragrances in the air, with the land all around being dedicated to orchards, fields, groves, and gardens. Even now, in the fall, the air was rich and full of life. In addition to all the life, Henry also noticed the distinct aroma of horse manure, which, naturally, made him wonder how Bentley had slept. He picked a wildflower and wondered what strange magic flowed through Harriet's veins.

Chapter Nine

Henry was quite near to the Minister and the young woman he was with when he realized that the two of them were unaware of his presence. To make matters worse, they seemed to be talking about him.

"I think you did the right thing, Eli. And you can't expect him to have known the consequences of his actions. In his mind, he was just killing horse thieves."

"Yes, but now we've lost people because of it."

"They knew the risks," said the lady.

"I still don't even know if he's going to help us."

Henry cleared his throat loudly, not wanting to lurk like a snake.

The Minister jumped at the sound, but the young lady just turned and gave him a somewhat forced smile.

"Everything else is forgivable. But eavesdropping?" She clicked her tongue in mock disapproval. "Eavesdropping is a bridge too far."

Henry smiled and nodded, thankful that the Minister's friend possessed more humor than he did. "I hope one day you can find it in your heart to forgive me."

"We'll see," she said with her smile seeming more natural by the moment. "As you might have guessed, the Minister and I were just talking about you. I'm Grace."

"A pleasure. My name's Henry, as I'm sure you already knew," said Henry, extending his hand.

"He had mentioned it," she replied, shaking it.

It was the first time Henry had gotten a good look at the Minister. He had a fine build in face and body, and he didn't seem as uptight as he had the day before.

"So, what's your role here at the ranch, Grace?" said Henry, taking out his pouch of tobacco.

"Horses are my business. Speaking of which, that's quite a beautiful animal of yours."

"I'll have to tell him you said so. Though I must confess, he's not exactly my horse." Henry rolled a cigarette absent-mindedly.

"I don't even want to know the story behind that one," Grace said, laughing.

"Where is the old bastard, if you don't mind me asking?" asked Henry before taking a long drag.

"Last I saw, he was stretching his legs over by the brook. I can show you if you'd like."

"Only if Eli doesn't mind. I didn't mean to disrupt your conversation," said Henry, examining the Minister in his peripheral.

It was the first time he called Eli by his name instead of what he was known by. He noticed the Minister closed his eyes and sighed inaudibly. Grace, who seemed as perceptive as she was good-natured, smiled jovially at Henry's jab and the Minister's displeasure.

"Shall we walk, Eli?" She smiled warmly at him as she spoke, and Eli's expression seemed to soften as she did.

"Lead on," said the Minister with an attempt at enthusiasm in his tone.

"This way then!" chirped Grace. "It's just on the other side of that far fence line."

She walked very quickly, almost a trot, a few yards ahead of the Minister and Henry.

"It's quite the place you have here. It's something special," said Henry.

"It is. I hope you can help us keep it this way," said the Minister.

Henry took a long drag.

"You don't owe me or the people here anything," the Minister continued. "But right now, you're the only person that can ensure this place's safety. I can't really offer you anything in return other than an open invitation."

"You don't need to offer anything. Lipton is already offering...too much," said Henry.

"*Too* much?" asked the Minister.

"Too much," Henry confirmed. "A million dollars and a hundred acres with a stream running through it."

The Minister shot Henry an alarmed look.

"A reward like that sounds like the kiss of death to me," Henry confided.

"I won't lie to you, Henry. It will be incredibly dangerous," said the Minister. "But I'll help you along the way. And Lipton said we'd find more help in Chico. I can't say I trust him, but if we don't at least make contact, he might get spooked."

"The bigger the party, the greater the chance of one of us dying," said Henry. "At least in my experience. And I still haven't agreed to anything."

"What are you two whispering about so secretively?" Grace asked cheerfully from ahead of them.

"Nothing at all, ma'am," said Henry good naturedly.

"You're already starting to wear off on him, Henry. He's usually so good at being secretive. You could learn a thing or two from him, you know."

"Oh, I don't doubt that."

The breeze picked up slightly as they crested a hill. It refreshed Henry. He could've sworn that if he was thirsty, a breeze like that could sate him more than a glass of water.

"How long have you lived here, Grace?" asked Henry.

"I was born here," Grace said, pausing for a moment to take in the scenery.

"Really?"

"Yes, my mother was pregnant with me when she came here with Aunt Martha. My father was, well...elsewhere. So, they came here from the north hoping that the monks could help deliver me. She had planned to move to the East Coast after I was born, but the birth was kinder to me than to her. The monks raised me. I was the first child they took in here."

"I'm sorry. I didn't know my mother either," said Henry, remembering the fact for the first time in a long time.

He noticed a momentary glance from the Minister when he said this.

"Don't be sorry," said Grace. "I may not have known my birth parents, but Martha and the monks gave me the happiest childhood I could have asked for, and they taught me about horses, for which I am eternally grateful." She glanced back as she spoke. Her bright eyes and fair hair were illuminated by the morning sun.

"Still, I can't imagine being raised by monks. They seem to be such dull creatures," said Henry, casting a smirk at the Minister.

"You'd be surprised. They have quite a good grasp of the importance of enjoyment and fun. I like to think that's why they live in places like this, away from all the nonsense that could distract them from fully enjoying the important things in life."

"I guess that depends entirely on what you believe to be most important."

Grace looked at Henry quizzically as she walked and opened her mouth to say something, but then seemed to decide against it.

Their course led them down into a glade of mature trees. They were far enough apart that the grass still grew thick and lush between them, but close enough together to create a canopy that shaded the light to an autumnal hue and held the breeze at bay. Henry could hear the stream splashing over the rocks on its banks. Dry leaves and twigs crunched under Henry's boots.

Henry stopped and took a deep breath of sweet air. "This glade feels full of magic," he said before he realized the words were escaping him.

"This is one of my favorite spots on the ranch," said the Minister. "If the land Lipton gives you isn't satisfactory, I'll have a cottage built for you right there." He pointed to an open spot near the creek. "You'd be able to catch trout seven steps from your front porch, and you'd never hear a hint of noise from the ranch."

For a moment, it was like gravity forgot about Henry's guts. He looked at the Minister, at Eli, and they locked eyes. Henry saw a mix of emotion, pleading, hope, and deep down, a kindness as sturdy as a stone house.

"I'd kill for that," said Henry.

The Minister and Grace both looked at Henry like they wanted something that only he could give them.

"You will? You'll help us?" asked the Minister.

Fuck it. "I will."

Eli smiled, relieved, and they shook hands.

Grace looked away to hide her relief, but Henry saw her heave a deep sigh and wipe a little moisture from her eyes. Then she took a breath and spoke. "Yes. I haven't seen much of the world, but I can't imagine how it could be much better than this."

"Where else have you traveled?" said Henry, happy to avoid any sentimental platitudes of gratitude.

"South a little ways. North to the mountains. That's about it. Though one day, I would like to go to Maine. I used to read about Maine when I was little. One day I'll go."

They came to the bank of the stream and stopped. Henry saw Bentley grazing and whistled to him. Bentley lifted his head, perked up his ears, and then thundered through the trees towards them.

"For not being your horse, he sure seems to like you," said Grace, watching the beast with admiration as he ran.

Bentley did not slow down at all when he reached the brook, displacing an inordinate amount of the water onto their faces and clothes. Grace squealed, Henry swore, and Eli couldn't help but chuckle.

Bentley nuzzled Henry, and he patted the horse affectionately in return. "Goddamn it, old boy. These were freshly cleaned. Yes, I am quite aware that you don't care. You've made that abundantly clear."

Grace looked at Eli with a look of surprised amusement. Eli continued to chuckle, this time at Grace.

"Would you two mind if I explored the ranch with Bentley for a bit?"

"Not at all," said the Minister, a little too enthusiastically.

"Just make sure you're back at Martha's house by three for dinner," said Grace with a smile. "She hates late-comers when her food is hot."

"Three is an odd time for dinner."

"Not if you're hungry at three," she replied matter-of-factly.

Henry considered this. "I like the way you think."

He jumped on Bentley's back and trotted away from the other two back through what was left of the stream and then eventually back across the pasture.

"What say we find you an orchard, old boy."

He clicked his tongue and tightened his knees as Bentley fell into a dead sprint across the field. There was something incredibly thrilling about riding bareback. It had always been one of his favorite things to do as a child. It had been years since he'd done it, especially in a place as beautiful and as peaceful as this. They rode through the pastures past the herds of various animals.

After a while, they found the orchards. Beautiful, well-groomed trees seemed to stretch on forever in perfectly straight rows. There was every kind of citrus tree. Apples, pears, peaches, and plums, each with several varieties. Olive trees and every kind of nut tree one could get to grow in the area. They found a cherry grove and paused for a moment as Henry plucked a handful of pretty autumn leaves from the branches. Most of the fruit was gone, but here and there they found a late apple for Bentley to munch on

"She would've loved to see a place like this. They both would've."

He let the leaves flutter and fall to the ground.

"Let's see the rest of this place."

Once again, Bentley broke into a run, and Henry tried his best to forget.

Chapter Ten

The Minister watched Henry tear across the pasture on his horse. Interesting what a paradox this man was—fierce, deadly, cruel, yet like a boy on his horse.

Grace turned to him. "What an interesting character your new friend is."

"I'm not sure that he is my friend."

"And that's not his horse, but he still rides it. And you will still have to work with him. I'm surprised you offered him a place here."

"I surprised myself," said the Minister. "If I'm being honest, I don't think he'll end up taking me up on the offer, but it seemed like the right thing to do in the moment."

"And it worked," said Grace, her eyes shining in a way that only hers could.

"It worked," said the Minister with a smile. They turned and started heading back the way they had come. "I must say, though. He worries me. He's a killer."

"He's not the only former Collector on the ranch," Grace countered.

"But he's not a former Collector. He's here on a job. If he actually wants to stay here..."

"Don't get ahead of yourself. A lot still needs to happen before this is over."

"You're right. But you didn't see him in Sacramento. He killed without a thought. Without a word. As easy as tying his boots." The Minister shook his head and frowned.

"Sounds like the sort of person that's needed for the task at hand. Barons aren't easy to kill. Especially Fairchilds," said Grace with a shrug. "And he's not all bad. I can see light in his eyes. And it was the thought of saving this place that made him say yes, not the reward Lipton offered. I think he'll surprise you."

"I hate surprises," said the Minister.

They walked in no particular direction, moving here and there from field to orchard. The weather was perfect, and the Minister knew that it was the last bit of time alone together that they would get for several weeks.

"I'm going to miss you," she said, her tone mournful.

"I'm here now," he said with a gentle smile.

"I'm sorry. I didn't mean to ruin it."

"You could never."

"Maybe when you get back, we could...talk?"

"We're talking now," he said with a smile.

"You know what I mean." She didn't return his smile.

"We'll see," he said, looking out over the landscape.

"Promise me. Whatever you choose, it doesn't matter which, but I can't keep living in the in-between." Her voice tugged at his heart.

"I'm sorry," he said. "You're right. I promise."

They held each other's gaze for a moment, and he wanted to kiss her, but didn't. He wanted a lot of things.

"I suppose I should meet with Lipton's man," Eli said with some reluctance.

"Can't it wait?"

"I suppose. I've been dreading it all morning."

"Then it needs to wait. You should never go into a meeting like that. On edge, I mean."

"I don't see it going well, no matter how relaxed I am."

She looped an arm through his and gave it a squeeze. "Well, at least let me tell you how I've been since you left. You can't pretend like you didn't hog the conversation all morning." He could hear the smile in her words.

"I suppose you're right. It can wait until after dinner."

After several more hours of walking and bantering, the pair decided to head back to Martha's house. It was nearly three.

The Minister did not feel talkative at dinner. Henry seemed completely at ease. He enjoyed the food, which looked and smelled delicious, but the Minister was not able to enjoy it, and his meal sat uncomfortably in his belly.

Once the feast was done, Martha began clearing the table with the help of Harriet and Grace. The Minister knew that now was as good a time as any to go speak to the soldier and excused himself. Much to his chagrin, Henry followed him out onto the porch and began rolling a cigarette.

"Where are you off to?" asked Henry as the Minister began to walk down the stairs.

"I...I need to have a conversation with someone."

"You're nervous about it."

The Minister shot a look at Henry.

"Who are you going to talk to?" Henry asked.

The Minister leaned against the railing and took a breath. "I need to speak to Lipton's soldier who is here at the ranch. I need to lay the ground rules."

"Let me come with," said Henry.

"No," said the Minister.

"I won't open my mouth. I give you my word."

The Minister considered this. "Why would you want to come?"

"I'm useful in negotiations. Your words will carry more weight if I'm standing beside you."

"I don't need help handling my business."

"I never said you did," said Henry, taking a long drag. "There's just something special about this place. If there's something I can do to help keep it the way it is, I'd be remiss to not do it."

"Not a word?"

"Not a word."

"Be ready to roll up your sleeves. Follow me."

They walked to the stables and one of the ranch hands pointed them toward the one that Lipton's man was in. They approached it. The Minister laid his hand on the door and exhaled. The man looked up from stropping his blade as Eli entered. Henry followed two steps behind.

"Evening, Baron," said the soldier as he stood up. He carried himself with the confidence of a man that had never found a fight he couldn't win.

Eli said nothing as he approached and took a seat on a hay bale across from the man. Henry stood just behind and to the left. He fixed his eyes on the soldier.

"Take a seat," said Eli to the soldier, forgoing preamble. "When do the rest of your men arrive?"

The soldier raised an eyebrow but complied and took a seat.

"Lipton sent them on their way three mornings ago. Should be getting here tomorrow late in the evening," the soldier replied, his expression hardening.

"We find ourselves in a precarious situation," said Eli. "I know that you were sent here as a means to ensure that I follow through with Lipton's orders. I can guess at what he's commanded you to do. I can guess at what you're prepared to do." He let the words hang in the air for a moment. The man's expression did not change.

Eli continued, "I imagine your orders were something along the lines of 'no one comes, no one goes, eliminate all if commanded?'" He leaned forward and stared at the soldier.

"Something like that," the soldier said after an uncomfortable silence.

"I'll make sure none of my people attempt to leave. They'll feed you well, but there's something I need from you in return."

The soldier looked hard at Eli, measuring him. "Though I appreciate your...generosity, me and my men are not in need of it."

Eli pulled up his sleeve past his elbow, revealing the tattoo on his forearm. Henry followed suit. "These are not uncommon among my men."

The soldier leaned back, and just for a moment, his mask of a face dropped.

"I know what you're thinking," said Eli. "'Maybe they aren't those kinds of Collectors. Maybe they're just men like me.' And that is a valid question. But a better question is, are you willing to truly find out?"

The soldier looked at his hands for a moment, then returned his gaze to Eli. "I've heard all sorts of stories about Collectors. I don't think I believe most of them. I don't believe in magic, or elves, or the travelers in the trees, or any other bullshit like that. And I certainly don't believe Collectors can hear heartbeats through walls or interfere with signals in the brain." The soldier took a breath and regained his bearings.

"Well trained, yes. Hard to kill, certainly. But no one can move without sound. No one never misses. Not even *those* Collectors."

"Maybe. But you never heard any of those stories first-hand, did you?" Eli asked.

As he spoke, he noticed that Henry began tapping a finger on his leg. It seemed to be in the rhythm of a heartbeat. The soldier did his best to hide the fear in his eyes. *He is, after all, one of those Collectors.*

"As I was saying, I have something to ask of you in return for our cooperation. There were some complications in Sacramento that have led me to believe that Thorpe will be sending men here to the ranch. All I ask, is that by whatever means you find necessary, you keep them away."

The soldier glanced nervously at Henry's tapping finger and then back to Eli and nodded his head. "No one goes, no one comes, not even Thorpe's men. If your people cooperate, I don't see why there will be any problems."

Eli nodded. "Trust me when I say, my people staying safe is in your best interest."

A sheen of sweat appeared on the soldier's forehead, but he maintained his bearings, and Henry's tapping sped up ever so slightly.

"You will be fed well," continued Eli. "I'll have my people convert this barn into a bunkhouse. You will be given rations of beer, not liquor. You will also be given rations of tobacco. And you will be granted reading privileges if you want them. We have a phenomenal library, though the library keepers will observe you while you are there. With any luck, Thorpe won't send anyone, and this will simply be several weeks of good food and easy duty for you and your men."

"That's very generous of you," said the soldier.

Henry's tapping slowed and steadied.

"How many men will you be? I'd like to have bunks set up before they arrive," said Eli.

"Fifty."

"Are all your men soldiers, or are some just common thugs?"

"Soldiers." There was an air of pride in his tone at that.

"What's your name, soldier?"

"Dom."

Eli was still for a moment. "Dom, if any of your men give trouble to the people here, you will be held personally responsible. Do I make myself clear?"

Dom hesitated before he spoke. "Sir, the men, they can sometimes be unruly."

Henry's tapping sped up again.

Dom shot another nervous glance at Henry.

"There's no such thing as unruly soldiers, Dom," said Eli, "only poorly led ones. I will make sure my men know the consequences of your faulty leadership if any of them decide to go rogue. Make sure you do the same."

"Yes, sir."

"Do we have an understanding, Dom?"

"Yes, sir."

Eli stood to leave but turned as he reached the door.

"You're on my land, Dom. The nature of our next interaction is entirely in your hands."

Dom nodded and was almost able to hide the fear in his eyes.

Eli led Henry back out into the breeze. He took a breath and exhaled deeply as he pulled his sleeve back over his forearm. "Mirroring the heartbeat was a nice touch."

Henry nodded and pulled his sleeves down over his wrists.

The sun was going to set soon. It cast golden light and

long shadows across the landscape, and the Minister felt a preemptive pang of homesickness as he and Henry walked back to the house.

The two men stood on the porch of Martha's house for a moment before they entered. Voices could be heard inside. They sounded cheerfully unburdened, and the Minister's homesickness only grew worse.

"I don't think you have anything to worry about with that soldier," said Henry.

"I hope you're right."

Henry looked out over the ranch and nodded. "I know there will be conditions for me staying here, if I do decide to when this is all said and done. I'm not sure that I will. But there is something about this place. Something I can't quite put my finger on. I can see why you love it so much."

"There's nothing I wouldn't do to protect this place and the people here."

"Nothing?" asked Henry.

"Nothing," said Eli.

"It'll be dark soon."

"Yes." The Minister sighed. "Let's say our goodbyes. We've got a lot of ground to cover."

They entered the house and found Grace, Harriet, and Martha chatting in the living room. They did not sit down.

"How did it go?" asked Martha.

"As well as it could have, thanks to Henry," said the Minister. He quickly relayed his instructions to Martha. She nodded, taking a mental inventory of everything he said and afterwards assuring him that she would have no trouble keeping fifty boys in check. "I have quite a little experience with such things." She had a rosy confidence.

"Thank you, Martha. I don't know what I would do without you."

Martha hugged the Minister tightly and patted his back.

"Is it that time?" Grace asked, doing her best to conceal the sadness in her eyes.

"Unfortunately," replied the Minister. "I should be back in a couple weeks or so."

"What about you, Henry?" Grace asked as she stood up. "Will you be back in a couple weeks or so?"

"Only time will tell," Henry said.

Jack entered the room, sleeves pulled to his wrists. "I've readied the horses."

"Thank you, Jack," said the Minister. "Henry, shall we?"

"If you insist," said Henry. "Martha, Grace, Harriet." He looked at each individually as he addressed them. "This has been one of the finest days I've known in years. Thank you."

"Oh, come here," said Martha as she pulled him in for a hug, whether he liked it or not.

Grace smiled at him as she leaned against the Minister.

The breeze was picking up, shuffling the first of the fallen leaves across the ground.

Outside, Henry patted Bentley on the neck. "Hey, old boy. How's your day been? Just as good as mine? Better? Well, I think you're lying, you old bastard. But I won't hold it against you."

"Are you ready?" asked the Minister.

"I guess so," said Henry, swinging himself in the saddle.

The Minister mounted his horse, a proud, black beast no less than sixteen hands tall. "Well, off we go then."

A moment later, the Minister clicked his tongue, and Henry gave Bentley an easy kick in the flank. They began trotting down the lane away from Martha's house. It was nearly dark now. Light burned orange and golden on the horizon, finding new lives to cast its warmth on. Henry had always loved sunsets.

"Beautiful," Henry said.

"Indeed."

"It's a nice thing you've built here. These are good people."

"They are."

The night creatures were out and vocal. The two men rode past orchards and vineyards of other small barons, their branches casting long shadows across the road. The Minister felt an onset of drowsiness overtaking his thoughts. Henry drew Bentley close and handed him a small pile of coffee beans from his saddlebags. He nodded gratefully and they crunched on them without speaking. As the sun cast its last hues of light across the landscape, the Minister looked back in the direction of the ranch. He said a quiet prayer. Then Eli repositioned himself in the saddle and readied himself for what was to come.

Chapter Eleven

E li drifted easy into consciousness. He laid there with his eyes closed for a moment. He couldn't remember his dream, but he remembered how it made him feel. Safe, excited, content. If only he could just fall back asleep, but he knew he had rested long enough. It was time to open his eyes.

Henry and both horses were gone.

Eli sat up and stared around in disbelief. "Surely not."

He stood up and ran a hand through his hair. "He wouldn't have."

He checked his pockets. Everything was still there, as was the canteen next to him where he'd set it down before he fell asleep. He searched the ground around him for tracks.

They had made their camp in a small clearing of very thick manzanita, making it impossible to see very far in any direction. Spotting some faint tracks, he quickly began following them. They became clearer after a few yards, and he began to run in hopes he might catch a glimpse of them cresting a ridge.

"I should have tied myself to his horse," he said out loud to himself.

"He's not my horse."

Eli nearly jumped out of his skin at the sound of the voice coming from the left of him.

"How did you get over there?" he asked as Henry emerged from the thicket.

Henry's expression was quizzical. "What do you mean? I walked."

"But your tracks led that way," said Eli, pointing.

"Leave the tracking to me, Eli," said Henry, patting Eli on the shoulder.

"What were you doing wandering off with both horses?"

"Both horses looked thirsty."

"Oh. I thought..."

"You thought what?"

"Nothing. It's unimportant."

"You thought I was running away, didn't you?" A smile broke across his face.

"No! I mean...maybe."

"You had a rough relationship with your father, didn't you?" said Henry with a sparkle in his eye.

"Fuck off."

"Oh! The Priest swears!" exclaimed Henry with glee.

The Minister shook his head and headed back to camp with the reins of his gelding in hand. "He's not one for laughter, is he, old boy?" he heard Henry say, chuckling to himself.

"That man has issues," Eli said to his horse, and then realized what he had done.

He reached their little camp a few minutes before Henry, who was apparently taking his time about things. He pulled a biscuit out of his saddle bag, along with a thick leather-bound journal, and sat down with his back to a rock. The journal fell open to a very old entry, and his eyes fogged up as they met the page.

> *Sunday morning, 10 am, he is dead. Nothing here remains. This old house may still be in perfect form, but it's only the remnants of a home. Only a shadow of what it was. Its heart died this morning, as did mine. I always wanted to leave here and never look back. Now I feel I have no choice but to do so. Tomorrow, I ride for Seattle.*

He closed the journal and placed it back in his saddle bag. *I don't know why I carry that old thing around.* Henry came clambering up the bank sopping wet, grinning, Bentley trailing a few paces behind.

"There's a fantastic little stream just over there," he said. "Apple?" He took a bite out of one and tossed another to the Minister without waiting for a response. Nodding to Henry, Eli took a bite.

"It would be safer to stay off the roads till dusk," Eli said.

"You might be right, but if the rat's on the move, we need to cover twice the ground. And we can't do that if we travel only by night."

"If we ran into any Fairchild thugs, there's a good chance they would try to stop us," cautioned Eli.

"Why would they harass two lone travelers?"

"The Fairchilds control the territory by controlling the roads. Merchant caravans or traveling barons almost always hire a Fairchild escort. Sometimes traveling without one isn't an issue, but usually...well, usually its best to either have a Fairchild escort, or avoid being seen."

"I don't understand you western folks. Back east, our

criminals are criminals, barons are barons, and soldiers are soldiers. The distinction seems so blurred here. Everything seems blurred out here. But blurred or not, we have ground to cover."

"Lipton's East Coast, and he seems just as blurred as the Fairchilds," said Eli, taking another bite from his apple.

"I suppose you're right on that account. Even so, we have a lot of ground to cover."

"Unless you plan on killing half a dozen soldiers today, we're going to have to wait till this evening to start moving."

"Half a dozen?" said Henry, tilting his head to one side. "Is that all? What say you, Bentley? Want to open some veins today?"

Eli looked at the horse and half expected it to say something back.

Henry said, "He says he wouldn't mind doing some violence today. Does your god have any objections?"

"He lets men make their own choices."

"Perfect." Henry took another bite out of the apple. "I'm choosing to make some progress."

"You aren't overly cautious, are you?"

"I kill people for money."

"Sure. I'd just like to not die in the process."

"Please," scoffed Henry. "You can handle yourself despite the persona you wear. And don't be deceived by my charm and good looks. I'm handy when I need to be."

"If we ride openly through the country, it is nothing but a matter of time until we're confronted by some of the Fairchilds' soldiers. I understand that you have an Ask to carry out, but I'd like to have minimal collateral damage along the way. I'm not keen on the unnecessary spilling of blood." Eli spoke with conviction, standing up and punctuating his close by throwing his half-eaten apple into the brush.

"Keen?" spat Henry. His eyes flashed with anger and his body seemed to swell as he spoke. "For a man so focused on survival, you seem pretty keen on wasting rations."

Suddenly, Eli was afraid. The man standing before him was not the same as the one who had given him an apple a few moments before.

"Let's take a breath," said Eli.

"Who goes there?" The third voice ripped through the air from the direction of the road. The Minister turned about, and a moment later a pair of men emerged from behind a barrier of manzanita. The two men bore the insignia of the Fairchild family on their coats.

"Who are you talking to, Father?" asked one of the men.

The Minister, confused, looked around, but Henry had seemingly vanished into the brush. He then replied, "I was... praying."

The man's brow furrowed. "Where are you going?"

"North," said Eli. "My parish in Seattle summoned me. And you?"

"South," said the soldier. "Thorpe summoned us."

"Thorpe," said Eli. "I know the name. Doesn't he have his own men?"

"There's been some trouble. He needs a little backup."

"How many are you?" Eli asked. As soon as the words left his mouth, he knew he had made a blunder. It was something in his tone. Something in his body language.

The soldier tilted his head, then looked at his companion. "Come to think of it," said the soldier as his hand drifted to his sidearm, "Thorpe mentioned that he was having trouble with a priest." He whipped out his pistol and belted Eli across the face with it, sending him staggering backwards.

"I don't know what you're talking about," said Eli, raising his hands in an attempt to stall them.

"Why do you have two horses?" asked the second soldier, cocking back the hammer of his pistol and training it at Eli.

"That one there, it's not mine."

Eli caught sight of Henry as he emerged noiselessly from the brush behind the men. He brandished a large Bowie knife.

"Then whose is it?" snarled the soldier.

Henry was moving quickly towards them. He was almost close enough.

"To be honest..." Eli said slowly as his hand drifted to the handle of his whip.

Henry's knife caught the sunlight and plunged into the side of one soldier's neck, slashing forward, nearly severing his head. The other soldier turned, but before he could fire, Henry hacked his hand clean off, slashed his throat, and plunged the heavy blade into the man's heart.

"...I don't know," finished Eli.

Henry stood over the bodies for a moment as he regulated his breathing. The Minister stood perfectly still, almost hoping that Henry didn't see him.

Henry cleaned the blade on a dry part of one of the soldier's uniforms before returning it to its sheath. Then he swung himself into Bentley's saddle and looked back to his companion. "There are ten more of them on the road. We need to get out of here quick and quiet."

"They're headed to the ranch. We need to stop them," said Eli fervently as he pulled himself into his saddle.

"No, we need to get the fuck out of here right now. Dom can handle them at the ranch."

"But—"

"Ten men, Eli," said Henry. "Ten men in broad daylight. Follow me, or stay and die. It's up to you, but I'm going to Chico."

Henry urged Bentley through the brush before Eli could

respond. He knew Henry was right, but the thought of ten soldiers headed towards the ranch, towards Grace, was almost enough to make him break his vow. He could hear the other soldiers calling to their now-dead companions. Henry was out of sight through the brush now. Eli released his grip on the handle of the whip and heeled his horse in Henry's direction, trying to make as little sound as possible. After a moment, he heard shouts in the distance behind him, then rifle fire began tearing through the brush. He was quite sure they couldn't see him, but even so, some of the rounds rattled by too close.

He couldn't see Bentley or Henry anywhere. The brush was almost too thick to navigate, catching his clothes and skin, making him bleed. The bullets stopped, and after a few more minutes, he could no longer hear the soldiers, but his heart was still pounding out of his chest. Eventually, the only clear way through led him back to the road. Off in the distance, he could make out Bentley galloping away from him. He put heels to hide, and his gelding slipped into a gallop, running like the wind.

He thanked God that the soldiers hadn't seen him re-enter the road and prayed that they wouldn't pursue.

Eventually, Bentley slowed enough for him to catch up. They slowed to a trot as Eli pulled up beside. He clenched his jaw and tried to let his heart rate subside.

"Next time I save your life, do as I say immediately," said Henry.

Eli said nothing.

"You don't have to thank me," said Henry looking straight ahead, "but when I say we need to run? You better fucking believe me. Us dying in the street won't help keep the ranch safe."

Eli nodded. "You're right. Thank you. I'll keep my head on a swivel."

Henry didn't look over, still emanating displeasure. "I am but the sea."

They saw very few people the rest of the day, although they did pass a few more patrols and several farmers, none of whom gave them a second look, a fact that Henry went to great lengths to point out. Eli was genuinely surprised that none of the patrols had stopped them. This was unusual. Henry's mood improved with each patrol they passed without incident, and by the time the sun stooped low in the sky, he seemed as carefree as ever.

"I'm sorry I threw away the apple you gave me. That was kind of you. I shouldn't have done that." Eli spoke the words earnestly.

"It was only an apple," said Henry too quickly.

"It was a gift."

Henry looked at him somewhat surprised, but he smiled slightly and shrugged. "Think nothing of it."

They rode on for a little while in a pleasant sort of silence. Eventually Eli spoke up. "What made you choose this life, Henry?"

"Oh...well." Henry seemed almost uncomfortable, awkward even for a moment, unsure what to say. "Circumstances," he said shortly.

"Come now," said Eli. "You've seen my home. My friends. My life. All I know about you is that you kill. If you want me to trust you at all, you're going to have to give me something."

Henry didn't respond at first, and Eli did not press further. After a few minutes of silence, Henry sighed. In the last embers of light the sun would cast that day, Eli watched as Henry's face was overtaken first by conflict, then anguish, then smoldering determination.

"My mother left this world in the act of bringing me into it, so my father raised me. We lived in the great countryside of

Ireland. Those were good days. Just my father and me. We weren't rich, but I never knew lack."

"How did you end up on this continent?"

"On a boat," said Henry. "I'm too hungry for sad stories."

"I'm getting a little hungry myself. We can stop any time now. With the progress we've made today, we'll reach Chico tomorrow afternoon."

"I won't argue with you," said Henry.

They came upon an orchard near a stream and decided to stop there for the night. It was easy enough to find dry fall along the bank for a fire, and they ate hot food for the first time that day.

Eli knew Henry was hesitant to tell him about his life, but if he was being honest, it was a beautiful evening, and he felt like hearing a story, and there was one card he could play that might get Henry to open up a bit. He reached into his saddle bag and pulled out a pint bottle.

"Care for a drink?" he asked, uncorking it and holding it out to Henry.

Henry accepted the bottle and took a sniff. "I must admit, I didn't expect you to have whiskey on you."

"Irish monks invented whiskey," said Eli, "and distilling is a highly valued skill. Some of the best spirit makers in the West learned at the ranch."

Henry took a sip and smiled, then took another before handing the bottle back to Eli.

They drank a few swigs each and watched the flames slowly die before Eli spoke up.

"How old were you when you came to America?"

Henry took another sip of whiskey and gazed into the flames for a long moment.

"There are better stories for a fire than mine."

"I'll let you have the better part of the whiskey," Eli offered.

"The best part is always the first sip." Henry grinned and winked as he lit a cigarette with matchwood from the fire.

Eli leaned back and took a small sip of whiskey before tossing the bottle to Henry, who caught it one-handed. Bentley snorted.

"If he's not your horse, then whose is he?" asked Eli, admiring the beast.

Henry did not respond at first. Then he took a swill, what looked to be the better part of the bottle before tossing it back to the Minister, who caught it one-handed.

"My daughter's."

"You have a family?"

Another pause, "Once," said Henry.

"Once," Repeated Eli to himself. He felt sad, and suddenly very tired.

They unrolled their blankets and lay down after banking the coals. The night was growing cold, and Eli was exhausted after a day of riding. The whiskey sat warm in his belly, and he knew the sun would come all too soon.

Once.

The Minister began to think less of the two corpses miles behind them and more about the man that had put them there.

Chapter Twelve

H enry woke with a start the next morning, just like every morning. They had made it to the small farms around the outskirts of Chico the night before. He got up and strode through the orchard where they had slept. It was the end of apple season, and the smell of the fruit and the branches filled the brisk morning air. Henry plucked an apple from a tree as he passed and took a few bites. He handed the rest to Bentley, who followed a few paces behind.

"Nothing like fresh apples in the fall, eh boy?"

Bentley munched happily.

They walked up and down the perfectly straight and organized rows of trees.

"Yes, I suppose you're right," said Henry as he rested his hand on Bentley's shoulder. "It is about time to head back."

Eli was awake and rolling up his blanket when they reached him.

Henry plopped down with his back to a tree and rolled a cigarette. "What was the name of that hotel you said Lipton mentioned?"

Eli sat back on his heels and took in a breath of the sweet, leafy air. "The Hotel Madison. His contact there should be able to instruct us once we arrive. I'd say about two hours once we get back on the road."

"Care for a smoke?" asked Henry.

"I don't smoke cigarettes," Eli said with a mild look of disgust. "We're going to need to be cautious when we get there. Do our best to keep a low profile. If word gets out of our task, the Fairchilds won't hesitate to start shooting people in the streets if it means eliminating a threat."

"If you say so. One thing's for certain. I could do with a hot meal and a cold beer."

"Agreed."

Henry nodded. "First order of business will be finding the Hotel Madison, though."

Eli nodded.

They finished packing up their camp and headed back to the main road. The ride passed with ease, and soon they were entering the city. Chico was drastically different than Sacramento. The latter produced copious amounts of opiates and other smokable items, while the former consumed them. Chico had come to be a place sought out by artists, brawlers, and those who wanted to discover what it was to live.

They rode slowly down the center of the streets. Everywhere there were people laughing, drinking, and smoking. There were beautiful women, wealthy men, and every convenience that Henry could imagine. Trees grew thick in parks and beautiful front lawns. The breeze gently carried the scent of food and drink through the streets, mixing with the dry, fresh smell of autumn leaves.

"It's not even lunchtime, yet these people are already drunk. Don't they have jobs?" asked Henry.

"People don't come to Chico to work. The bars never

close, and the streets are never empty. People come here to bathe in all the impulses of humanity."

"There's so much food here," Henry said, amazed at the amount and variety of restaurants everywhere.

"Chico has an ice factory. It's steam powered. It works much the same as the ones from antiquity. It's amazing what you can do with a bit of ice and a lot of money," explained Eli.

"How have I never been here before?" asked Henry rhetorically. "It's perfect."

"You and I have very different tastes," said Eli. "The hotel should be this way, if I remember correctly."

They made their way through the full but not crowded streets. Henry noticed a young man sitting at a table with three attractive, empty-looking girls standing behind him. One handed him a cigarette, another lit it for him, and the third caught Henry's eye for just a moment before looking away. The man never even looked at the women or thanked them or offered them a seat. Henry thought he'd like to teach that snobby bastard a lesson in manners, but he was soon distracted by a group of lads stumbling down the street. They had their arms over each other's shoulders, singing a shanty of some sort. It brought a smile to his face. He leaned forward and mused quietly to Bentley.

"It's incredible, old boy. So many people in the same space, yet each one doing something so different. Some are just waking up, others just going to sleep. Twenty people in the same cafe, each eating a different meal. Some drinking coffee, others whiskey, others tea. What an interesting cacophony of different lives, dreams, desires, and intentions. Look at all the emotions. They are just noise to the individuals, they all mean nothing to each other, but as a whole, they make each other possible. Isn't it beautiful?"

Bentley huffed and jerked his head a bit.

"Yes, I know I can be long-winded."

"It's just here." Eli turned his horse down a side street, at the end of which stood a huge brick building. The front yard was elaborately planned. Each tree had a purpose, each stone deliberate, each blade of grass disciplined and in place.

"Good God, it's gorgeous," said Henry with an enamored smile.

"Truly," said Eli. "There will be a valet to stable our horses. If the Fairchilds are still here, I recommend getting a feel of this place before moving on them. It would be a shame to have to leave without Bentley."

"I'm not leaving without Bentley," said Henry resolutely.

"Oh, and Henry," said Eli, dismounting.

"Yes?"

"I imagine Lipton told you about the tattoo on the back of the Ask's neck."

"Sure."

"Well, I'm going to need that."

"What?" asked Henry in surprise as he slid to the ground.

"I need to take that tattoo to the Vault," explained Eli.

"Why are you telling me this?" inquired Henry in a blank tone.

"So, you don't shoot him in the throat. The skin on the back of the neck must stay intact."

Henry raised an eyebrow. "And you accuse *me* of being fucked up."

"Do you understand?" asked Eli.

"And he thinks *we're* fucked up," Henry repeated to Bentley.

"Henry, do you understand?" pressed Eli. This time his voice was tight, and he had a serious look about him.

"Yes, of course. Square between the eyes," said Henry in a cool tone.

The valet emerged from a small gatehouse as they approached.

"Good day, sirs. Do you have rooms reserved?"

"No, but spare no expense on the care of our horses," replied Eli quickly and deliberately.

"Yes, sir. Just follow the path to the front door. Your saddlebags will be delivered to your rooms."

The valet quickly led the horses around to another gate, and Henry almost followed them but took a breath and trusted that Bentley would not be stolen. So, he turned and followed half a pace behind Eli as he approached the front door. Henry noticed that Eli's shoulders were tense and his back stiff. He guessed that talking details of their mission had brought up some unpleasant emotions. *I think there may be a beast beneath that gold cross.*

"I'll talk when we get inside, Minister. You just do your best to keep looking uncomfortable and superior. I'll be my naturally suave self."

Eli rolled his eyes but did not protest. A few leaves crunched under Henry's boots as they made their way up the path. The heavy wooden doors clicked, then were slowly pulled open by doormen in formal black and white valet uniforms. The doors were solid oak, but there were tall, thin windows at either side of the frames that the doormen must have been watching through.

Henry and Eli stepped into a massive, lavishly furnished foyer. A concierge stood behind a counter immediately to their right. Two staircases led up the left and right sides of the room. Between the stairs was a large open breezeway leading to the back.

Both men's eyes swept the room and took in everything at once. All the male staff were dressed like the doormen, and all the female staff wore slim black gowns. All the guests wore

whatever they thought would best portray their wealth
without overtly indicating they needed people to know they
were rich. Music played quietly from various synchronized
record players.

The girl behind the counter smiled at Henry. "Reserva-
tion?" She had long dark hair, big eyes, and what Henry
thought of as incredibly kissable lips.

"Afraid not, love. Any vacancies?" he inquired good-
naturedly.

"Of course. Shall I put you down for two separate rooms,
or one master suite?"

"Two rooms should do just fine."

Henry paid upfront and left a generous tip. He winked at
the concierge as he paid. She smiled mischievously as she
slipped two numbered keys across the counter.

"I'll have some fresh clothes sent up to you. We, of course,
have a full menu and bar here at the Madison, but I'll gladly
give you recommendations for other establishments about the
town. Just let me know if there is anything else you need." She
smiled again at Henry as she spoke.

"I most certainly will," said Henry with a smile of
his own.

"Just up the stairs and to the left, sir," spoke one of the
doormen as the pair left the counter.

"This way, Minister," said Henry as he directed a stone-
faced Eli towards the stairs.

Henry admired the paintings hanging in the second-
story corridor. The red carpet made him feel more important than he knew he was. Their suites, numbers six and
eight, were near the end of the hall. He unlocked and
pushed open the heavy wooden door. The room was
exquisite without being lavish. Two leather wingback chairs
stood in front of the small fireplace. There was a large bed

against the wall, a door leading to a small bathroom, and French doors that opened out to a balcony that was scarcely more than just a place to stand. He stepped out onto the balcony, and a moment later, Eli stepped out onto the adjacent balcony.

"Not too bad, eh, Eli?" said Henry enthusiastically as he looked around, taking it all in.

"Should work," said the Minister, casually impressed. "Why didn't you ask about the Fairchilds?"

"They're already gone," said Henry, "I didn't see a single soldier anywhere."

"What if they were dressed in civilian clothing?"

"You tell a soldier by how he carries himself and what he's drinking, not what he's wearing. Tonight, the mission is twofold. One, find Lipton's man. And two, get drunk."

"Preferably in that order?" Eli queried.

"Absolutely not. My best Collecting work is nearly always done five drinks in."

"Normally, I would try to argue, but I actually believe you, and..." Eli's voice dropped off.

"And?"

"And I'm thirsty," conceded Eli.

"Finally. Signs of life."

Henry took a bath and was about to lay down to take a nap when a knocking came at his door. He opened it, and Eli brushed passed him, breathless. He walked straight over to the side table and poured himself a glass of water, chugging it quickly.

"Come on in," said Henry.

"Another group of soldiers is headed to the ranch. Apparently, the Fairchilds approved action against me. We need to do something." Eli had a frantic look in his eyes, and beads of sweat were breaking out across his forehead.

"But I was going to take a nap," said Henry in genuine remorse.

"This isn't the time for your pointless jokes," spewed Eli. "Fifteen more men are headed to the ranch. That's on top of the ten we passed yesterday."

"Why wouldn't they all travel together?" asked Henry.

Eli clenched his jaw and took a breath. "The Fairchild army is dispersed throughout their territory. They operate in cells. Sometimes they're in big groups and they all travel together, sometimes they are not." He enunciated every word. "Get dressed."

Henry reluctantly complied, and a few minutes later he met Eli in the lobby. "They're staying at a small inn a few blocks away, the Latch. Based on what the innkeeper said, they'll be leaving in the morning," said Eli, stepping out into the front lawn of the Madison.

"Hold up a minute, Eli."

Eli stopped and faced Henry with a look of impatient questioning.

"Are you expecting me to barge in there and start shooting? What's the plan here?"

Eli ran his hands through his hair. "I don't know. We need to find a way to keep those men from reaching the ranch. We could steal their horses."

Henry shook his head. "They'd be able to find new mounts, and I have no idea what I would do with fifteen horses."

"We could bar the doors and burn the inn down," said Eli.

"That could be catastrophic. And I'd hate to do that to the innkeeper. Do you have any poison?" asked Henry, disgusted with himself for even thinking it.

"Nothing lethal," said Eli, shaking his head.

"What *do* you have? And do you have it on you?"

"I have a heavy paralytic in my room," said Eli apprehensively.

"I have an idea. Go get it. I need to fetch something out of my saddlebags. Then you stay here. I'll be less conspicuous by myself."

"What are you going to do?" asked Eli.

"I'm going to do you a favor and take care of this problem for you instead of focusing on the task at hand. And you are going to buy me as many drinks as I can hold when I'm done and not ask me anymore pointless, fucking questions," Henry said.

In his room, Henry took out of the pouch of diamonds he'd carried in his saddlebags since New York and emptied about half of them into a handkerchief, hesitated, put half again back into the pouch with the others, and then tied up the handkerchief. He sighed regretfully, remembering what he had gone through to earn them, but told himself that it was the right thing to do. In the hallway, Eli handed him four vials of clear liquid and asked again what Henry's plan was.

"What did I say about questions?" said Henry, which silenced Eli, and then he made his way out to the street.

So much for a nice nap.

It didn't take him long to find the Latch. It was a stand-alone, wooden structure, and Henry thanked his luck. He peered in through the windows and saw the soldiers carousing inside. There didn't appear to be any civilian patrons, and then he walked around to the back of the building. There was a door leading into the kitchen which Henry entered.

The innkeeper tried to wave him away. "We're all full until tomorrow, and this is not an entrance," he said in a non-friendly tone.

"Are you the owner?" asked Henry.

"Yes, now kindly get out of my kitchen."

Henry looked around the room. There was a large barrel of lard, one barrel marked "brown high proof" and one marked "clear high proof." *That will do.*

"I've got a proposition for you, innkeeper," said Henry, pulling the handkerchief of diamonds out of his pocket and untying it. He placed it on the counter and watched the innkeeper gawk at it for a moment.

"This would be your payment. Are you interested?"

The innkeeper chewed his mustache and stared first at the diamonds, then Henry. "I'm not going to kill anyone for you, and my daughter is not for sale, so if that's what you want, then you can get out right now."

"Oh, I don't need anything so nefarious from you," said Henry, tying up the handkerchief again. "All I need you to do, is serve a round of shots to those soldiers out there, then leave and forget you ever saw me."

"What are you going to do?" asked the innkeeper, barely taking his eyes off the handkerchief.

"I'm going to give you a life-changing amount of money and disappear. Just do as I ask."

"And what if I say no?" asked the innkeeper.

"I hope for your daughter's sake that you don't," said Henry, looking unflinching into the man's eyes.

"Oh," said the innkeeper. "Then I'll do it."

"Good choice," said Henry, picking up a mostly full bottle of whiskey. He found a large stack of clean shot glasses and laid fifteen out on two trays. He poured the vials of poison into the whiskey bottle and shook it up, and then he split the contents equally between all the glasses.

"Are there any exits other than the front and back doors?" he asked the innkeeper.

"No. Just those two," said the innkeeper, starting to realize Henry's plan.

"Serve these to the men out there. Make sure they all drink it down. Then come back to me."

Henry sat on a stool and waited. A moment later, the front room erupted in loud cheers and applause, and then the innkeeper returned, trays empty.

"It's done. Now what?" the now-sweating innkeeper said.

"Go around front and bar the door as firmly as you can, then leave the means for me to bar this back door. Then go away for a day or two. There's no one else here aside from the soldiers?"

"No, my wife and daughter are away with her sister for the week. It's a nightmare running this place without them," said the innkeeper.

"Good." Henry held up the handkerchief. "Go bar the front door, and then you'll get this."

The man nodded and left, returning a few minutes later, during which time, the sounds of merriment in the dining room started to grow quieter. "I just need to grab a few things from upstairs," said the innkeeper.

"No," commanded Henry. "If you don't lose everything in the fire, it will look suspicious. You'll already be under scrutiny by having the means to rebuild so quickly." He tossed the handkerchief to the man.

The innkeeper nodded and walked to the back door. He paused in the doorframe and looked back at his kitchen. "This is not the way I thought today was going to go."

"Yeah," said Henry, "I was supposed to be taking a nap right now."

"Hmm," said the innkeeper contemplatively. And then he left without another word.

After another twenty minutes of waiting, the dining room was completely silent. Henry got to work. He maneuvered the barrel of lard out to the dining room filled with paralyzed soldiers and upset it, spilling the slick contents across the floor. Then he did the same with the other two barrels of high-proof spirits. He shoveled a bucket of red-hot coals from the oven and carried it into the dining room. The fumes were enough to choke him, and he hoped he would have enough time to get out before the whole place was engulfed. He tried not to look at the sedated soldiers, and he couldn't help but feel like a coward for using poison. He tossed the coals in a glowing arch through the room, and the majority of them landed in a pile of lard. First there was nothing. Then in an instant, a liquid blue flame alight around the coals, and with a breathtaking whoosh, the whole place seemed to ignite at once.

Henry ran through the kitchen stamping the flames off his boots as he exited, slamming the door behind him. He barred it with a heavy cut board placed there by the innkeeper, and then he sauntered around to the street, walking quickly away. A moment later, the windows shattered and smoke billowed from the building, the flames flicking and reaching high into the sky. Some people screamed, others cheered, and a few sober ones started running, calling "Fire! Fire!" but there was nothing they could do to stop the blaze, only keep it from spreading to other buildings.

As Henry walked away, he noticed the young man he had seen earlier with the girls. This time, the man was looking at him, and he smiled a wicked, knowing smile.

Henry's stomach turned, and he hoped with every fiber of his being that he hadn't been made.

Chapter Thirteen

By the time Henry made it back to the Madison, he was grimy with smoke, grease, and sweat, undoing all the good work of his bath earlier. He had just decided to take another one when a knock came at his door. He opened it to see Eli waiting in the hall.

"Come in," said Henry, stepping aside.

"How did it go?" asked Eli, pacing into the room.

"As well as it could have. Though I'm not used to losing money when I do a job."

He quickly summed up the events to Eli, who sat back in a chair, looking deeply conflicted yet utterly relieved.

"They were all in there?" Eli asked.

"I probably should have counted," said Henry. "I'm sure they were all there."

"Well, that's not entirely comforting. And no one saw you?"

Henry thought of the young man with the girls. "No. I got out free and clear."

Eli nodded. "I do wish there had been a less violent way, but..."

"Oh, fuck off," interjected Henry.

"But..." continued Eli, "I recognize the circumstance. Thank you."

"Thank me at the bar. Now if you don't mind," said Henry as he stood and opened the door.

"Right," said Eli, taking his leave.

Once Henry had gotten cleaned up and changed into fresh clothes, he knocked on Eli's door and the pair walked down the stairs to the lively mob and music below. What Henry thought was just a lounge turned out to be a full-fledged casino. There was a very large indoor area with game tables, bars, places to sit, and places to eat. The room opened up to an even larger courtyard that they had observed from above, with a floor for dancing and a stage for the talented, albeit chaotic, band that occupied it. The whole place was full of people sitting on the patio that surrounded the courtyard, dancing, eating, drinking, smoking, and, most refreshingly, laughing. The pair approached one of several bars and leaned on the counter.

"What can I get for you?" the barman asked from beneath his illustrious mustache.

"Two shots of gin," said Henry.

"And two beers. Your hoppiest," added Eli. "It's been a while since I've had gin," he added to Henry as they waited for their drinks.

Henry thought about responding, but he was annoyed and tired, and he felt that Eli was to blame, so instead he rolled a cigarette.

The bartender returned with two shots and two beers.

Eli picked up his shot glass and looked at it like a chemist examining a new and potentially dangerous compound. "What are we drinking to?" he asked after a moment and a resigned sigh.

"The next one," said Henry in a flat tone.

The shot glasses clinked, tapped the counter, and were thrown back. Henry signaled the barman for two more.

They stood and sipped their beer for a few minutes, taking everything in. At the tables, some people were losing, others were winning, and none of them seemed to care too much either way. A bad run wasn't going to stop them from laughing and shouting. A good run wouldn't keep them from turning to the bottle. Outside, some laughed and danced. Others sat alone and played the part of spectator.

Henry noticed one young couple at the far side of the dance floor moving together slower than the music beckoned. He felt Eli staring, but for the moment, he just didn't care. The young woman was beautiful, but it was not just her physical appearance that reminded him of someone else. It was the look on her face. Her slight smile was so subtle that if you didn't know the look, you might think that she was looking right through you. In a way, she was—at least, that's what everyone else saw. She didn't see the face and body in front of her; she saw the man they belonged to. Rarely looked upon, even more rarely seen. She not only saw it, she loved it. Not in ignorance of its flaws—in spite of them.

"She's taken."

Eli's words kicked Henry's thoughts from his mind. It took him a moment to respond.

"Sorry, yes, I know. She...she reminded me of someone," said Henry, dismissing the deep memories and returning to the present moment.

Eli looked thoughtful for a moment, and he handed Henry another shot of gin.

"What say we do our best to make tonight worth being reminded of. I'd say you earned it," said Eli, holding his glass up.

"Worth a try, I suppose," responded Henry, raising his own glass.

"Blackjack?" suggested Eli.

"Blackjack."

The glasses clinked together, tapped the bar, and were thrown back.

They made their way to a table and started playing. They were both up after a few hands.

"I can see it's not your first time at the tables, eh, boys?"

Henry looked over at the young man who had addressed him, and his heart dropped. It was the young man he had already seen twice that day, the one with his three girls. He took a seat, his women standing behind him, posing with blank expressions.

"Nope," he responded shortly.

The young man extended a hand. "The name's Kyle. Kyle Crenshaw."

"Good to know," replied Henry as he placed his bet.

Some of the other gentlemen at the table chuckled. The young man seemed flustered but said nothing for a few hands. He started winning. Eli was chatting quietly with the gentleman on his left about different aging and distilling methods for whiskey and brandy.

"You're new to Chico, aren't you?" the young man continued to press Henry.

"What was your name again?"

"Kyle."

"Kyle. Is there something you would like to talk to me about, or do you just have an inability to recognize when you are yammering mindlessly to people too sober to find you interesting?"

The anger boiled into Kyle's face, but he quickly brushed it away and nodded to one of the girls. She leaned over, and he whispered something in her ear. She set her eyes on Henry as she listened. Then she moved like silk in the wind, and Henry found her pressed ever so gently against him as she whispered in his ear, "He says he saw you. There have been rumors, and you should mind your manners if you want to live."

A chill ran down Henry's spine. It wasn't just her hot breath in his ear, or the smell of her hair brushing against his cheek, or the view that her leaning in had afforded him. It set off the primeval alarm deep within him. It made him want to mount up and move out of town straight away.

She moved away from him as gracefully as she had approached and resumed her demure posture of absolute indifference with her companions. Henry looked at her, but Kyle snapped his fingers, drawing his attention back.

"It's me you're talking to, not her."

"What do you want?" asked Henry.

"Entertainment! Money! Cold drinks and warm bodies! I want everything. The question is, what do you want?" Kyle gushed with illustrious gesticulation.

"I want to have a drink and a game in peace," Henry said in a low tone.

"Really? And here I thought you wanted Fairchild soldiers to die in a fire." Kyle spoke just loud enough for everyone at the table to hear.

All eyes were on Henry. Eli gave him a deadly look. Henry was used to pressure. He had his tells, but he could fool a casual observer.

He presented a dismissive expression, an amused and unbothered expression, one he had seen on the faces of many a guilty man. "My cup's nearly dry," he said, beginning to stand.

Kyle twitched his fingers, and one of his girls placed a

hand on Henry's shoulder, gently pushing him back to his seat while one of the other girls moved in the direction of the bar.

"No need to fetch your own drinks when you're with me," said Kyle. "That's what these are for."

Henry ignored the comment. "Hit me," he said to the dealer, who turned up a ten, putting Henry at twenty-three.

"Oh, that's tough. Looks like your luck may be running a bit thin," Kyle sneered.

"I've never relied on luck all that much," said Henry.

"This table's cooling off," said Eli. "Maybe we should move on?" It came out as more of a command than a question.

"You must stay for at least one drink," said Kyle. "I insist."

Just then, Kyle's girl returned with an unopened bottle of gin. Kyle made a sweeping gesture towards himself, Henry, and Eli, then she poured the clear liquid into each of their glasses.

"One more hand won't break me, I suppose," said Henry.

"That's the spirit," said Kyle, raising his glass out towards them. The glasses clinked, tapped the table, and were thrown back. The liquor began to work on Henry.

"So what brings you two to my city?" asked Kyle.

"We're traveling north," said Eli, placing his bet.

"Ah, north. What does the north hold for you?" He showed a mirthless smile.

"I've heard there are fewer annoying little shits up that way," said Henry, pushing a few chips forward. He was dealt the Jack of Hearts.

A few of the other players did their best to contain chuckles, and Kyle motioned for one of his girls to lean in close for him to whisper something to them. Then she came to Henry as she had before, but this time her presence was less intoxicating, Henry felt an anger begin to rise within him. Even so, her breathy voice was soft on his cheek. "I remind you, that if you do not mind your manners, I will inform the remaining Fairchild soldiers who is responsible for the deaths of their comrades."

As soon as she had finished speaking, Henry leaned towards Kyle. "I really wish you would. In fact, I'd like you to go inform them right now, in person. I'll accompany you. Being there all together will make my day all the brighter."

It caught Kyle off guard.

"Bet's to you. Are you in or out?" asked Henry.

Kyle pushed a few chips towards the dealer.

When Kyle turned his focus towards the cards, Henry glanced at Eli and winked at him. It was a shot in the dark, but he hoped Eli knew where he was going with it. Then he gently took the bottle of gin from the girl that held it and poured himself a glass. He looked Eli square in the eyes and handed him the bottle, "One last drink before we go."

Eli nodded and poured himself a glass. Henry leaned forward to obstruct Kyle's view of Eli and the bottle. Then Eli handed the bottle back to the girl, who he could have sworn had the slightest glimmer in her eyes for the first time that evening. She filled Kyle's glass.

"Not yet," he said, irritation poking through his tone. "Cigarette."

One girl placed one in his lips, and another lit it for him.

"Never learned to use a lighter?" asked Henry, lighting a cigarette of his own.

The music from the stage began to swell. More people moved to the dance floor, and the energy at the table began to shift. The other players stopped trying to hide the fact that they were paying more attention to the exchange than the game.

Kyle opened his mouth to speak but Henry cut him off.

"Let me guess, that's what *these* are for?" He looked at the girl holding the lighter. "What's your name, love?"

She smiled, surprised and amused. "Lena."

"That's what Lena's for," Henry said to Eli. And then he raised his glass. "To Lena, and her lovely companions, and the essential service they provide."

Kyle's superior smile had turned sour.

"Come now," Henry said to Kyle. "I thought we were drinking." He jiggled his glass.

Kyle begrudgingly raised his own.

The glasses clinked, tapped, and were thrown back. The gin went down easier than before, and Henry felt the pleasant tingling of it in his ears and the back of his head. He could feel Eli's heartbeat increase, and he patted him on the knee.

The dealer dealt Henry the Ace of Spades.

"Well, would you look at that. Turns out I still had a little luck left after all," he said, turning to Kyle. "Feeling alright there, dear boy? You're looking a bit pale."

Kyle swallowed hard and put down his cigarette, "I think I may have drank a little too..."

Then more vomit than Henry knew could exist in a single human ejected itself so quickly and forcefully from a horrified Kyle that there was scarcely a clean spot on the entire Black-jack table. There were a few gasps, but for the most part, everyone who witnessed the fiasco just laughed and raised a glass. Kyle looked around, shocked and horrified. He wiped his face with a handkerchief.

"What the fu..." He was abruptly interrupted by another heave.

"Sorry, what was that?" said Eli, calmly. "Come now, Henry. Let's end on a win."

Henry nodded in agreement and stood, collecting his chips, which miraculously had avoided Kyle's mess. The men at the table laughed and cheered. Kyle's girls were struggling to maintain their emotionless expressions, and Henry took Lena's hand and kissed it. "Thank him for the drink once he's recovered," Henry said to her.

She nodded and almost smiled.

"We need to move fast," Henry said just loud enough for Eli to hear.

Eli nodded, then they headed towards the lobby.

Chapter Fourteen

Henry's head was buzzing from the excitement and gin, but his legs were working just fine. He didn't see the concierge anywhere as they passed through the foyer. *Pity.*

"I would've liked to drink and possibly sleep with her."

"What?" said Eli in a somewhat confused tone.

"What?" Henry added, also confused.

"You said you wanted to sleep with who?"

"Was I speaking out loud?" His tone was mildly aghast.

"Afraid so."

"I hate it when that happens."

They hit the streets and walked until they found a small, inconspicuous-looking pub. They sat down at an outside table with a clear view of the street, while still being obscured by shadow. The air was a perfect combination of brisk and balmy. Lanterns lit the sidewalk, and mirth filled the streets.

"I'm glad you knew where I was going with that last drink," said Henry. "It was quick thinking."

"Good on you for creating the opportunity," replied Eli as if it was required of him. "But Henry..."

The waitress approached. "What can I get for you?"

"Light beers. And some meat and cheese sandwiches, and maybe some kind of potatoes if you have them."

"Fried okay?" she asked.

"That would be grand," said Henry with a polite smile.

"She looks like she's led a long, hard life," said Henry once she had gone.

"Don't change the subject. I asked if anyone saw you. I asked if you killed them all, and you lied about both." Fumed Eli.

"I thought I did get them all."

Eli rubbed his face and took an irritated breath with his eyes closed.

"Listen, what was the point of threatening that soldier at the ranch into defending it if we're just going to kill everyone before they even get there? The ranch isn't unprotected, and we did kill thirteen of fifteen," said Henry.

"*You* killed thirteen of fifteen," Eli corrected.

"With poison that you gave me, and upon your request," Henry reminded him. "I say we mount up and leave town right now. It seems like every time we stop moving, I have to kill people, and you get pissed at me for not doing it right."

The waitress barely stopped walking as she dropped off their beers, "Food'll be out in a minute."

"This place isn't even busy," said Henry, picking up his beer. "The service here could use some improvement."

"We can't leave until we find Lipton's contact. We don't even know where we need to go," said Eli, picking up his beer.

"Cheers," said Henry holding out his glass.

"If you say so," said Eli raising his own to clink with Henry's.

But Henry pulled his glass back and gave Eli a look of genuine disapproval. "You can be nasty with me about business, and you don't have to like me, but drinking is sacred. When I say cheers, either cheers me back or decline to drink. None of this half assed, passive aggressive, greater than thou bullshit. Not when it comes to drinking."

"I'm sorry," said Eli, and Henry could tell that he did mean it.

"Cheers," said Henry, again holding out his glass.

"Cheers," said Eli, clinking his own against it.

The waitress brought their food and walked away without a word.

They started eating, and it was very good. It was not as good as Martha's cooking, but Henry found that his annoyance at the lackluster service diminished a little more with every bite and sip.

"Does all this bother you?" asked Henry.

"Does what bother me?" responded Eli, conversationally.

"All this excess with starving families a few days' ride away."

"It's not excess that bothers me," said Eli, taking a sip of beer and savoring it. "It's lack. Frugality is a poor substitute for generosity. The reality of the situation is that most of the people partying here live hard lives. Though they may never know hunger, the trials they face are from a deeper chamber of hell. I don't blame them for letting themselves be free and lavish in this place. There are truly evil people in this world, but most people are just trying to avoid pain."

Henry nodded. "So, instead of berating the wealthy for their greed, you go and feed the poor."

"I wasn't always this way," said Eli, avoiding the compliment.

"I know," said Henry. "People that have always been good don't keep an arsenal of poison on them. And they certainly don't have one of those whips you've been carrying around. I know what it is."

"I haven't used it in many years," said Eli, taking a bite.

"But I reckon you still remember how."

"Do you ever think about retiring?" asked Eli.

"I think about a lot of things," said Henry. "But not all of us have a ranch and a lady like Grace waiting there for us."

Eli shot Henry a look he had not yet seen. It was some cross between confusion and offense. "Grace isn't waiting for me. What would make you think that?"

"Of course she isn't.," Henry said. His tone was patronizing.

Eli's expression turned dark. "We need to find Lipton's contact."

"Do we even know who we're looking for?" asked Henry.

"No, but..." Then Eli froze.

Henry's head snapped in the direction that Eli was looking. The two Fairchild soldiers walked down the street, talking to one another. They passed the tavern Henry and Eli sat at without noticing them and entered a building that did not look like a pub at the end of the street on the opposite side.

Eli put down his sandwich and placed a thin silver coin on the table. "Let's go."

"I'm eating," said Henry, but Eli was already on his feet. Henry stuffed as much of the sandwich as he could manage into his mouth and followed, unsure of their plan.

They reached the front door of the building. Henry realized it was a brothel. They entered. The room was lit sparingly by electric bulbs hanging above the bar and in the center of the room, leaving the tables and booths around the edge of the room in shadow.

"Whoever owns this place must be doing quite well for themselves," noted Henry as he looked at the impressive lights. "It's got to be expensive to have enough electric mills for all these lights."

"Indeed, it is, and indeed we are."

Henry turned to see who was speaking.

Kyle Crenshaw was standing up from a corner booth with a sneering grin slowly overtaking his features. "Let me buy you boys a drink."

Henry noticed the Fairchild soldiers standing from the same booth Kyle had been at.

"Oh, that's quite alright," said Eli, slowly backing towards the door. He bumped into someone who was entering.

"I insist." As he spoke, Kyle snapped his fingers, and a few uniformly dressed men who were scattered about the bar snapped into action like toy soldiers and stood at attention with their backs straight and their hands in front of them, left over right.

"Don't worry," said Kyle as he forcefully directed them towards an empty table. "I don't poison my guests. I have a reputation to uphold."

There didn't seem to be any customers in the front room, but with all the shadows around the edges, it was hard to tell. Henry and Eli exchanged glances and proceeded to the table. Kyle waved his hand, and Lena brought over a bottle of gin and three crystal glasses on a tray. There was a horrendous bruise forming across her face, and one of her eyes was almost swollen shut. She set it on the table and turned to walk away when Kyle aggressively grabbed her by the wrist.

"You're fucking stupid, aren't you?"

"Yes," she said nervously.

"Yes, sir," Kyle said threateningly.

"Yes, sir." She corrected her reply while trying to discreetly remove her wrist from his grasp. He only tightened his grip.

"Why didn't you pour our drinks?"

She looked pleadingly at Henry and Eli.

"They aren't talking to you. I am," snapped Kyle.

Her hand was turning blue.

"Answer the question."

"I didn't know you wanted me to, sir," she said with pain in her voice.

"What do you do here?"

"What I'm told." Her hand was nearly purple.

"Pour the fucking drinks," said Kyle, squeezing her wrist so hard his knuckles began to turn white.

"My hand." Her face began to go pale.

"Use your other hand!" roared Kyle.

Henry's hand began to move to his coat pocket.

Eli's hand stopped it.

Lena yelped and choked back a sob.

"Allow me," said a steady voice.

All eyes looked to see who was speaking. Henry immediately recognized her as the gorgeous concierge from the Madison. She was sitting casually at the bar, a glass of whiskey in one hand, a half-smoked cigarette in the other. No one had been at the bar when they had entered, and Henry was shocked that he hadn't seen her come in. She wore a long black trench coat and had a red handkerchief tied delicately around her neck. Henry knew it was just because he was drunk, but he couldn't help but notice how her legs looked in that trench coat.

"God, I'm such a pig."

Eli shot him a look.

"Was that out loud?" whispered Henry.

Eli's face said it all.

The concierge drained her glass of whiskey and walked towards the table.

Kyle's eyes darkened with lust as the concierge approached, and he released Lena's wrist. She scurried away, massaging the blood back into her hand and wiping tears away.

The concierge reached the table, uncorked the bottle of gin, and filled the three glasses. She then poured some into her own empty glass.

"What's your name?" asked Kyle flirtatiously.

"Moraya," she responded in kind.

"I know you're not one of mine. Where do you work?"

"Does it really matter?" she said in a tone of voice that made Henry hot under the collar. "I'm here now, your glass is full, and I've got a drink on the house. Why don't you boys just carry on as you were? Don't mind me here."

"Oh, I don't mind at all," said Kyle, sweetly, before he turned to face Henry and Eli. "It's so hard to find good help these days. At least that's what my father says. Luckily, I've got a knack for improving work ethic. That's why I'm in charge."

"You're in charge because of your father," scoffed Henry.

"I might have been given power because of my father, but I've kept it through my own power. My reputation."

"Reputation as what exactly?" asked Eli.

"As Kyle fucking Crenshaw!" shouted Kyle. His face reddened, and the veins in his neck bulged.

"Sure, sure. But what does that mean, you know?" Henry asked. "I'm new to town, and you must enlighten me."

"What does it mean? I'll tell you what it means," spat Kyle as he worked up a fury. "It means what I say, happens. It means that my father's second only to the Fairchilds. It means that I'm the one that decides who gets pussy when they visit, and who gets a bullet when they poison me."

There was silence for a moment. All the uniformed men,

seven by Henry's count, including the two Fairchild soldiers, drew a revolver and a knife.

"A bullet?" asked Moraya dryly.

Everyone in the room looked at her as if they had forgotten she was there. Kyle seemed too dumbstruck to respond.

She continued, "If your men used bullets right now, not only would none of the guests in the back return, but they would leave without paying. What's more, there's nothing you could do about it because you would also be killed by some of the bullets, just like these gentlemen here. Next time, if you plan to have an enemy shot, you shouldn't sit in the trajectory of the exit wounds. Instead, you should just cut their throats." Her voice was no longer sultry and inviting. It made Henry's blood run cold. She smiled cruelly. "Like this."

Everything happened so fast that it was not until a few moments afterward that Henry pieced together what exactly took place.

Right as she finished speaking, Moraya elegantly produced a thin double-edged blade from her left sleeve with her right hand. Before Kyle could react, the blade was lodged in his throat. His men reacted, but too slow. Moraya released a hailstorm of bullets from two magazine-fed pistols. Some of the guards managed to get a shot or two off before being peppered by Moraya's rounds. The sound was deafening. Screams erupted from the back rooms. Some of the guard's shots must have made it through the walls.

Henry looked back at Moraya. She was already tucking the pistols back into their holsters inside her jacket. He looked at the guards. All seven lay twitching on the floor, hands clutching their necks, chests, or groins. The whole thing happened in less than five seconds. Henry had only ever seen one other person move that quickly.

Eli was speechless, but he clutched the handle of his whip.

Henry spoke for both of them. "Holy shit. I thought shooting with both hands only happened in fairy tales."

Moraya holstered both her weapons and responded coolly, "Well, I guess that makes me your fairy godmother." She removed her blade from Kyle's throat, cleaned it on his cuff, and returned it to its sheath somewhere within her trench coat. "Let's move."

Lena lay dead on the ground, cut down by stray rounds of the men Moraya had dispatched. Eli and Henry were stumbling after Moraya as fast as they could, but people were flooding out from the back rooms, jostling them violently. She led them out of the chaos, down the street through the gathering crowd and up another, through a narrow alley and out onto another avenue where the energy was fueled by music and liquor instead of fear. She kept walking at a steady pace, occasionally checking to make sure the two men were still in tow. After a few blocks, she ducked into a small dive bar with only a few stools taken. The bartender nodded to her as she made her way to a table in the back room and sat. Henry and Eli joined her, and a moment later the bartender set down a tray with a bottle of water, a bottle of gin, a bowl of ice, and six glasses. Three short, three tall.

"Lipton said you would be here before now," she in a matter-of-fact tone, once she finished a thorough examination of both of them.

"What the fuck, woman?" said Henry as he attempted to regain his bearings.

Eli leaned back in his chair and shook his head, eyes wide.

Moraya pushed the water glasses towards the two men. "Drink those."

Henry and Eli complied.

"Now these. They might calm your nerves." She slid small pours of gin towards them.

They once again complied.

"Are you ready to listen?" she asked.

They nodded.

"The Fairchild entourage left two days ago, though I know they did not go far. I never personally saw Clarke, but I did see three of the top Fairchild advisors. I also saw the whole unit of elite bodyguards, which is rumored to always be within earshot of whichever Fairchild they're assigned to." She paused to let them catch up. "Somehow, they heard rumor of your arrival on the West Coast, so they took Clarke to the safest, most secure family stronghold they could think of. It's not far from here. A few days' hard ride. Getting there and finding it is not the difficult part. It's called the Haven, but, in reality, it's more like a fortress. It's in the mountains, outside a little town whose name was forgotten centuries ago. Stealth is your only viable course of action. There are over fifteen men in Clarke's elite guard, and I imagine an entire battalion of the Fairchild army is stationed in the barracks at the Haven. I will help you get inside, but after that, you'll be entirely on your own."

"Wait," interrupted Henry. "What do you mean, you'll help me get inside?"

"I'm coming with you."

"Okay," said Henry with a boyish grin and then quickly thought twice. "You work for Lipton, that slippery bastard. How do I know you won't stab me in the back as soon as I've done my part?"

Moraya stretched an exquisite leg out toward and flipped open the bottom part of her trench coat, revealing a scandalous amount of it. It took Henry a full two seconds to realize that she was showing him a tattoo of her own on the upper thigh. "I would never kill another Collector. We all know how that ends," she said firmly, then covered it up again, much to Henry's disappointment.

Henry studied her for a moment. "I wasn't expecting that, though I can't say I'm surprised. I knew you were too quick." He leaned back and thought for a bit. "I'm not splitting my reward with anyone."

"I don't want your money!" spat Moraya indignantly. "I owe Lipton a debt. Once I help you kill the Fairchild, it will be paid, and I will be free."

Henry looked at Eli.

Eli shrugged.

"Works for me," said Henry with a shrug.

"We need to move now," said Moraya. "Crenshaw the elder will be turning the whole town inside out to find you."

Thirty minutes later, they were on the road again. Henry was hungry and exhausted, but they had to put some distance between themselves and Chico. By the time they finally stopped for the night, Henry scarcely had time to pull off his boots before sleep took him. There was the house, the porch, the impact from behind, and he woke with a start, scarcely feeling like he had slept at all.

Chapter Fifteen

On their third morning of riding, Eli awoke before the others. He took some bread, a bit of dried meat, and a piece of hard cheese from his saddlebag and walked up the road from where they camped. Eli let his mind wander as he walked along that ancient, indestructible highway. In the five hundred years or so since the Crash, it had gained barely a scratch. *Not rock nor glass, not metal or gas...* He never fully understood old brother Lewis and his long-winded soliloquies on lost technology, much less his lectures. In that particular moment, he liked to think of it as a parting gift from a world past, something to remember her by.

He walked along for a while as the sun softened the frost on the octagonal pattern of the road. He saw some smoke from beyond the next rise. It was still early enough for him to scout ahead and make it back to the others before they were awake and ready to move. The closer he got, the thicker the smoke became. There was a well-kept gravel drive leading towards it. He took the last bites of his breakfast and cautiously approached. He stepped off the crunching gravel path and into the trees, his footsteps muffled by years of pine needles deep upon the earth. After a few minutes, he reached the top of the rise and looked around. His heart nearly stopped. In the gully around a farmhouse were rows upon rows of tents, makeshift corrals, and stock wagons; it was a whole army.

There was a sentry posted on the road, but he didn't see Eli in the trees; he didn't seem to be paying much attention to anything, in fact. Eli could see the Fairchild insignia on his breast. He wanted to go question him, but decided that it would be too risky, so instead he slowly and quietly began making his way down towards the camp in the hopes that he would be able to overhear some bit of useful information.

Thankfully the trees grew thick, and reached to the very edge of the encampment, providing him sufficient cover to get close. There must have been close to three hundred soldiers, he estimated, and none of them seemed to be talking about their plans or their direction. He had almost given up hope of overhearing anything other than crass talk and friendly jostling when he spotted two soldiers at the edge of the tree line. They sat with their legs outstretched and their backs to thick tree trunks, smoking, and they looked a bit older and wiser than most of the young men Eli had seen thus far.

"Who knows if it's even true," one said.

"From what I heard, Thorpe seemed quite convinced of it," said the other.

"Either way, at this pace we'll be at the Haven the day after tomorrow."

"Hopefully not too late. I hate marching through dinner."

"I'd rather have a late dinner and a good pace than run myself into the ground."

It was all Eli needed to hear. He slipped away as he had come. His mind was racing, but he breathed deep and tried to steady himself with the knowledge that three on horseback can cover ground much faster than three hundred with carts and supplies.

It took him longer than he had hoped to reach camp, and as he approached, he could smell a fire and coffee. He saw Moraya and Henry, but they did not see him, and despite the urgency of the situation, he paused for a moment to observe as Henry poured himself a cup and then one for Moraya. She sat with her eyes closed, taking in the morning sun. He approached her cautiously, almost like a child about to ask a stranger for directions home, then he held the cup out to her. It took her nearly five seconds to realize that he was there and open her eyes.

"Thank you." She looked at him almost quizzically as she took a sip.

"Of course."

She smiled absentmindedly.

"Do you mind if I smoke?" he asked as he pulled out a cigarette.

"Not if you brought enough to share."

He drew out a second cigarette from within a case.

"Lipton said he had a *man* in Chico," said Henry after a moment.

"I'm sorry to disappoint," said Moraya as she ashed off her cigarette.

Henry ashed off his own cigarette. "No, I'm just surprised, is all."

"I suppose the Crenshaw boy was an Ask?" he added after another short silence.

"Does it matter?" she asked.

"I'm not sure if I should thank you or congratulate you on a job well done."

"A job well done wouldn't have involved the death of seven extra men, an innocent prostitute, and the injury of bystanders," she said, her eyes fixed on something other than Henry.

"It can be tough to get someone alone."

She looked at him with a raised eyebrow.

"For me," he added and took too a big gulp of hot coffee that left his eyes watering. It was almost endearing.

She blew on hers and took a small sip.

"What's the nature of your...employment with Lipton?" asked Henry.

Moraya sighed. "Complicated. And with any luck, nearly over."

Henry looked into his cup and frowned. "I've never heard of a Collector in long-term employment."

"And I've never heard of Collector receiving a million dollars for an Ask," she replied.

The stump of Henry's cigarette burned his fingers, and he threw it on the ground with a twitch and an involuntary expletive.

"You should really stop burning yourself," she said with an amused half smile.

Eli decided not to lurk any longer and walked into the camp, being sure to make enough noise to be noticed as he got close.

"Where did you run off to?" asked Henry.

Eli poured himself a cup of coffee. "We'll need to get moving and try to keep a low profile for a few miles. I have bad news."

"You?" Henry jabbed.

"There are about three hundred Fairchild soldiers headed towards the Haven." A memory flashed through his mind, the sickening crack of breaking bones and the smell of blood and gunpowder. He suddenly needed to breath and drew in a deep drink of air as the words landed on Henry and Moraya.

"They expect to arrive there the day after tomorrow...in the evening."

Moraya stood immediately and began packing up her things. "We can get there before them. We could be there tomorrow night, and that's with a good rest in a village tonight."

Henry dumped the grounds out of the small, improvised coffee pot and tucked it into his blanket as he rolled it up. "Where are they now?" he asked.

"Just up the road a ways. With any luck, we'll have long passed them by the time they start moving."

They saddled the horses and eased up the terrain back onto the road. Eli remembered the last time he had killed. *Never again.* He couldn't seem to catch his breath long enough to hold it. He could feel his heartbeat in all his extremities. It wasn't faster than usual, but was it always so strong? Perhaps he just hadn't noticed it before.

Henry was loose in the saddle, letting Bentley do the walking. "Eli, calm down before you give yourself a heart attack. It's making it hard to feel for any other pulses."

Moraya's eyes darted to Henry for a moment. Eli tried to empty his mind. But he just couldn't shake that feeling.

"You're one of those Collectors," Moraya said to Henry in a low tone.

"You're not without your talents," said Henry, "and I'm not without mine. Now be quiet."

They were nearly to the gravel path leading to the Fairchild encampment when Henry pulled Bentley up short and raised his fist to the others. "We're just travelers. Keep moving." He carried on at a trot. A moment later, a Fairchild sentry appeared in the road before them. Two others sat on stumps just off the gravel path playing dice. The sentry motioned for them to stop, and they complied.

"Stretch your legs for a moment, travelers," said the sentry in a polite but firm tone.

Eli wanted to put heel to hide and be gone from there. But then they would send riders to pursue. *We're just travelers.* He dismounted with his companions.

"What brings you folks up the road today?" asked the sentry.

"All different reasons, actually," said Henry as easily as if he were chatting with a tavern keeper. "We only met on the road last night and decided to hold pace for a while. It's always safer to travel in a group."

"That's very true," said sentry.

"What brings you to the road, soldier?" asked Henry conversationally.

The sentry's faced grew stern. "You still haven't answered my question. Why are *you* going north?" He was much smaller than Henry but had so much more to prove.

"I'm visiting my uncle," said Moraya. "I rarely see him and he's not well, so I'm headed north to see him one last time." She gave the sentry a sad look. A look that certainly didn't ask to be comforted yet needed to be comforted just the same.

"I'm looking for work, and then a boat ticket," said Henry.

The sentry looked at Eli. His heart was in his throat. The Minister never got nervous like this. But he was back at the ranch, and Eli's hand instinctively drifted to his belt. "I'm headed to a parish in Seattle. There are rare works there, and I've been wanting to study."

The sentry's eye's followed Eli's hand all the way to the whip. "You know," he said in a relaxed tone. *Too relaxed.* "I heard about some trouble with a priestly type down south."

The other two had stopped their game of dice and were listening. They less than twenty feet away. *I could reach them.*

The sentry either didn't notice or didn't mind that Moraya had taken a step towards him as he continued, "I don't suppose you know anything about that."

Eli's mouth was dry. "Nothing comes to mind."

"Nothing," said the sentry. "That's an interesting whip you're holding onto their, padre." His hand resting on his sidearm. "Why would you need a whip to read?"

It was like the breeze shifted, but the wind lay still at that moment. Before the sentry's hand could even twitch to grip his sidearm, Moraya hand opened a thin line in his forearm with a knife she had slipped from her belt inside her coat. He froze first in shock, then with something else, then he convulsed.

The other two sentries were on their feet.

Eli gripped the handle of his whip. *I could reach them.*

They had their rifles in hand when Henry sent his Bowie knife thudding into one of their throats. Then the air split with the crack of a rifle, and Eli threw himself to the ground as a bullet whizzed past his torso. He heard pistol fire as he rolled to his feet and saw Moraya and Henry both holstering their weapons before the body had even hit the ground.

The three companions did not waste a second. They were back in the saddle and riding at a full sprint before Eli even noticed that he had scraped his hand. He knew that the sounds of gunfire would draw investigation, and he knew that riders would mostly likely be dispatched north and south to try to overtake them. But he did not know exactly how fast the riders would be dispatched, or how many. Or how fast they could ride.

They pushed the horses as hard as they could without endangering them. Then they gradually slowed to a trot which they maintained until well after noon. They heard a stream just off the road and reined the horses towards the sound of it.

They drank and refilled their skins and canteens with the fresh water and took a moment to stretch and rest before getting on again

"What did you do to that soldier?" Henry asked Moraya.

"I'm not without my talents," she replied.

"If only the Minister could have lent his talents, maybe that last one wouldn't have gotten a shot off and set a whole damn army on our tails. Or have you forgotten how to use that whip?" Henry said. He did a decent job masking his disgust when he looked at Eli.

"I haven't forgotten," said Eli.

"Well, that's a comfort," said Henry in a resigned tone. Then he stood up very straight as if listening. "Fuck."

"What is it?" whispered Moraya.

Henry crouched. "There are five of them. We're safe to use guns. I doubt there's anyone around to hear them."

Moraya nodded, drew a pistol, and seemed to evaporate into the dense trees.

"You stay low, Minister. Wouldn't want your whip hand cramping," said Henry as he concealed himself behind a large rock.

Eli could hear them coming through the trees. Their horses were probably thirsty too after half a day of hard pursuit. He found a large evergreen that would keep him out of site. There was no time to hide the horses.

After a moment, the five riders came out of the trees onto the low, rocky bank of the stream. Upon seeing the horses, they drew their weapons and dismounted, using their horses as cover as they tried to spot threats. But the three companions made no move at first.

"Where'd they go?" one of the riders asked his comrades.

"They can't have gone far. Eyes up, boys," said another.

A tense minute passed before the riders lowered their weapons and led their mounts to the stream to drink. One of them started walking towards Eli's tree, unbuttoning his pants as he approached.

Eli held what little breath he had.

The soldier began to relieve himself, shoulders relaxed and eyes closed for a moment, and Eli began to think he was in the clear. But then he opened them.

"Wait a minute," said the soldier, not yet done with his business.

Suddenly, Eli's nerves were quite calm, and he had two lungs full of air. He leapt out from behind the tree, drawing his whip, just as Henry stood and raised his weapon. Moraya was the first to fire, concealed by the trees still. Eli smashed the handle of his whip into the soldier's face, sending him sprawling over backwards, and out of the corner of his eye, he saw that another soldier had his rifle raised at Henry. Eli lunged towards him as his whip uncoiled in a silent arc, licking out and wrapping around the rifle, and then he yanked it back as the shot broke, missing Henry and setting the soldier off balance. Henry sent two rounds through the man's chest. Then the rider who had spotted Eli sprang at him from the ground and tackled him and began pummeling him. Eli managed to get a hold of his wrists, but the soldier was on top of him. A few more shots rang out as Eli and the soldier locked each other in a stalemate, and a moment later Henry was standing above them, razor in hand, and then Eli felt a spray of wet across his face as the soldier jerked and ceased to struggle. Eli threw the man to the ground and rolled to his feet, trying to gain his bearings.

All five soldiers lay dead. Henry looked unscathed. Moraya reappeared from the trees. Aside from a sore spot on his back from being tackled onto the rocks, Eli did not seem to have any injuries.

The three companions looked at each other as they caught their breath. Eli recoiled his whip; he had used it without waking it up fully. He still hadn't broken his oath.

"I guess you do still know how to use that thing," said Henry, who was bleeding slightly from his temple. A bullet had grazed him.

"Thanks for the help with that one," replied Eli.

"I had to return the favor somehow," said Henry, his voice shaky.

"Wash your face, Eli," said Moraya as she replaced her spent rounds. "You too, Henry. Jesus, you had a close call."

They nodded and went to the stream

"Let's hope they don't send out any more parties after us," said Henry after he had splashed water on his face.

"I doubt that they will," said Eli after he washed the blood off. "The main force won't make it this far by the end of the day. They'll grow suspicious when this group doesn't return, but the soonest they'd find the bodies is tomorrow morning, and even then, it will only confirm that we are moving north."

"That will give us enough time," said Moraya.

"I hope we can find an inn tonight," said Henry as he unsaddled the fallen soldier's horses.

Moraya looked through their saddle bags once Henry had gotten them on the ground. "I may know just the spot."

Chapter Sixteen

Henry knew how close he had come to death. He tried to dismiss the thought, but every time he checked on the scab forming across his temple, he knew that a single crack of the whip was all that had kept him out of a shallow grave. He rode as hard as he could, knowing but trying not to think about what pursued and what still lay ahead. Chatting with Moraya helped. He had expected her to be rigid, but she was a rather laid-back character with a gift for small talk and getting men to let their guard down. Henry had decided that he liked her very much. She was a beautiful force of nature, and he was pointedly aware of the fact that he hoped to never be counted amongst her enemies. They didn't talk much as they rode, but the on-and-off banter served as a pleasant distraction and helped calm his nerves from almost being shot in the face.

More hills began rising from the landscape, and the trees grew dense and crowded together. The mountains looming off in the distance looked to Henry like lesser gods kneeling before their queen, Mount Shasta. It was breathtaking. Henry had seen mountains before, many times, but there was something about a magnificent, angular, snow-capped peak that never ceased to invigorate him.

That evening, they reached a small town. There was not much left of it. From what Henry could tell, there was never much of it to begin with.

"If memory serves, there should be a good place around here to stop for the evening," said Moraya.

It did not take them long to find a small saloon. The sign had long since disappeared. They tied their horses out front, dusted themselves off, and moved towards the door. Despite the outside being in shambles, the inside was quite clean. The bartender was a tall, broad man with a dark, short beard, glasses, and the easy manner of movement and speech that all good bartenders possess.

"What'll it be?" he asked as the three of them sat down at the bar.

"Tequila," said Moraya quickly.

"Shit," said the bartender, grabbing four very large shot glasses. Filling each of them to the brim, he slid three of them in front of the trio and held the fourth up in front of himself. "What are we drinking to?"

"The good times," said Henry, "and that they may find us again."

They clinked their glasses, tapped them on the bar, and threw them back.

The room was nearly empty, aside from them. Only a few individual patrons were hunkered down alone in their various booths along the wall, each one looking lonelier than the last.

"There's only one thing to drink with shots of tequila—light beer," said the bartender, filling four-pint glasses.

"What's your name, good sir?" asked Henry as he gratefully accepted the pint.

"Wendland."

"Is this your establishment?"

"The fuck d'you think?" responded Wendland with a laugh. "I've been working here since I was...well, I was a boy. Came here when I was young and left here for a while to travel and find myself in the world. I never forgot this place, though. The previous owner willed it to me when he died."

"Does it have a name? I didn't see a sign," said Henry before taking a long drink of the cold beer.

"Never figured it needed one. Names seem a bit irrelevant when a thing's purpose is so apparent. Once the sign fell down, well, I saw no need to put up another one."

"Mind if I smoke?" inquired Henry, pulling out his tobacco.

"Not if you share," replied Wendland with a cheeky grin.

"Hear, hear," said Moraya.

"Eli?" asked Henry, looking at his friend. Eli nodded.

Henry began rolling four cigarettes.

"Hungry?" asked Wendland.

He received a resounding yes from all three.

Smiling, he walked around to the back room. A moment later, he returned with three plates on a tray. Each was piled high with roast chicken, mashed potatoes, and fried onions.

"Wendland, you're a saint," said Henry.

"I'm an atheist actually, but I appreciate the sentiment," he said with a jovial smile as he tipped back his glass for an articulate sip. He continued, "So what brings two men and a beautiful lady to my little establishment?"

"Common interest in self-preservation," said Eli after he realized the other two had mouths too full to speak with.

"Right," said Wendland with a knowing smile. "Is that why you all have your left forearms covered, or is that just due to the chilly weather we've been having?"

The trio looked up from their meal in unison. Wendland

smirked and held up his hands in front of them as if to stop their suspicion before it left their mouths.

"I serve drinks, not judgment. God knows I've no right to do that."

"I thought you said you don't believe in God?" said Eli, a devious twinkle in his eyes.

"I don't believe He's real. Doesn't mean I don't think he's useful as a figure of speech."

"Fair enough," said Eli with a shrug.

A few minutes later, after they had cleaned their plates and he had delivered a few cocktails to other guests, Wendland came back to the three.

"Leave any room for pie?" he asked.

"Had I known there was any, I would've," said Henry, a hint of disappointment in his tone.

"Oh, there isn't any. I was just wondering if you saved any room."

Moraya scoffed and rolled her eyes. "I saved room for more tequila."

"I like this one!" declared Wendland, grabbing a few more oversized shot glasses.

"What're we drinking to this time?" asked Eli.

After a moment of consideration, Henry raised his glass. "To the future. May it be just as bright as the past, so that we may forget the present."

The glasses clinked, then tapped the bar, then were thrown back.

"So, if you won't tell me who you're here to kill, or why three of you are required for it, how about at least telling me where you're all from? Starting with you," he said, gazing deeply at Moraya.

As he spoke, it was as if the rest of the world went quiet. There was the slightest bit of pressure in Henry's ears, like they needed to pop, and then remembered his old teacher. *I wonder if Wendland ever crossed paths with Rust.* The mysterious barman slid her another glass of tequila. She held his gaze and her eyes smiled as she drank her shot.

That seems like a lot of tequila.

"I was born in Australia, actually, though I wasn't there long," she began comfortably. "My father moved us to the States to be an accountant for a handful of barons in Rhode Island and Connecticut. My mother was a whore, though my father never knew it. For being an accountant, he wasn't very good at piecing together how mother had so much money for new clothes.

"He was a good man. I almost pitied him for it. He knew how numbers worked, but he never seemed capable of comprehending the other parts of life. He loved to watch me draw, and I loved to draw for him. It was always our special time.

"Eventually...inevitably, one of the barons he worked for made a military advance on another, which failed. The baron who survived was convinced that my father had been aware of the other's plans to attack him and intentionally had not warned him. After all, how could my father not have known? He oversaw all the financial accounts, which included those involved with hiring an army. So, as punishment, the surviving baron sentenced my father, mother, and myself to death.

"But a third baron my father worked for negotiated for my life and sent me to learn at The Vault in Seattle. I was nine years old when I began studying to be a Collector. I was eleven when I got my tattoo. When the baron that paid for me to live sent me to Seattle, he made it very clear that until the debt was paid, until he felt I had earned my freedom, I belonged to him. And now I'm so close to being my own master."

"So...you're from Australia then," said Wendland after a moment of silence.

Moraya laughed, somewhat embarrassed. "Jesus, Wendland. What did you put in that tequila?"

"Nothing. That's why it worked so well," he said, pouring four more comically large shots of the stuff. "What are we drinking to this time?"

He looked at Henry, who replied, "To death. May it find us at peace, drinking with those we love."

Glasses clinked, tapped, and were thrown back.

"So what's your story, preacher boy?" asked Wendland, shifting the weight of his attention to Eli.

"Oh, nothing too interesting. Sad, mostly. I don't know if I'm quite drunk enough to tell it."

"Sad?" said Wendland as he poured himself a quarter pint of beer. "You want to hear something that will make you cry?"

The trio nodded with expectancy.

"Okay. Shit, you guys caught me on a bad week. I'm usually, I don't know, joyful, exuberant, and here you've got me talking about my saddest moments. But anyways, I've lost both my parents. They were great. Raised me well. I got along good with my father, but I really loved my mother. Really loved her. My father died a year before. Nearly to the day. But on this particular day, my mother was dying. The doctor was basically just trying to keep her out of pain. It wasn't working very well. Mom was pretty out of it. Delirious. But for a minute, she was all there. She didn't seem in pain, and I was actually talking to her. The real her. Not the fading shadow of herself she had been for weeks. And in that moment of the real her, she looked at me, and she asked me in her clear strong voice, 'Why are you crying?'

"And the only thing I could think to say was: 'Because my heart is broken.'

"Because my heart is broken..." Wendland repeated as he refilled the shot glasses. "Tomorrow's the anniversary."

Henry handed Wendland a cigarette and lit it for him. He felt the knot that had been in his chest all afternoon begin to loosen, and he felt alive. Maybe not happy, not really sad, but definitely alive. Once they had all got their cigarettes lit, and Wendland had refilled all the glasses, they raised their tequila. No toast was necessary this time. They had entered the sacred, unspoken contract of the bar top. They were going to drink, and talk, and not take anything too seriously, nor too lightly. They drained their shots, and once they had recovered themselves, Eli spoke up.

"An odd concept, your heart being broken," said Eli.

"How do you mean?" asked Moraya.

"I guess it's just that...it's not that your heart breaks. Your heart keeps beating. It's something else that breaks. Something subtler. Something deeper. It's almost as if...well, bear with me. Admittedly, the drink is beginning to work, so this might only make sense in my head, but picture a mansion. Endless rooms, each larger than the last. Each more beautiful and dynamic. Now imagine that you are the mansion, and each room is part of you, but all the rooms are locked at first. When you're born, you're in the entryway."

"Wait," interrupted Henry. "How can you be born if you're a mansion?"

"Okay, so picture the mansion as your personality, and your soul as the being that inhabits it. Got it?"

"Sure. You're definitely drunk, though," said Henry, smiling around his smoke.

"Shut up and listen. So, when your soul is born into the mansion, you're just in the entryway. And you don't have any keys to any other room, at least at first. Other people do. They can unlock new parts of your personality.

"Your parents are the first ones that start unlocking doors. When they show you a new room, they hang their portrait on the wall. Every time you enter that room, every time you experience that part of your personality, whether consciously or subconsciously, you know they showed you that part of yourself, because it's their portrait that hangs on that wall.

"And some rooms lead to other rooms, and so on, and each new person you invite into your life, if they're any good, will unlock a few more doors and hang a few more portraits. But to reach those sections of the mansion, you have to pass through rooms and corridors. Each one with a portrait of its own."

Eli paused for a sip of beer, Wendland leaned in, and Henry noticed the strange pressure of silence again. Eli continued with a faraway look in his dark brown eyes. "Then one day, your father dies in a fever. Since your mother was a good-for-nothing who your grandparents sent away the day you were born, it was your father who opened all those first doors for you, and so many more after that. Every time something happens that requires you to pass through a door he unlocked for you, you're acutely aware of it. You realize that he will never unlock another door for you again.

"Somehow, the room feels empty. Somehow the fields that he walked you through as a child seem so empty. So painful. They seem only to remind you that never again will he walk with you through the rows of grain.

"So, you just sell the field. You sell it and you move to Seattle, put the money in a safe, and learn to kill."

"Wait," interrupted Henry. "You lost me right at the end there."

"Oh," said Eli, snapping back to reality. "Forgive me, I lost track of my metaphor."

"I'll say."

"I guess what I meant to say, before I drown in a personal recollection, is that grief is not a heart that is breaking. It's that for a while, everything you feel is only going to seem like a monument to that which you've lost. A stopped heart kills you. Grief makes you wonder how you'll survive."

"You could've just said that," said Henry, reaching for an empty drink.

Moraya and Wendland both shrugged and nodded their heads in agreement.

Eli frowned at his empty glass. "I think I'd like another one of these, Wendland."

"I think we all would," said Wendland, pouring another round of tequila. "What are we drinking to this time?"

"Sobriety. May it stick to better men than us," said Eli.

The glasses clinked, tapped, and were thrown back.

"How old were you?" asked Moraya.

"Me?" Eli responded.

"Yes. How old were you when your father died?"

"Seventeen," he said, nodding slightly.

"Why did you go to Seattle?"

"My father owed people money. I had to pay the debt," said Eli, not breaking eye contact with his pint glass.

"You're lying," she said, though she spoke it as an observation, not an accusation.

Eli looked a bit caught off guard and did not respond. He just clenched his teeth with his pint glass between his hands.

"Why would you lie about becoming a Collector?" she inquired gently.

He sighed. "Sometimes, it just seems easier than explaining the truth."

She placed a hand on his shoulder. "Explaining is easy. It's justifying that's difficult. You don't need to justify anything to us." Her voice was like deep, warm water, or a fire on a cold day. Hearing it made you feel as though you could wrap yourself in the words and be safe.

Eli looked at her, and Henry could've sworn he could see a tear gathering in the corner of his eye.

"I was angry," Eli said. "His death was unexpected, and out of my control. I felt powerless. I couldn't stand to be at the old house without him, so I sold it. I knew about the Vault, and Collectors, and in my grief, I deceived myself into thinking that killing would numb the pain and make me feel like I was in control again. Of something. Eventually, the guilt overpowered the grief, and I stopped."

"What overpowers the guilt?" asked Henry.

"For a long time, nothing," said Eli. "Then, in a few experiences that are so meaningful that saying them out loud would cheapen their worth, I met God. And He led me to the monks. They taught me about grace. About how it is the only thing that can truly heal. The only reason we could ever forgive."

Moraya looked away, hiding her expression, and took a few sips of her beer.

"Then you met Grace," said Henry.

"Yes," said Eli with an absent smile. "Then I met her."

"You found peace in your faith?" asked Moraya.

"Yes," Eli said with a smile.

"I envy you," she said. "Faith brought me nothing but pain. Hope only brought...disappointment."

"I'm sorry. I wish I had an answer for you, but I don't," said Eli truthfully.

"You don't?" mocked Moraya. She was somewhat surprised but clearly wanted to cover it. "Usually, people of the faith always have an answer. Aren't you going to tell me that everything happens for a reason?"

"Everything definitely happens," said Eli matter-of-factly.

"So, you don't think that your god makes everything happen?" Moraya practically sneered the words out.

"Certainly not. But I think He can use everything for good."

Henry felt a small surge of anger rise in him when he heard those words, but he decided to drown it instead of giving it breath to speak.

"I'm going to check on Bentley," he said rather abruptly and walked towards the door in as straight of a line he could manage.

He was glad for the cold night air once outside. "How're you doing, old boy?"

Bentley chopped his bit contentedly.

"You ever wonder what she would look like now? Nearly all grown up. I don't say it often enough, Bentley. I'm sorry I couldn't save her."

Just then, he heard the door open behind him, and all three of his companions shuffled out.

"Cigarette!" ordered Wendland.

Henry quickly rolled one for each of them.

"You've got a really fine-looking horse," commented Wendland to Henry.

"It's not his horse," said Eli almost instinctively.

"Oh, is it one of yours?"

Moraya and Eli both shook their heads, then laughed outright.

"Then whose is it?" asked Wendland with a grin.

All three turned to Henry, who took a long drag on his cigarette and looked from face to face before lowering his gaze to his boots. He said he was never going to speak of it, but that was years ago. Maybe it was time to break his rule. He glanced at Wendland and caught his eye. The strange silence again. He felt compelled to break his rule. *Fuck it.*

"Her name was Scarlet. She was my daughter. Bentley was her horse." He paused and dragged his cigarette, but no one else filled the silence. It was as though it had made a blanket of itself and wrapped around them.

Just saying her name to another human lifted a weight off his chest he sometimes forgot he carried.

"She picked him out when he was just a colt. It was her sixth birthday. I advised her to choose a mare, but she insisted on a stallion." Henry sighed. "Scarlet was born on a rainy May morning. My wife, Lily, asked me to quit collecting and take up the plow, but I was young and still too ambitious and refused to listen.

"Those were good years. We had a little house in a clearing on the top of a hill in upstate New York. Just the three of us. I would take about one Ask a month. We stashed away all the cash, which now I wish we never had done. I wish I had spent it all on pretty things for her. For both of them.

"Eventually, a group of knockoff triggermen set up shop in the town near our house. Why they chose that town, I'll never know. They would take a life for a few hundred dollars. When the cost of a soul falls to an affordable price, chaos replaces consequence. The men, there were six of them, knew that I was paid well and lived cheap, and figured that I must have amassed a stash of money hidden somewhere on our property. Which I did. So, one night in early October, they decided to do something about it. Get rid of the competition and score a huge haul all in one take.

"I was sitting on our little porch smoking a cigarette before bed. When I finished, I tried to go back inside, but the door was locked. It was a little joke Lily had been playing on me since we bought the place seven years previously. I had a spare key hidden in the woodshed, which was a little ways from the house. I started walking towards it and looked up at the stars. I realized that I never wanted to leave that little patch of heaven with my two perfect devils ever again. I decided right there and then to never take another Ask. I was going to use the money we had been saving, buy all the land adjacent to us, and take up the plow.

"Maybe we would even try for another kid. I built this little scene in my mind. Me on the porch, Scarlet in my arms reading the *Odyssey* to me. Lily in a chair beside me holding a baby, a son. For the first time since I was a boy, I felt like the demon inside me was gone. I decided that I was going to tell Lily the very next morning. Wake her up with a kiss and the news that I would never have to say goodbye again. I let my guard down. I didn't realize that I had already said goodbye for the last time.

"Something hit me from behind, and the world went green and black. I don't know how long I laid there. When I woke up, it was still the middle of the night. The back of my head was sore and sticky with blood. Then I remembered my family. I stood up, dizzy and nauseous, and looked back towards the house. The door was kicked open. I tried to run towards it, but I stumbled a few steps before I fell and vomited. That happened twice more before I finally reached the porch. I called to them, but they didn't call back. I didn't want to go inside for fear of what would greet me, but I couldn't just stand there on the porch. So I went in, and there they lay. The fire in the hearth ensured that I saw all that I did not want to see."

Henry's voice had been calm and soft as he gave words to his heartache. He sighed and continued.

"They were dead. Both of them. Butchered with my own

razor, which sat bloodied beside them. I held them for hours, then I buried them. When the sun rose, I picked the razor up off the floor, put a saddle on Bentley, and rode into town. I stopped outside the apartment the trigger men had been using as a base camp. I walked in and found them playing billiards, my gold strewn across the floor. They recognized me, but there was nothing they could do fast enough. I killed them with the cue ball and my razor. Sometimes I wish I'd made them suffer more, but most times I'm glad I didn't. I don't think my rage could have been tamed.

"Later that day, I packed a bag, burned my little house down, and rode south."

He tried to take a drag, but his cigarette was out. The other three stood absolutely speechless. Henry wondered what they were thinking, but he couldn't bring himself to look at them. He felt a firm, gentle hand squeeze his shoulder, and he looked up to see Eli. He had rarely seen eyes as under- standing and full of compassion as Eli's were in that moment.

Moraya ran her fingers down the back of his neck. He felt it all the way down to his toes. She took his hand and led him back into the saloon. They sat down at the bar as Wendland readied four more shots.

"What are we toasting this time?" he asked all of them but looking at Henry.

Henry didn't feel like toasting, nor did he want to talk anymore. But Moraya's hand was warm in his. It calmed the storm slightly.

"Well?" asked Wendland, holding up his glass.

Eli cleared his throat. All eyes turned to him.

"To Henry."

"To Henry," replied the other two.

The glasses clinked, tapped, and were thrown back. And inexplicably, Henry felt at ease.

The rest of the evening was a bit of a blur. Wendland had their horses stabled and let them stay in a guest room above the bar, free of charge. Henry, in his stupor, still made a point to drink as much water as possible before falling asleep.

That night he dreamt that he was on the porch of his little house, smoking and smiling at the stars. After a few minutes, he went inside, and his daughter was sitting by the fire with a book. He took a step towards her and then snapped awake with a falling sensation.

Chapter Seventeen

I t was still early. Henry was sprawled out half on the floor, half on a mattress on the floor. Moraya and Eli were both sleeping deeply on their larger and much more comfortable beds. He vaguely remembered drawing the short straw on that situation the night before. He got up and crept downstairs quietly so as to let his companions sleep off the tequila.

There was a steaming pot of coffee on a stove, but no one to pour him any. So, he just sat and began stropping his razor.

"Coffee?" a friendly voice behind him asked.

"Please."

The voice belonged to a plump young lady with kind eyes. She slid a steaming mug towards him. Henry graciously accepted it.

"Wendland's not here this morning?" Henry asked.

"No, off on another one of his excursions," she answered over her shoulder.

"I see. Where does he go?" asked Henry, taking a sip.

"Oh, who's to say? Always comes back with mad stories. If

you ask me, I'd say he's not all there. Some of the things he talks about from his excursions, you just wouldn't believe."

"Oh?" said Henry, somewhat mystified. *What an odd place this, is but this coffee is phenomenal.* "How much do I owe you?"

"Nothing. Wendland insisted," said the young lady with a smile. She was bustling about, preparing food and polishing bottles and just generally looking quite busy.

"Bit of an odd character, isn't he?"

"Aren't all the best ones?"

Henry couldn't deny it.

When he was on his second cup of coffee, he heard the door open and turned to see a short, tan fellow walk in. The man nodded to Henry as he approached the bar and sat down. He wore strange clothes that did not seem suited to travel, and under his jacket, on his hip, Henry could see the telltale bump of a sidearm.

Henry had left his revolver upstairs but still had his razor.

The man took off his jacket, more of a dress coat really, and hung it on the hook in front of his stool and asked the waitress for a cup of "kafe," in an accent that Henry found ridiculous.

She gave him a confused half smile and poured him a cup. "One cup of coffee. Will there be anything else?"

"Not at the moment," he said with a wink, then he turned to Henry. "Well, mon frère, I'm beginning to think my time has been wasted in coming here."

"How far have you come?" asked Henry.

"Oh, incredibly far. You would not believe it if I told you," said the man with a flourish. "But travel can be quick if you know which door to leave by."

"I've been hearing that a lot today," said Henry, rolling a cigarette. "Would you like one?"

"No, no, merci. I have my own," said the man, patting the breast pocket on his vest.

Henry nodded.

After a moment, the man shrugged and looked at Henry again. "Are you not going to ask me why I am here? Or my name? Or occupation?" he asked with too much intonation.

Henry let out a long exhale. This was far too much talking for how little coffee he'd had after how much tequila he had drank. "Why are you here?"

"Let me start with my name," said the little man. "I am Emil Boucher. I am a Collector, and I am here for the killer of one Kyle Crenshaw."

"Are you now?" said Henry, turning on his stool to face the man, open posture, hands on knees.

"Come, come, mon frère, there is no need to show your hackles like some great beast. We are civilized men. And to my original point, I believe I have wasted my time in coming here. Because," he said the last with even more flair, "I believe that you too are a Collector, and I never known a Collector to pick traveling companions that do not also share the mark." He finished with a satisfied smile.

Henry said nothing but raised an eyebrow at the man.

"And as you know, Collectors do not Collect their own," Emil added.

"I'm aware of the codes," said Henry.

"Right. Well, you must forgive me for asking, but I would just like to hear it from you directly that the two with whom you travel are also indeed Collectors." Emil let the words hang in the air. Not a threat. Not quite.

"Yes, Emil. We are three Collectors. I'm on an Ask, and they have a vested interest in my success."

"Excellent," said Emil with gusto.

Henry sparked up his cigarette and turned his attention back to his cup of coffee.

"Well then, I shall leave you to it and trouble you no further," said Emil, standing up. "But I should warn you, Mr. Crenshaw of Chico is none too happy about the death of his second-born. Though I dare say he would be far more perturbed if it had been his first or third born." He chuckled a little.

"I appreciate the professional courtesy, Emil," said Henry.

"I would avoid Chico for the foreseeable future."

"Got it," said Henry, raising his glass to the little man.

"Right," said Emil, standing awkwardly for a moment. "I... better be getting back."

"You do that," said Henry.

"Farewell, mon frère," said Emil Boucher.

Henry gave a non-committal, over the shoulder wave and then heard the door swing open and close. *What the hell was that?*

It was about forty-five minutes later when Eli and Moraya joined him. They ate toast, eggs, and ham, then they began riding. Henry didn't mention the strange interaction he'd had with the odd, little Collector. The recollection of it felt more like that of a hallucination than a memory. It was bizarre, and Henry made note to avoid Chico if he was lucky enough to pass that way again. If he made it through the night.

The land was more wooded now. Vast forests reached endlessly on either side of the ancient highway. It was beautiful, almost mystical. Henry thought back to before the Crash when this place would've been nearly overrun by people and machines. He couldn't even fathom what the noise would've been like. Thousands of cars screaming up and down this now-so-peaceful highway. And he thought about before that, before all the cars and roads, before the rise and the fall of the last great civilization, before the highway even existed. He would've liked to have seen that. But this was the next best thing.

He felt some nervousness in his body and mind. Tonight was the night. With some luck, twenty-four hours from now, he would be on his way to receive a fortune. Then he would be rich, deeply and truly rich. By most standards, Henry was already quite wealthy. But it was a dispersed, nomadic sort of wealth. It was common for Collectors to open accounts in the cities and towns they visited, as well as rent or buy flats in such towns. They lived fairly transient lifestyles, but they would often revisit the same towns over and over again, so it was practical to set up accounts along their routes and migrations. Henry had many such accounts.

He let himself dream for a moment about the little glade on the ranch and imagine what it would be like to wake every morning to the sound of a stream. He looked at Moraya, the way her raven black hair caught the sun and cast about her fair cheeks, and he wondered what she planned to do when this was all over. Then he banished the thought from his mind.

They rode single file, none of them really feeling like conversation. Moraya led, Eli was in the middle, and Henry brought up the rear.

"What a forest, old boy, and just look at that mountain out there. I've seen a lot of peaks, but that one just might be my favorite."

Bentley snorted happily.

They came out of the walls of the trees to an open place. On one side of the road was a long hill rising up out of the trees. On the other side of the road, the right-hand side, was a broad open field stretching up before them. The wind rushed through the golden expanse. Henry's eyes rested on a red barn at the far end of the clearing just before the trees started again. It was pretty, in its own, lonely way. Henry wanted to stop and look at it more, but he knew that examination would ruin its simple beauty.

Moraya had gained a bit of a lead on them. Henry clicked his tongue, and Bentley glided, as if riding the wind, up towards Moraya.

"How much farther?" he asked, reining in Bentley as he approached her.

"A few hours." She pulled out her canteen. "We should be at the Haven an hour or two after dark." She took a drink and handed the canteen to Henry.

"What say we get there a bit sooner and take a rest before we move in tonight?" he asked before taking a swig of her water.

She fastened it back on the saddle. "If that's what you would prefer. You're the one going inside, after all."

Henry turned back to Eli. "Want to do some real riding?"

Eli put his heels into his horse and sped past the other two.

Not about to be outdone, they followed suit. They rode hard for about forty-five minutes before slowing to a trot. Bentley fought when Henry tried to slow him.

"You'd run yourself to death if you had the chance," said Henry. "Crazy bastard."

Chapter Eighteen

Henry sat, checking his weaponry. Six in the cylinder, sixty spread throughout various pockets and across his gun belt. The Bowie knife was ready to go, and the razor was nearly there, a stubborn burr reluctant to let go of the edge as he stropped it. It was a natural result of the last time he used it for something other than shaving.

"Nervous?" asked Moraya, stepping around the trees to sit next to Henry.

"I am but the sea. Nothing but a consequence," Henry said, not looking up from his work.

"But are you nervous?"

"I've been killing since I was eight, Moraya. I'm not nervous." He looked at her, his eyes empty. "I smell blood, and I'm thirsty."

Moraya flushed slightly. "I still get nerves sometimes before a Collection."

"It's because you still have them. I can't lie. I'm somewhat jealous of that."

"Don't be dramatic. You have them too. You just don't

listen to them." Her voice seemed softer than it usually did. Her heart rate was slightly elevated. *She actually is a little nervous.*

He cautiously put a palm on her shoulder, as if he was calming Bentley. "You're too pretty to die. Me, on the other hand? I guess let's hope I'm too damn mean."

She smiled at him and her heart slowed back down.

Henry refocused on stropping his razor. The burr was now gone. He plucked a hair from his head, held it over the blade and let it go. It floated gently towards the edge; there was not a breath of wind to deter it. Then, ever so softly, it met the steel and the edge loosed its two halves from each other. Satisfied, Henry snapped the blade shut.

"It's nearly dark," Henry said. "We wait thirty minutes after night falls, then we move. I'll use blades to reach the Asked, but I'll collect the rat with a gun, so you'll know when I'm on my way out. Don't cause a ruckus until you hear my shot fire."

"I'll be as silent as death herself."

Eli opened his eyes. "I'll be nearby with the horses. We may have to leave in a hurry."

Aside from the full moon, it was fully dark now, and Henry was feeling impatient.

"Let's move," he said. "It's as dark as it's going to get, and I'd like to study the grounds before I go in."

They mounted up and started moving.

Henry patted Bentley's neck. "This is it, old boy. What a crazy fucking week,"

The night was cool with clear skies. The moon and stars cast their silver blue light across the land. The trees loomed ominously above them like dark spectators of some morose game. They left the road and started up a long gravel lane.

"Wait here with the horses," Moraya said to Eli in a low

voice. "Once you hear gunfire, get as close as you can without being seen."

Eli nodded.

They dismounted, then Henry held Bentley's face close to his own for a moment. "Wish me luck, old boy."

"This way," said Moraya just above a whisper.

They quickly made their way through the trees and soon saw it: the Haven. It was a fortress complete with a stone wall surrounding the ancient and angular steel, concrete, and glass complex. It was commonly known that it was built before the Crash. It was beyond opulent, and whatever technology had been used to build it was lost in the Crash itself.

"How many men you think there are?" asked Henry.

"No less than eleven in the elite guard. They'll be in the house with the Fairchild. Beyond that, I'm not sure. We'll have to get on top of that wall to see how many are encamped on the grounds."

"Let's do it," said Henry.

They scanned the open area between the trees and the wall. There was nothing. And from what they could see, there were no sentries anywhere but at the main gate house. It was about a hundred yards to the wall from where they were. They left the concealment of the trees and moved quickly to the wall.

"Boost me up," said Moraya.

Henry obeyed. "What do you see?"

There was a pause. "There are..." She counted under her breath for another moment. "Ten three-man tents plus all the other tents. No doubt that the larger one is a mess hall. Another one looks to be an armory, and there are a few supply tents as well. If I had to guess, I'd say there are no more than thirty or so regular soldiers. We're lucky we got here before the reinforcements."

"Sentries?"

"A few, but not in our path. Looks like most are bedded down for the night. Let's get this over with."

She swung a leg over the wall and pulled Henry up after her. They sat there, straddling the wall, facing each other for a moment. She took out a dagger, the same one she had used on the sentry the day before. It was something he had only seen one other time. It was about ten inches long with one sharpened edge and a very slight curve.

"Do you know what this is?" she asked as she unscrewed the small pommel and inserted a vile from her coat.

"Yes. It's a fang. The blade is made of a porous metal of unknown origin. The venom you just inserted into the handle paralyzes and kills almost instantly unless the antidote is administered," said Henry, unconsciously leaning back a little to create distance from the deadly thing.

"Very good. But there's no need to keep your distance. It only cuts if I mean it to. Kind of like you and heartbeats."

Henry gave her a quizzical look.

"I'm not without my talents. I have two of them. There will be no more soldiers left when we meet again." She pulled a flask from inside her jacket and took a long pull. "Finish it." She handed it to Henry. It was less than half full.

He set it to his lips and then handed it back empty. "I will."

"Good luck." She slipped the empty flask into the inner breast pocket of his coat.

"Thank you." He looked at her for a brief moment, taking her in and knowing that she might be the last beautiful thing that he would ever lay eyes on. He did not want to look away. Then he turned to the task at hand. The wall was about eight feet tall. He pushed himself off.

His mind flooded with thoughts as his body left the ledge.

Thoughts of his childhood and his father. Thoughts of Eli and his ranch. Thoughts of Moraya. He thought of the day Scarlet chose Bentley. He thought of Bentley. He thought of Scarlet and Lily, and then his feet hit the ground, and he thought of nothing except his next moves.

Chapter Nineteen

Henry didn't look back at Moraya, but he heard her feet hit the ground an instant after his did. There was a ground-level entrance into the building a hundred yards in front of him. That's where he had to go. He felt the whiskey tingle in the base of his skull as he moved like a shadow across the garden. He saw two sentries in the distance, standing under lanterns by the main gate, blissfully unaware of the fate they were doomed to.

He reached the door. Finding it locked, he pulled out a few delicate tools from a coat pocket. A moment later, the door was open. Now in a small entry room, he kicked a small pair of shoes and boots out from under his feet and looked through a door that was already ajar down a hallway. A guard stood at the end—no doubt one of the "no less than eleven" elites that protected the Fairchild at all times. He pulled the Bowie knife that Preston gave him out of his belt and checked its weight and balance. It felt quite comparable to a knife he worked with when he was much younger.

Five rotations distance.

Henry stood. He inhaled and swung the door open,

stepped into the hallway, and poised holding the knife by the blade. The elite looked at him as the knife left his hand. Thump. Henry exhaled as he quickly traversed the hallway. He had just cleaned the knife on the elite's shirt when the door directly in front of him opened, and two elites stepped into the hallway. He still had the Bowie knife in his hand, and they did not expect him there. He slashed at one man's throat, and the other let out a stifled shout as Henry smashed his head into the wall with his left hand plunging the knife in and out of his chest. The one with a slashed throat threw himself at Henry in a dying effort to choke him from behind. Henry landed one, two, three elbows into his gut, then the man fell back hard against the opposite wall and slid to the ground. A moment later, Henry was at the top of the stairway at the heavy door waiting for the sound of coughing and gurgling below him to stop.

Ten seconds. Twenty seconds. It stopped.

He was slick with blood, but not his own. Not yet at least. He cracked open the door and looked into a large room. One elite on a couch with his back to the door, another on the balcony through the glass wall. He switched the Bowie knife to his left hand, point down, and opened his razor with his right. He quietly pushed the door open and moved towards the couch. He was halfway to the couch where the one elite rested when the guard on the balcony turned. Immediately their eyes met. The man shouted, and Henry knew that his strategy was about to change. The guard on the couch jumped to his feet and turned in time for Henry to leap, razor first, over the couch and tackle him onto the ground. There was a struggle, and Henry's hands were so bloody he lost his grip on the handle of the razor, but its work was already done and Henry took the man's gun. The guard from the balcony rushed into the room with a handgun raised, firing. One shot smashed through a vase near Henry's face, sending water and bits of glass at him. Another shot grazed his shoulder, and a third thudded into the head of the elite with a gash in his throat as he tried to get his hands around Henry's neck. Henry fired three times quickly, center mass, and then sent one more through the man's face.

"Fucking shit," said Henry.

Noise. The noise of men's voices and footsteps. Henry snatched up the gun from the other corpse, then looked at the door at the far end of the room and listened with all his sense. He had enough time to feel more than one heartbeat on the other side, but he couldn't figure out how many before it swung open. There was a barrage of gunfire. It shredded the couch he dove behind, bullets whizzed by him and smashed into the floor and everywhere else, sending dust and debris into his eyes, nose, and mouth. He looked over the remains of the couch, holding a gun in each hand, to see four of them coming through the door. Henry unloaded both guns in their direction as quickly as he could pull the triggers. Nine bullets, four targets. One of the guards fell dead, while the other three were still on their feet and charging at him with metal studded clubs.

He dropped the two empty pistols and fired the last two rounds of his own revolver into the chest of one elite. Then he pulled out his Bowie knife and lunged over the couch at the other two.

He protected his head at the expense of the underside of his upper arm, but the impact was still enough to send his senses reeling as he thrust the blade into one of the guard's chests and then spun, ducking a club while slashing at the other guard. They were still up, and he heard more footsteps coming. He punched one in the face. The cross guard of the Bowie knife punctured the man's forehead, then Henry ripped it out and smashed the man's face again. Taking a blow to the back, he spun, swinging, and the pommel met the temple of the remaining guard with a sickening, cracking thud.

His heartbeat began to hit a canter. He quickly scanned the room, looking for cover, and found it behind a short half wall, which he slumped behind as he reloaded. He heard more elites entering the room.

"Where are they?" a voice shouted.

He heard gunfire outside and an alarm bell rang out one halfhearted chime.

He snapped the cylinder back into position and leaned over the half wall. Three more elites, all out of cover. He fired one, two, three rounds, before ducking back behind the wall as a hailstorm of lead and shards of stone from the wall ripped and pelted and fell all around him. They were on him. But he was on them, too. He barely stopped a blade with his left hand as he emptied the revolver point blank into the man that held it. Another soldier launched into him, driving a shoulder hard into his gut, knocking the wind out of him as they sprawled on the floor, kicking, punching, and thrashing about. The man had enough hair for Henry to get a hold of it. He yanked man's head back so hard he felt a crack, and the soldier let out a pitiful screech and his hands went limp, then Henry leapt to his feet. The man was still alive, glaring at him as he laid motionless on the floor. The sound he made was awful. Henry snatched up a club and made the sound stop.

Three deep breaths. Heaving them in and out, he reloaded as he steadied himself, then walked into the next room. There were three gray-haired men—terrified, well dressed, and each with a conspicuous bump on their hip under the jacket,

One of them stepped forward, hands raised. "What do you think you're doing? Let's talk! We can—"

Henry sent a bullet through him, then into each of his two companions. Clean shots. They didn't suffer. He approached and found pistols on their belts. Then he took a moment to refresh his spent rounds.

There was a staircase in the middle of the room leading to the third and final floor. He stopped for a moment and listened as he reloaded. He closed his eyes. *I am but the sea.* He felt his heart slow. He felt more pulses in the room above. Six more. All of them elevated, one alarmingly so. They were ready for him. But he was ready to die.

There was a liquor cart in the corner, and he walked over to it. Three mostly full decanters of stuff strong enough to burn. There was a small towel. He ripped it into three pieces and then heard a sound behind him. He spun around in time to see the shins of a man coming down the stairs. In an instant, he sent a bullet through one shin. The man screamed and crashed violently down the stairs. Henry sent one more round through his head, replaced the bullets, then went back to his task with the bottles. Four more plus the Asked. He tried to not think about Moraya. He soaked the bits of rag and then stuffed them into the tops of the decanters. Then, standing at the base of the stairs, he closed his eyes and felt where the remaining elites were above him. He lit the rags and began throwing the bottles. He heard them shatter and the familiar whoosh of flames taking light. Henry took a breath and charged up the stairs.

Everything happened quickly. The flames were spreading, and the air was filled with smoke. Four elites turned and saw Henry there, covered with blood, sleeves rolled up, his face as calm as the reaper. One of them was within arm's length of Henry. Henry's razor flashed, then the man clutched his throat. Henry used him as cover as his companion's shots tore through him. There was a heavy impact on the left side of Henry's chest, sending him sprawling to the floor, and for an eternal instant, Henry was sure his heart would not beat again. But it did. He whipped up his revolver and returned fire. One, two heads were scattered on the walls behind them. Henry rolled to his feet to face the last elite whose back was to him.

He was pulling, by the hand, a small figure, hair in a tight bun, with a small tattoo on the back of its neck. The revolver went off again. Before the last elite had even fallen to the ground, Henry steadied his .45 at the back of the last head— Clarke Fairchild's head.

She turned around.

Henry stopped. She. How could it be her? It was not an evil face that stared into his; it was his daughter's.

He blinked hard, breaking the mirage, and he no longer saw his daughter's face. It was a face he didn't recognize—a scared, innocent face. She was young, too young to die. The barrel of his revolver began to shake. *Do it.* He tried to steady his aim, but his hands would not obey him. He was going to be sick. There she stood, Clarke Fairchild, a girl who could not have been much older than nine or ten years of age, still clinging to the hand of her dead protector. *Is this how Scarlet looked before they murdered her?* The thought overwhelmed him. His stomach turned, and he doubled over, retching up blood and whiskey on the floor.

Still pointing the barrel in Clarke's direction, he looked back at her. She had welled up with tears. *Just pull the trigger.* Her eyes began to brim over. *Just pull the fucking trigger.* She began to sob and pulled a knife out of her dead protector's belt.

He couldn't do it.

He lowered his revolver.

She ran at him with the knife, but he took it from her, tossing it across the room, and then he held her firm by the shoulders until she stopped struggling and glared at him through tears of rage and fear.

"Do you have a coat?"

Confused, she slowly stopped crying and pointed to a small coat tossed over the back of a nearby chair the flames had not yet reached.

Henry fetched it and walked back to her. She seemed utterly confused. He offered his large, bloody hand to her. Her hands were bloody too. She took his hand.

"Well, let's go then."

He headed towards the stairs, and she followed half a pace behind, tightly gripping his hand. The flames were running out of things to burn in the stone room. Her eyes darted from one body to the next, seeing but too shocked to fully comprehend.

"Don't look at them," he said, taking his own advice.

Henry had to walk slower than he was used to. She stared blankly at the corpses they passed. When they finally reached the door Henry had entered, Clarke stopped and mechanically pulled on the small pair of shoes Henry had nearly tripped over on his way in.

The darkness and breeze welcomed them.

"This way."

She kept up half a pace behind. They walked towards the gatehouse.

"Did Thorpe send you?" she asked. "They were afraid that he would send you."

Henry stopped and looked at her "Who was afraid?"

"My advisors," she said. "They were my teachers."

"The old men?" he asked.

"They were my friends." Her voice quaked with grief, and a rage Henry recognized.

He caught his breath. "Thorpe didn't send me." They started again towards the gatehouse.

Moraya stepped out of it when they were a few paces away. "About time," she said. "I was beginning to think..."

She stopped dead in her tracks, looking from Clarke to Henry.

"Moraya, this is Clarke Fairchild," said Henry in as calm a tone as he could manage.

Moraya seemed catatonic.

"What's going on?" All three turned and faced Eli, who had just stepped through the gate, horses in tow.

Time seemed to stop. Henry was overwhelmed by the circumstances. If he did not kill Clarke, Moraya would lose her chance at freedom, and Eli's ranch would become a war zone. If they did manage to fight off Lipton's army, it would be at a staggering cost. They might not ever regain the progress they had worked so hard for. He had seen the hope in Moraya's eyes when she spoke of freedom from Lipton, but then he looked at Clarke, and it was all he could do to keep from seeing Scarlet. He was capable of numbing himself to a great many things. But not that. Not her.

"Henry," repeated Eli. "What's going on? Who is that?"

Henry tried to seem steady, but he felt the shaking in his tone as he replied. "This is Clarke."

Eli's fist clenched around the handle of the whip, which was coiled and hooked to his belt.

Henry's fist clenched around the handle of his revolver. It still had one round in the cylinder.

Moraya was still frozen.

Eli eyed Henry's gun hand.

Henry's mind flashed to watching Scarlet chase butterflies. Then to burying her. Then he remembered Clarke, and his veins turned to ice.

Eli released his grip on the whip and sighed. "I guess...our plans have changed."

Henry felt a flood of relief and threw his arms around Eli, who was surprised, but after a moment embraced Henry before patting him on the back.

Henry stepped away. "I don't know what I expected."

"I wouldn't do that," said Eli. "I won't do that."

"Fuck," said Moraya under her breath. "I was so close."

"I'm sorry, Moraya. She's just a kid," said Henry, looking down at the little face, her eyes wide, staring back at the Haven.

"There will be serious repercussions for this," said Eli.

"You have no idea," said Moraya.

"No. There will not. Because I'm going to kill him," said Henry. All three looked at him. "I'll go back to New York the way I came, and I'll cut his throat."

"He's in Portland," said Moraya.

"My warden is on his way to Portland," said Clarke. "He's probably there by now. He went by rail a few days ago."

All three looked at her. The shock began to clear from her eyes.

"Your warden?" asked Henry.

"Evan Thorpe. My *advisors* were alarmed that he left Sacramento." She looked at Henry with the kind of malice he had only ever seen in a mirror.

"Look at me," said Moraya, pulling Clarke's icy gaze away from Henry. "Did you say Thorpe?"

"Yes. My warden."

"The Thorpes designed Sacramento to be what it is," said Eli in a tone Henry had not heard from him before.

Moraya spoke up. "Lipton let that name slip once." She

appeared to have a moment of realization. "You can't trust that man, Clarke. He's been feeding Lipton information."

"I can't trust anyone since Grandpa died," said Clarke.

"Did Thorpe say why he was going to Portland?" Moraya asked.

Clarke scowled, thinking hard. "They said he was meeting with generals. And they were afraid he might have sent someone like you after me." She looked back at the Haven. "I guess they were right."

"But Thorpe didn't send me," said Henry.

"Who did?" asked Clarke.

Henry glanced at Eli and then looked back at Clarke. "Lipton."

Clarke took a sharp inhale through her nose. "Grandpa's Lipton?"

Henry shook his head. "I don't know. Charles B. Lipton."

"He was Grandpa's friend. Grandpa was his teacher." Bewilderment briefly wiped the grief and scorn from her face, then she seemed to recall something.

"They're in Portland," said Henry, trying to make sense of the situation.

"At Hotel Kex. At least Lipton is," said Moraya. "If we play our cards right, he won't know our plans have changed. We can get close."

"Only if we maintain the element of surprise," said Henry. "An unstable element at best. But it's the closest thing to a plan that we've got."

They all looked at each other for a moment, unsure of what to say next. Clarke broke the silence. "You're going to kill them?"

They all looked at Henry. He spoke as he reached for a cigarette. "Yes. I will. It's the only way to keep them from killing us."

"I don't see any better options," said Eli.

Moraya nodded. "That would certainly be one way to clear my debt with him."

Clarke said nothing.

Moraya motioned to her right. "There's a clean tent that can accommodate us. That one there, farthest out, closest to the mess tent."

Eli looked at Clarke and approached her gently. "I can take you if you'd like. We can get you cleaned up before you go to sleep."

"I don't think I can sleep. I am a mess, though," she said, looking at the blood spattered across her hands and arms.

"Come on," said Eli, leading her along.

Henry and Moraya followed a few paces behind.

"I didn't hear too many shots from out here," he said.

"They were asleep when I fell on them. Your shots woke the last few up, but it was quick work. Less experienced men out here. They didn't sleep armed. They weren't expecting a woman. They weren't expecting anything at all except rein-forcements."

They walked along for a moment longer before Henry felt the ache in his chest and remembered. "Oh, I meant to give this back to you." He pulled out the flask she had given him. There was a bullet lodged in it.

She looked at it, and then looked at him, and then looked away for a moment.

He held it out to her, and after a couple of steps, she took it from him, her fingers stroking his ever so slightly as she did. It was probably an accident. It was dark out, after all.

She said nothing, but Henry reached out with his mind and felt her heart racing. They were a few paces away from the tent and she stopped him.

"Henry."

"Yes?"

She looked at him, and he at her, and they were quiet for a second. "Will you help me with the bodies?"

It took nearly two hours, but they made two piles of them, and logs for burning, and canvas from some of the smaller tents. They soaked the whole bloody mess with oil and lit the piles ablaze. They took care of the horses, then they walked wordlessly back to the tent and washed themselves with a barrel of water just outside of it. Clarke and Eli were both asleep already.

Henry pulled off his clothes and slipped between the soft, fresh covers of the small cot. Weariness hit him like a ten-foot wave. His body hurt from all the cuts and bruises, but it was nothing compared to the relief of once again facing inevitable death and somehow still making it to bed. He thought of the little glade on the ranch and disembarked from consciousness.

He dreamt of a porch, but a different porch than usual. He was sitting watching the sun peek up over the trees, and he couldn't see anyone else, but he was not alone. And he was at peace.

Chapter Twenty

The sun woke Henry up the next morning, glowing orange and yellow through the walls of the tent. Henry's whole body cried out from the injuries of the previous evening. Sitting up off the cot was enough to pull a painful grunt out of him, rattling loose some new and unpleasant sensations through his chest. Nevertheless, he got dressed and stepped out into the morning as first light crept towards him over the mountains, and through the trees.

The Haven looked different in the yellow light. He noticed a horse stable with a corral beside, containing the mounts of the deceased. Henry walked over and opened the gate, stepping aside as the horses meandered out into the grounds. Satisfied, he entered the stable. There were a handful of highbred stallions, and in the farthest stall, a small gelding.

Henry freed the stallions on his way to the gelding. It greeted him over the gate, and he wished he had an apple to give it. It was already well groomed, but Henry still ran the brush over him for good measure. Then he tacked up the gelding and brought him out to meet Bentley. Once they were introduced, he took his time brushing not only Bentley but Eli and Moraya's horses as well. Eli woke up next, then Moraya, who promptly went to arouse Clarke.

With no food, aside from the coffee beans Henry passed around, they hit the road. It was a grueling day. The wind blew occasional gusts of spattering rain into their faces, and then it would stop as it started. What little food they ate was cold. Please and thank you were about the only words Clarke spoke to Henry all day, and only when he offered her coffee beans. He knew she was too young for them, but it was the only thing that paused the proactive silence she warded against him.

Aside from one lone, old man traveling south, they didn't see another soul. Dinner was quick and cold, and sleep came on fast to all of them. Henry slept just below the surface as he often did.

Click.

For a moment, he didn't know why he had woken up. The stars peeked through tree branches and cast a pale glow across the fallen leaves and dried pine needles that invaded Henry's bedroll. Then the shadows shifted with a rustle and he saw her.

No less than three feet away, Clarke stood, pointing Henry's .45 directly at him, center mass. Her hands were steady, but her heart was racing. Even in that light, Henry recognized that the hammer was cocked. But her grip was off.

"You'll want to move your hands up to the top of the grip if you plan on pulling the trigger," he whispered so as to not wake up the other two. "Otherwise, it'll fly out of your hands."

She adjusted her grip, barrel still trained at Henry.

"Very good," Henry whispered. Then he waited.

There was enough light to see the anger in Clarke's eyes, enough light to see the glint off the barrel.

Then came a sound.

Bentley huffed as he awoke and stepped gingerly over to Clarke. He nuzzled her.

She brushed him away with one hand and then steadied her aim back on Henry without a word.

Bentley stamped the ground and nuzzled her again, huffing right in her ear this time.

Clarke glared at him, lowering the .45, but Bentley refused to be ignored. He pressed his forehead into her chest and huffed again.

Henry watched as the rage in her eyes began to melt. She hugged Bentley's head to her chest for a moment, and Henry began to breathe a little easier. He didn't see her cry, but her heart slowed down to a calm pace.

After a moment, she released Bentley, then looked over at Henry. "You're lucky your horse wants to protect you."

Henry sat up with slow cautious movements. "He's not my horse. And I don't think it's me he's trying to protect."

"You were riding him. And you're the one I was going to kill."

"I know. If you had pulled the trigger, I'd be dead. Being dead's easy, kid. Being the one to walk away..." His voice trailed off.

"Why would he protect me?" asked Clarke. Her voice wasn't murderous, but it was far from warm.

"I think you remind him of his owner. My daughter. Scarlet." The words kept falling out of his mouth without him trying. "We lost her a while back, but Bentley stayed with me."

Clarke looked back at Bentley and rubbed his velvet nose, then she directed her eyes at Henry. "I don't trust you."

"I don't expect you to, but let's make a deal."

She kept looking at him.

"If you don't kill me, I'll make sure no one kills you."
Henry meant it.

She looked at Bentley and thought about it for a moment,
then with both hands, she let the hammer down easy, set the
.45 at Henry's feet, and went back to her bedroll.

Henry was so relieved he didn't even notice his pain for a
full thirty seconds. He took his revolver and checked it and
put it back in its holster by his head. Then he eased himself
back down to horizontal. He didn't think he'd be able to sleep
again, but he closed his eyes anyway. Next thing he knew, the
sun was coaxing him awake.

Stiff. Cold. Hungry. It did not matter. They still had
ground to cover.

Chapter Twenty-One

Eli did his best to focus on the task at hand. After breakfast, they got back on the road. It was even windier that day. A chilling breath from the north faced them as they made their way through the foothills of southern Oregon. If they were lucky, they'd reach Ashland before dark.

Eli was eager to find a place to eat. Riding that day had been especially strenuous for some reason. He knew the air was thinner than he was used to, but he had forgotten how much that actually affected him. Or maybe it wasn't the air. *One day at a time.*

They came to the city and entered. Ashland had always given Eli a strange sort of feeling. He loved it. He didn't put too much stock in mysticism, but this place always made him question his stance on the matter. The damp cold clutched his hands and nose, and the dense clouds made the air hazy to the point of, almost, misting slightly.

"I know of a good lodge just up this way," Moraya said, motioning with a toss of her head as she turned up a side street.

Clarke was the first to follow. Henry's face betrayed nothing, certainly not pain, as he directed Bentley up the side street.

In a previous world, the old stone building they approached had been part of a university, a bastion of knowledge in ages past. Now it was nothing but a monument of the fallen society. And a lodge.

They tied the horses out front and entered through a heavy wooden door. A young, clean-cut man with a broad smile greeted them from behind a desk.

"What can I help you with?" he asked congenially.

"We'll be here for the evening, stable fares for four horses, and four rooms will be all," said Moraya in a firm but polite tone.

"Of course." The attendant began making marks on his ledger. "It appears that we only have three available rooms, but one of them is a suite. It should be more than comfortable for two ladies like yourselves."

Moraya and Clarke shared a glance, shrugged, and nodded in agreement.

"Thank you," Clarke said. "You may send the complete bill to number three Graphton Street in Seattle."

"Of course," said the attendant with a nervous glance over his ledger. "Here are your keys. All three rooms are up the stairs and down the hallway to the left."

After they had washed up, they headed back down to the main road. Ashland was a very small town but had never felt like one. It was an oasis of sorts for travelers. There were farmers that worked the surrounding land, and, though technically in Fairchild territory, soldiers rarely spent time there. It had a sort of calm about it that was hard to find in most places.

"I'm starving," said Moraya. "I know of a good place just up the way."

"Lead on," said Henry.

She led them up the road and walked so quickly that Clarke was nearly running to keep up. After a few minutes, they stepped inside a brick building a few yards up a side street. The place was packed full. As soon as the bartender saw Moraya step through the door, he rushed to the nearest table, said something to the occupants that they seemed to find upsetting, and they quickly but quietly stood and left, their plates still half full. The bartender frantically flagged down a barmaid, and she had the table empty and clean before Moraya could even reach it.

"Moraya, my little bird, what a delight!" said the short, round, Italian bartender. He spoke in a warm gregarious tone as he took her hand and kissed it with a bow.

"Ezio, it's good to see you. Though I will say, you really didn't have to kick that poor couple out."

"And have you wait for a table like some kind of peasant? I'd sooner serve a Fairchild. May they all die a thousand deaths."

Moraya laughed at the irony.

Clarke seemed lost somewhere between anger, confusion, and amusement.

"Who are your friends?"

"This is Henry, Eli, and Clarke. We're traveling to Portland."

"Oh, I love Portland. Though I must ask, what is a group like you doing traveling together?"

"Ezio..." clucked Moraya patronizingly.

"Oh right, of course, of course. Your business is forever your own, as is my hospitality. Please sit."

They did.

Ezio's hospitality gave Martha a run for her money. Five courses later, Eli felt like more than his belly had been filled. After the meal, they sat and sipped coffee. Clarke insisted on taking hers black like everyone else, though she shuddered with every sip.

Moraya gently teased her, "You really can use sugar if you'd like, Clarke." She was more at ease here than Eli had seen her.

"No, I like it black," insisted Clarke, choking back a cough, which brought a smile to Henry and Moraya.

"Does the young lady not like the coffee?" observed Ezio, pulling up a chair with his own small cup in hand.

"No, I do. I promise," assured Clarke.

"Here you are, my little flower," said Ezio, dropping a sugar cube and a little cream into her cup. "There is no shame in not liking bitter things."

Clarke seemed disappointed until she took a sip, then she couldn't help but smile at the difference it made.

"So how is business going, Ezio? Still importing all that cheese from the old country?" Moraya asked the man.

"Of course. I actually just received a very large shipment yesterday. Several barons and generals have sent men to collect some."

"You sell cheese?" asked Clarke.

"Oh, it's so much more than cheese, my little flower. I sell the product of thousands of years of Italian practice and passion passed down from generation to generation. I sell the heart and soul of my home country. I sell the reason God blessed us with cows. My little lady, I sell perfection."

"Parmesan mostly," said Moraya, interrupting Ezio's dramatic pause.

"Psssh. You lack heart, Moraya," scolded Ezio.

Moraya shrugged and pursed her lips. "You more than make up for it, I'm sure."

"No amount can make up for how much you lack," jested Ezio.

"Who are some of your buyers for this shipment?" asked Moraya.

"Oh, come now, Moraya. I don't ask who you Collect, or who your friends are, or why you seem to have kidnapped a well-behaved young lady. Let me have at least one secret."

"If you insist, dear Ezio, if you insist."

The restaurant had calmed down significantly since they had arrived but was still far too busy for Ezio to sit for very long.

"Tell you what," he said. "You come back later this evening for drinks, and I'll let you sample some of the better cheeses from this shipment."

"Deal," said Moraya. "We'll meet back here, let's say, eight o'clock?" She turned to Eli and Henry.

"Sure," said Henry with a forced smile. "I'd like to see what perfection looks like."

"Where will you be until then?" Eli asked Moraya.

"Revisiting old haunts and savoring a few moments without you three constantly lurking about."

"There's a beautiful park not far up the road," said Ezio to Clarke. "It's a wonderful place for a walk through the trees, especially this time of year."

"Can we go?" she said, looking at Eli.

He glanced at Henry, who nodded. "Of course,"

Clarke had requested for the bill to be sent to number three Graphton Street, but Ezio refused to let them pay for a thing. They stepped out of the restaurant into the moody weather. Moraya took a left while the others turned right upon Ezio's direction. The meal had put Henry and Clarke

very much at ease, and the two walked a few steps ahead of
Eli in a leisurely silence.

A stone's throw down the street from them, a figure
walked quickly across the cobblestone and entered a store
front. Henry stopped walking. Clarke took a few steps more
before turning back to look inquisitively at him.

"What's wrong?" she said as Eli passed Henry and
glanced at his face. The calm was gone.

"Henry?" said Eli, placing a hand on his shoulder.

Henry snapped back to life. "Sorry, I thought I recognized someone. Just my mind playing tricks on me." He
pulled out a cigarette and lit it urgently. "Let's go then." He
attempted to try to sound as calm as he had been a moment
before.

He started walking again.

Eli noticed that Henry's hand was trembling slightly. It
made him feel uneasy.

Henry took a long drag of his cigarette.

Eli noticed Clarke glance at Henry's quivering hand. He
watched her begin to reach out with her own small hand and
then stop and pull back.

They walked all throughout the park, and very little was
said. Clarke was more at ease when Moraya was around. Eli
enjoyed the quiet. He enjoyed watching the heavy mist wash
over the town from the mountain. The sun was setting, but
the park was full of lampposts, casting a warm glow
throughout the wooded paths. Clarke sat down near the little
stream on a rock and watched the water.

Her silence became pensive when Eli and Henry perched
on rocks near her. She was hugging her knees, staring intently
at the water then spoke. "I've never really had friends before."

Eli looked at her, surprised.

She continued, "People always protected me and served

me and told me what to do because of my last name. You two are helping me in spite of it. I'm not used to that."

"You must've had friends," Eli said. "People that you played with."

"I had servants. They only spent time with me when they were paid to. I had my advisors...my teachers. They were good to me." She looked at Henry. "They're dead now."

"I'm sorry about your teachers," he said in a sincere tone. "I didn't have many friends growing up either."

"Nor I," Eli chimed in.

Clarke hugged her knees a little tighter. "I think I'd like to make more real friends when this is all over. I think I won't even tell them my last name just to be safe."

"Safe from what?" asked Henry sincerely.

"It's amazing how nice people can be when they think they might get something out of it."

Eli pondered for a moment what she had said. It made him sad. "What will you do once this is all over?"

She tossed a small stone into the stream. "I don't know. My family is all gone now. And my teachers. I don't want to be in charge. I think I'll sell all the land. Or give it away. My parents wanted me to be a strong heir, but I don't want that. What will you do?" Her face showed the depth of her thoughts, while her mouth puckered just a bit.

A large crimson leaf fell from a tree and landed gently on the surface of the water.

Eli watched it sail its course for a moment. "I'll return to the ranch. My ranch. You're both welcome to come with me."

"What's it like there?" Clarke inquired.

"It's beautiful and peaceful. There are a lot of people there your age. They all learn and work and live together. Most of them end up leaving together when the time eventually comes."

Clarke cocked her head to one side. "Where do they all come from?"

"Sacramento. We rescue them from the city."

She seemed surprised at this. "Why do they all need to be rescued? What keeps them in the city?"

Eli felt his jaw tighten. "The conditions in the city...they aren't good. I help people escape. I help them find their reason to live once they're out."

"I see," Clarke said thoughtfully. "I didn't know that. What's it like in Sacramento?"

Another leaf landed on the water.

Eli inhaled deeply, flaring his nostrils a bit as he did. "The people are always hungry, working every day from the age of four or five onward. They live in tenements, and they are perpetually intoxicated by the haze of poppy and herbs that burn constantly in the city. They're born, they're miserable, and then they die."

Clarke's eyes brimmed now with tears of shock and disbelief. "That's how my people live?"

"They aren't your people," said Eli, his words ripe with quiet conviction.

Clarke looked back down at the water. "I never knew. Grandpapa never talked to me about Sacramento, and father never talked to me at all. I never knew."

Eli quietly stared at the leaf as it drifted down the stream.

"If I live through this, the first thing I'll do is stop that," Clarke said. "I always knew that Sacramento was good for business, but I never knew how. I never knew Thorpe would..." For one so young, she seemed to understand the gravity of it all. "They never leave the city?"

"Not unless we get them out," said Eli.

"I'm so sorry." A few tears brimmed up in her eyes. "I'll fix it."

A dozen thoughts flashed through Eli's mind, not the least of which was how much time he had spent hating the people that had raised this little girl. "It's not your fault." He heard himself say the words, then he saw his hand rest on her shoulder to comfort her.

Then something he did not expect happened. She moved from her rock to his rock and buried her face in his shoulder. He had a soft spot for orphans, and he put his arm around her and hoped that she would keep her promise.

Chapter Twenty-Two

Henry wasn't paying much attention to Eli and Clarke's interaction. He rolled a cigarette. *It couldn't have actually been him, just some person that looked like him.* Either way, he was a bit rattled.

It started raining, lightly at first, then in great driving torrents. Thankfully, they reached Ezio's before they were completely drenched. It was mostly empty when they entered. The dining room was warm and well-lit by grain-shine lamps that flickered on walls and tables. The rotund little man smiled and directed them to a booth in the back corner of the establishment.

The door opened behind them, and Moraya walked in.

"Good evening, fellas," she said with a genuine smile.

"You seem rather chipper," responded Henry in kind.

"Give it twenty minutes. I'm sure I'll be sick of all of you again."

"Make yourselves comfortable. I'm just with a customer. I'll join you in a few minutes," said Ezio as he headed into the back room.

"As you wish," Moraya called back.

They found their way over to the booth and settled in.

"So how did you all spend your evening?" asked Moraya.

"We went to the park and walked around," said Clarke.

"It is beautiful there," said Moraya.

A barmaid brought dark beer to the table and water with cordial to Clarke.

"What are we drinking to?" Eli asked, looking at Henry.

Henry raised his glass, "To clear skies and open roads."

"Here, here," Moraya said.

"Cheers," added Eli.

Clarke raised her glass, but her smile seemed forced.

Henry wondered who had made the beer. It was fantastic. Dark, rich, and chocolaty, yet not too sweet or too heavy, and it was very cold.

"Where's the water closet?" asked Clarke once everyone had returned their glasses to the table.

"Just down the hallway and to the left," Moraya said.

She stood quickly and skipped in the direction Moraya had pointed.

Henry remembered a time he and Lilly took Scarlet into the little town they lived near. She had pranced through the restaurant exactly as Clarke just had. It was one of the only times she had been out into the town.

Suddenly Henry wanted to drink. He pulled out a flask, but it was empty. So he finished his beer. He put his hands on the table and waited for the room to begin spinning. It didn't. In fact, he started to have a very uneasy feeling.

The same barmaid brought out bread, butter, and sharp cheese. He began munching on a thin slice of warm bread with a cold slab of cheese crumbled on top.

"Quite all right, Henry?" inquired Eli, as Henry tipped back another full pint of beer and set it back down empty.

"Yes. Just thirsty is all."

"I think your thirst has inspired me," joined in Moraya, taking a long pull from her own pint.

Eli looked at both of them. "Did I miss a cue or something?"

"Generally, yes," said Moraya, setting her mostly empty glass back on the table.

"At last, I can join you," said Ezio from behind them. "I was just finishing up with a client. Allow me to introduce you."

Henry turned around to look. *It can't be him.*

"Meet my guests," said Ezio to his client.

"This is Moraya and her companions, Eli and Henry. Friends, this is... Oh sorry, I seem to have forgotten your name."

Henry spoke, "Preston."

All eyes were on him, including Preston's. It seemed like a lifetime ago that he had been in New York. A lifetime since Preston had slipped that Bowie knife into Bentley's saddlebags.

"It's good to see you, Henry," said Preston, extending his hand. "Moraya," he said, nodding politely.

"The pleasure is all mine," replied Henry, taking his extended hand.

Preston smiled good naturedly. "Still drinking, I see."

"Perpetually, if it can be helped," said Henry.

"I'm glad to see you survived the Ask," he said sincerely.

"Yes. It was riveting," said Henry, shifting uncomfortably in his seat.

"I didn't know you two were friends!" exclaimed Ezio with all the stereotypical energy of a full-blooded Italian. "You must stay and have a drink."

"Oh, I rarely drink anymore," said Preston, "but thank you."

"Sit. I insist," said Ezio sincerely.

Henry could feel the blood begin to run cold in his legs, and the air seemed to be clutching his throat.

"Okay. Just one drink," agreed Preston. He slid into the booth next to Moraya, across from Henry, blocking her exit, and Ezio pulled up a chair. The barmaid brought fresh drinks for everyone. Preston stared at Clarke's half-drunk cordial water.

"Is there another traveling with you?" he asked, nodding toward the glass. "Lipton was only expecting three."

"No," said Moraya before Ezio could say anything. "I'm just doing my best to stay hydrated." She took a sip of the beverage.

"Expecting?" asked Henry.

"Yes." Preston turned to Eli. "Lipton sent a soldier to your ranch. He should have told you that Lipton expected to see you on your way to the Vault."

"I spoke to a soldier," Eli said, "but he made no mention of that."

"That's strange," said Preston thoughtfully.

"He seemed a bit scattered when I spoke to him," Eli responded. "I think he was expecting something different of me."

"Something different?" asked Preston with a good-natured chuckle. "And what did he receive?"

"I wasn't always a Minister," said Eli flatly.

"I see," Preston said with a knowing smile. He tipped back his pint.

Henry touched his own pint to his lips but did not drink any of it.

"How's that knife I gave you holding up?" Preston asked Henry, as if just remembering he had given it to him in the first place.

"Quite well," said Henry, taking it out and setting it on the table.

Ezio began looking worried and shot Moraya a concerned glance.

"I need to visit the water closet," said Moraya as Preston smiled at the Bowie knife on the table.

"Wait," ordered Preston.

Every muscle in Henry's body tensed. He could see the pulse on Eli's neck.

"Before you go, let's all have a shot, then I'll be on my way."

"Of course," said Moraya. "Tequila!" she called to the barmaid, who quickly brought over a tray of brimming shot glasses.

"What'll we drink to, Henry?" asked Preston, glass in hand and a broad smile on his face.

"May we all be as lucky as we are drunk."

The glasses clinked, tapped, and were thrown back.

"That burns so good," declared Preston.

"Indeed," agreed Henry.

"You know, Henry," said Preston, settling into his seat, his cheeks flushing from the alcohol. "I honestly didn't know if you had it in you."

Henry struggled to maintain his calm, "What's that?"

"Well, you Collectors always talk about being nothing but a consequence, but that last Fairchild, Clarke was her first name, she was just a little girl. I didn't know if you would be able to pull the trigger. I don't think I could've. I mean sure, her grandfather really fucked over Lipton when he offed half his family. Fuck, offed his *whole* family. Nearly killed Lipton, even after they grew up in the same tutoring house. Brothers in every way but blood. But even with knowing the whole story, I don't think I could've killed the little girl regardless of who her grandfather was."

"I am but the sea who catches those who fly too close to the sun," replied Henry, in a flat tone, his eyes growing colder.

"Right," said Preston.

Just then, one of Preston's men came out from the back to see where his boss had disappeared to.

"Tell the others I'll be right out," Preston said firmly to the young soldier.

"I really need to go to the water closet," said Moraya again.

Preston stood for a moment, letting her out, then sat again. "Before you go, I must confess," he said, gently taking Moraya's hand in his as he spoke. "You are truly one of the most beautiful things I have ever had the joy of seeing. I'll be gone before you return."

Moraya's gaze softened. Her shoulders relaxed slightly, and she smiled. "Thank you."

Preston smiled.

"Who are you?" asked a kind voice from behind them.

Preston turned and looked squarely into the eyes of Clarke Fairchild. The smile faded slowly from his face, and he turned to Henry. He did not wear an expression of surprise or anger, but of understanding and even kindness. "What does a man have if not his choices?"

"Everything else is lent to us. Everything will be taken as it was given," said Henry calmly.

Preston did not look away from Henry as he replied, "Every choice I ever made was my own."

Henry nodded. "Are you going to call for your men?"

Preston's expression did not change. It was not malicious, not scared. But it was cold. "I'm sure they'll hear the gunfire."

There was a moment of complete silence. Utter serenity. All present knew that none present were responsible, and those responsible really only left them with one choice. This was a moment of consequence, not of choosing.

Then, as if by an unspoken agreement, everyone started moving. Preston, who still had a grip on Moraya's wrist, jerked her downward, ruining her balance. Henry reached for the Bowie knife on the table. Moraya's free hand was moving towards her gun. Eli clutched the handle of his whip as he began rolling out of the booth, clearing Henry's exit.

Preston's fist reached Moraya's skull, and she went limp. Somehow, he already had her pistol in his hand, but Henry had the Bowie knife in his right hand, and with his left, he kept the pistol from pointing at him. He lunged at Preston, who fired two shots before the blade met his throat.

There was commotion from the back, and men began coming through the door. Henry was standing now, revolver raised and ready for them. The first one through the door caught two rounds in the chest before he could fire. The second one got a poorly placed round off before Henry shot him through the neck, then two more burst through. Henry was close now, and he shot one through the chest before taking a heavy blow from the butt of the fourth soldier's rifle. He stumbled back, his head spinning, but he managed to empty the final two rounds into the soldier's gut and groin before he could do any more damage.

Then there was the fifth soldier. He leaned around the corner just long enough to pull both triggers on a sawed-off double-barreled shotgun. By some miracle, Henry had the wherewithal to fall to the ground before the shots broke. Some of the pellets seared into his shoulder as he fell. The fifth soldier had disappeared behind the door again almost as soon has he had fired. Henry glanced at his wound as he got to his feet. The pain barely fazed him, and he leaped to pursue when a small hand upon his forearm stopped him.

It was just a moment that he stood before chasing the last shooter. No more than two seconds in reality, but to Henry, it was an eternal moment. He looked down. Clarke was white as a sheet. Eli had moved her out of harm's way and had shielded her with his body. Now he was checking her for wounds. She seemed to be entirely in shock, too horrified to even be scared. Too surprised to even seem caught off guard. Henry felt his stomach turn slightly when he saw her. Then he took in the rest of the room. Moraya was sprawled out by the booth, unconscious and bleeding from the side of her head. Preston was slumped lifeless and face-down upon the nearly saturated table. The barmaid had caught the worst of the shot from the double barrel in the face and the neck. She was crumpled in a pile of broken glass and blood. Ezio was slumped in his chair next to the booth, the two slugs Preston had fired from Moraya's pistol having left a gaping exit wound in his back.

He looked at Henry.

How is he even still alive?

Ezio tried to speak, but the only thing that left his mouth was a cough and a small stream of blood. His head began to nod, and his neck went limp. What was left of his white shirt was slowly turning red like the rest of it.

Henry looked at the bodies of the four soldiers on the ground before him, dead or about to be. Then he looked back at Clarke. Her eyes were glazed over. She had broken into a cold sweat. Physically she was unscathed.

Thank God.

"Watch her," he commanded Eli, who nodded.

Henry dashed to the back of the restaurant in hopes he

could kill the fifth soldier before he had the chance to return to Lipton and warn him of their coming. Everything was riding on the element of surprise. He ran through the kitchen and burst through the back door into an alley just as the soldier was rounding the corner out of view at the far end. Henry kept moving at a flat sprint, replacing the spent rounds one by one in his revolver with fresh ones.

Once out in the street, he saw the soldier get on a horse and begin riding away. Two other soldiers were already leading the way. He saw them each release, from cages attached to their saddles, pigeons. Reality crashed in around Henry as he saw the birds flutter up into the air, barely visible in the night sky, take a circle, and then start flying north as fast as their wings could take them. *Fucking homing pigeons.* They were out of range, as were the two riders that released them. They were going to warn Lipton, but the soldier from the restaurant was still in range, his back unprotected. Henry stopped, pulled up his revolver, and released all six rounds in quick succession through the soldier's back and out his chest. The horse kept galloping at full speed as the man leaned backwards and slowly shifted, then fell out of the saddle, colliding abruptly with the gravel. One of his boots was caught in the stirrup and he was dragged for a few yards before the boot came loose and he was left in a crumpled pile as his mount sped away in a frenzy.

Henry felt some of the rage leave his body, then he ran back inside. His stomach turned again as he saw the scene spread out before him like some nightmarish dreamscape. Moraya was conscious now and weeping bitterly next to Ezio's body. Clarke stood where he had left her, staring blankly at Moraya and Ezio as if she was in some kind of trance.

Eli had his jacket off and was pulling a few shotgun pellets out of it.

"Did any get through that jacket?" Henry asked him.

"No, it was made in the Vault. Even so, it will leave a mark." He looked at Henry, his voice somewhat shaky. "I'm sorry I wasn't faster. Thanks for taking care of them."

"You got between her and the shotgun. That's all that matters," said Henry. Then he shook his head. "We're fucked, Eli. He knows we're coming. Two soldiers got away. And they released pigeons." He picked up a mostly full glass of water off a nearby table and drank it. "We need to move."

Eli put his coat back on, but Moraya and Clarke seemed like they barely heard him.

"Now!" he shouted. "We need to move now, before word gets out. Let's go!"

Eli took Clarke by the hand and half led, half pulled her out of the restaurant. Moraya was still kneeling besides Ezio, weeping. Henry walked over to her. She was so strong, and so dangerous, that it undid him to see her undone.

"Moraya." He knelt and wrapped an arm around her waist. "Moraya, we need to go now."

She covered her face and tried to regulate her breathing.

"I'm sorry. We need to go." He lifted her as he stood and guided her gently away from the scene and out into the street.

People were gathering. The whole town would be out in a few minutes. They rushed back to the lodge, grabbing their things from their rooms, and fetched the horses from the stables themselves.

"We need to avoid the crowds," said Henry once they were all mounted.

"I know a way," said Moraya. "Follow me."

She took them up a side street that ran parallel to the main road that was now blocked with townsfolk. It was dark, and the rain was picking up again. That plus the heavy fog made it easy enough to get out of town and back on the main highway without drawing too much attention.

Henry's ears were ringing. His shoulder throbbed with pain. He was alive, but his plan to surprise Lipton was now hopeless, and it was all he could do to keep from giving himself in to despair.

Chapter Twenty-Three

They rode until they were nearly asleep in their saddles. They slept without food and woke up ravenous. They had a cold breakfast, and Henry passed around a pouch of coffee beans for them to crunch on as they rode. It was a wet, cold, monotonous day. Joyless and bleak.

That evening they were lucky enough to come across a small village with an inn. If they were well rested and dry, they probably wouldn't have stopped in there, poor excuse for a village that it was. However, as cold and wet and tired as they were, the ramshackle inn seemed like a blessing from beyond.

They ate simple stew and drank what the innkeeper called tea. Henry cleaned and bandaged his wounds, and they shared one small room with cots on the floor. Sleep came quickly to all.

Henry woke a little later. It was still dark, and there was a strange noise coming from the other side of the room. It was soft and muffled, but it was definitely there. He couldn't make out what it was at first, but it reminded him of an emotion he had forgotten how to feel. Slowly, the sleep wore off his mind, and he recognized the sound.

Crying.

Clarke was crying quietly to herself. So quietly, in fact, that Henry resolved that it must have been something else that woke him. He remembered that Scarlet would cry like that if she ever had a bad dream. Clarke was living a nightmare. She had seen too much blood and lost too many people for one so young. Henry felt his legs carry him over to her. He felt his hand rest upon her shoulder. Then words flowed from his heart and out of his mouth that he had not said in years.

"There, there, little blossom, all will be well."

She turned to him, sat up, buried her face in his chest, and wept, the sobs shaking her little body.

Henry picked her up and carried her out onto the little porch, where they sat on a bench, and he held her until she had spent all of her tears. He remembered this feeling.

Through her sobs, she managed to ask, "Why did Ezio have to die?"

"I don't know," he confessed. "Some things just don't have a reason."

"I'm not going to die, am I? I don't want to die."

"One day you will," said Henry holding her a little tighter. "We all will, but not today, not soon, and not by Lipton." This seemed to calm her somewhat. The sobbing slowed to a stop, but she still clung to him, one cheek resting where his heart was.

They sat for a while, looking out over the dark village. No windows were lit up, and all was quiet.

"I wish he hadn't died. He was kind to me," she said softly.

"Me, too. But if a person has to die, I'd say October is the best time to do it. I always imagined I'd be buried on a crisp

October day with the sun shining through the red, falling leaves. Then, a few months later, there would be spring flowers growing on my grave, still thawing from the winter." He sighed. "If a person has to die, October is the best time to do it. I'll die with the leaves."

Clarke wiped her nose. "I think I will, too," she said, and then they were silent again.

Henry held her until she slipped back to sleep. Then he placed her back in bed and went back to the bench on the porch. He rolled a cigarette and looked at it and then put it back in his pocket. There was a knot in his chest. He pulled the cigarette out again and tried to light it, but his hands wouldn't cooperate, so he crushed it into a ball and tossed it away. He wanted to go talk to Bentley, but even Bentley needed his rest, and it was cold out, so he returned to his cot and slept again.

Chapter Twenty-Four

On the third morning since leaving Ashland, the weather finally broke and they saw the sun for the first time in days.

"We should reach the city by one or two o'clock," Moraya said after several hours of riding.

"What's the plan?" Clarke asked.

Eli replied, "We'll find a safe place for you to lay low, then take turns guarding you while the other two do recon. We need to find out everything—where he's staying, how many men he has, if he has any other friends there that will help him or any enemies that will help topple him. We need to find his vulnerabilities. We need to know how to kill him."

Henry noticed something in Eli's eyes as he spoke. He could not tell what it was, but he knew Eli was not saying all that he was thinking.

"You might get a little stir crazy, but it can't be helped," Henry said to Clarke. "It can't be helped, and we can't risk having you anywhere but concealed. Let's just hope no one sees us on our way in."

"How long will it take?" Clarke asked.

"I don't know. Maybe a day. Maybe a week. Maybe they'll kill us before dinner. Maybe it will take a month."

He had a feeling it would take much less than a month. Either Lipton would kill them, or they would kill him. His man would've warned him by now, so Lipton would be searching for them.

Moraya seemed so far away. She had been like this since Ezio died. Though she was only a few yards to his right, her mind was somewhere else. She didn't even seem to hear their conversation.

The world felt like it was on the verge of rain. The air hung thick and low around their faces, and the clouds let nothing but the grayest of light seep through to the earth. A strong wind seemed to be driving them to reach the city.

Smoke from the chimneys of mills and houses was the first thing they saw. It was nothing like the haze of Sacramento, but it was also not so perfect as the mountain air they had been breathing the last few days.

Then they saw the city. The majority of the buildings were newer construction, but the city was still mostly brick and steel as it had always been. It was thriving. The port provided wares from up and down the coast, and even from far over the Pacific. It was a large area of land, and much of what had once been the outskirts of the city was now mostly abandoned ruins, for though it was thriving, there were still not enough people to occupy the whole place. There were more people there than most other cities, however, and the city center was bustling and vibrant.

"We'll be there soon," Henry said, more to himself than to anyone. "Try not to draw any attention to yourself." He looked at Clarke, and the girl nodded her understanding.

They rode on. Buildings multiplied and were closer and closer together. The outer sections of the city were still mostly abandoned. Most of the wooden structures had long ago been torn down and burned for fuel. The farther into the city they rode, the less derelict it all was.

Then the people began to appear. First, only one every few streets peeped through windows or over fences from back gardens. Then a few walking or riding here and there and smiling from front gardens. Before long, they were everywhere. They had seemingly driven all the silence from the city. By the time they had reached downtown, the streets and buildings were full. Eli looked collected, but not at all relaxed. Moraya wore the same vacant expression that she had for days. Clarke seemed unaffected by it all. If anything, she looked a little bored.

Henry felt uneasy. He could not tell what it was that had made him so. He did not feel as though he was being watched. It was not claustrophobia from the city or crowds. He felt like he was riding towards an unforeseen precipice. It was probably just the weather.

It was about 5 o'clock when they found a small inn to their liking. It only had four rooms and was somewhat run down but clean. The pub downstairs smelled of hot food, and the other patrons were mostly dock workers coming off their shifts. They booked two rooms, Clarke and Moraya in one, Henry and Eli in the other. They ate quietly and retired to their rooms, each of them eager for a hot bath and the comfort of a bed. It was a good day to call it an early night, and they agreed that their search would begin in the morning.

Eli was soon breathing heavily in the bed next to Henry's. Tired as he was, Henry could not sleep. He got dressed and walked back down to the pub and sat at the bar. There were several other patrons scattered around the room, a few playing cards, a few others having an enlivened conversation about the flaws of their respective foremen, and a couple others sitting alone studying the glass in their hands. They were all drunk, and Henry felt comfortably invisible.

There was only one girl behind the bar. She was plump, with a pleasant face and big, welcoming eyes. She placed a glass of water in front of Henry and gave him a tired smile. "What else can I get you?"

"I'd love a coffee."

She raised an eyebrow at him but returned a moment later with a steaming mug and set it in front of him, lingering for a moment.

"If I can't sleep, it might as well be on my own terms."

"I've never been much of a morning person either. What brings you to town?"

"My cousins and I are looking for another of our kin."

"Another cousin?"

"Yeah. Last we heard, he was working for a man called Lipton as a soldier. He said he was going to be in the city for a while, but he didn't say where, airheaded as he is. We have some rather bad news to give him."

The waitress stiffened. "Your cousin should know better than to work for a man like that. There are nasty rumors about that man."

"Yes, but he pays well, and my cousin has the foresight of a mole."

The girl sighed. "I didn't know Lipton was in town again, but it makes sense. There's an army gathering in the city. Hundreds of them. I bet Lipton is behind it. You won't find him or his anywhere around here."

"Do you know where I should look?"

"You can try where the Willamette and the Columbia meet. Rich people like that always stay on the western bank. But I can't recommend going up there, especially if Lipton's in town. Everyone knows he's paranoid."

"I just need to find my cousin."

"Well, if I were you, I'd try to find him tomorrow. The places on the western bank don't like uninvited guests any time. Least of all at night."

"Are there many other...people like Lipton up on the western bank?"

The waitress raised an eyebrow. "You've never been here before?"

"Not for a long time. And I didn't stay long."

"Well yes. There are a lot of other people like Lipton up there. It's not fenced off or anything, at least the streets aren't, but it's not a very welcoming place."

"It sounds as though my cousin has gotten himself hired by the wrong employer."

"He isn't the only one," said the waitress.

Henry felt restless. The other patrons got louder the more they drank, which did nothing to improve his mood. *I need to get out of here.* He didn't know where his feet would take him, but he stood, put a coin on the bar, and left.

Chapter Twenty-Five

Henry found his way to the stables. Bentley was reluctant to let him get the bit in.

"Oh, what's the matter now, old boy? Too tired for a little walk?"

Bentley snorted and pranced uneasily, but once Henry was in the saddle, he seemed to cheer up.

Only a few people walked the streets, and only a few lights flickered in the windows Henry passed as he made his way north.

"What do you mean, where are we going?" He patted Bentley's neck. "I told you, I couldn't sleep, and now I feel compelled to finish what we came to do."

Bentley huffed.

"No, I don't think I should have woken them," he said. "They got us this far, but I was hired to Collect, and I failed that, and now it's my job to fix it." He patted Bentley's shoulder again, but Bentley seemed unconvinced.

They came upon a bridge that led from the main part of the city to the "western bank," as the waitress had called it.

There were guards posted, but they did not wear the mark of Lipton.

"Stop right there," one of the guards commanded as he approached Bentley. "This part of the city is closed for the evening. If you have business, you can return in the morning."

"I do have business, but it will not wait 'til morning."

"All business can wait until the morning," said the soldier.

"Is that what you'll tell your master when he asks why you didn't let me through?"

The soldier squinted through the lamplight at Henry. "Why would Perry have business with you?"

He was close enough to cut. The other soldier hadn't even unslung his rifle from his back. Henry almost made a move, but Bentley turned his head and nuzzled the man's shoulder.

"Perry is a man of exceeding wealth," Henry guessed aloud, "and his interests expand beyond what you may perceive as usual." He pulled up his left sleeve as he spoke. "If you don't know why he would have use for a man like me," he leaned to make the tattoo fully visible, "then I would be more than happy to show you."

It worked. The soldier flushed white and took three full steps backwards. "I'm very sorry, sir, my deepest apologies."

"Don't apologize. Just stand aside."

The man nodded obediently and returned to his post, waving to some invisible watcher in some window across the bridge.

"Enjoy your evening, sir," said the soldier, looking at the ground as Henry passed.

The western bank was, as Henry anticipated, much nicer than the city proper. The roads were paved with stone instead of dirt, or oversized gravel. There were very few pubs, and those that were there seemed to be occupied mostly by soldiers, a few debutantes, and the occasional woman with more makeup than clothes; even they seemed too posh for most cities. There were some shops, and some buildings that Henry guessed to be barracks and housing for the help. But all the estates were set back from the road, even the comparatively small ones. They all had space for yards and gardens, and they all had hedges. Some of them even had gates with guards.

The streets had a handful of people walking about, and he suddenly felt out of place on a horse. Then he had a stroke of luck.

A little way down the road, Henry saw something. One of Lipton's soldiers. Even at a distance and in the lamplight, he could clearly recognize the insignia on the man's left breast and shoulder. He seemed to be walking very straight and intentionally.

He's been drinking.

Henry felt a surge of hope and started discreetly following him. He kept a safe distance, even more than what was necessary, but he never let the soldier get out of his sight. After a couple blocks, the soldier ducked into a pub.

"I'll be back, old boy."

Henry looped Bentley's reins around a hitching post on the street but did not tie them off and casually strode inside.

The soldier was on a stool with his back turned. There were five or six other patrons scattered about the place. Henry took a seat at one of the stools.

"Lager," he said.

"Yep," replied the bartender, who started pouring it almost before the words had even reached his ears.

This place must get pretty busy if they have service like this.

He glanced over and got a better look at the soldier. He was young. No more than eighteen or nineteen, and he had kind eyes. The beer was good, light and crisp. It didn't weigh down his thoughts.

"That's an interesting emblem on your shoulder," Henry said to the young soldier. "I don't think I recognize it."

"It's the crest of Baron Lipton," the soldier responded enthusiastically, springing at the chance for a casual conversation.

"Lipton? Is he a baron in these parts?" asked Henry conversationally.

"He has a large baronage in New York and has been a consigliere to the Fairchilds forever. But he'll own land here in a few days, too. He's been in the city for a little less than a week overseeing the transaction." The soldier smiled and ordered two more lagers, sliding one in front of Henry, who still had most of his previous pint left. "What's your business in the city?"

"Oh, same as everyone else, I suppose," Henry replied casually. "Just on the cosmic scavenger hunt of life. Also, I like the beer here."

"I'll drink to that," said the young man as he took a sip.

"How long have you worked for your baron...what was his name again?"

"Lipton. I've been in his service a month now. To think, less than 40 days ago I was pouring beer in New York. I had never left the city before. Now I've traveled across the entire continent." The soldier's eyes swam with intoxicated wonder.

"Well, that's cause for celebration, my young friend." Henry signaled the bartender. "Two whiskeys."

The bartender wordlessly filled two shot glasses and slid them over.

Henry raised his glass. "To your time in a baron's army. May it not disappoint."

"Hear, hear."

The glasses clinked, tapped, and were thrown back. The young man chased the shot with his entire beer.

"Gotta hit the head," he declared and standing somewhat shakily.

Good. Give it time to kick in.

A moment later, the young man returned and sat at the stool, looking rather wild around the eyes.

"So, this Lipton, you say? Is he buying a section of the Fairchild empire?"

"Not exactly. From what I've heard, the Fairchilds are having trouble with succession. Lipton was one of Grant Fairchild's closest friends and advisors. I think the heir, Clarke Fairchild, wants to let the whole empire fall into the ground, which would cause absolute chaos for so many of the regions. All the small baronages that have been paying homage to the Fairchilds would go to shit. They'd probably start killing each other. Who knows! I think Lipton is the right man to maintain the," he burped, "fragile order of things."

"I ordered this for you while you were away," said Henry, sliding over the full pint the young man had ordered for Henry a few moments before.

"Ah, you're a good man," said the lad, taking a heavy swig.

"I think you may be right about the small barons. They probably have no idea how good they have it. The iron hand of an empire maintains good order. Small folk can sometimes forget where credit is due."

"Exactly!" said the young man. "I think this new Clarke Fairchild is a jumped-up fool with ridiculous dreams in his head. Doesn't know his place. Doesn't know people need a strong man at the head of things."

"And you think Lipton is a good strong man?"

"Yep," said the young man, finishing his beer and waving to the bartender for another.

The bartender glared at him as he placed another one down in front of the young man and then turned to Henry. "Make sure he doesn't cause me any trouble."

"Won't cause trouble," said the young man. "Swear."

"We should probably get you back to Lipton's after that pint, my young friend," said Henry, patting the young man on the back.

"But it's still early!" the lad protested with an exaggerated scowl.

"It's not that early. And I'm sure you want to make a good impression on your new employer."

"Do want that. That'd be good. Make me a captain!" He raised his glass into the air, spilling some beer in the process. "Sorry!" he shouted to the bartender. "Sorry," he repeated to Henry.

"Better leave the man some silver. Money is the best apology for a bartender," Henry said.

"Smart," said the young man, fumbling through his pockets. "You're a smart guy." He said it with the forceful sincerity that accompanies too much drink.

"I think you're smart too," said Henry, patting him on the back. "Let's get you home."

"Home. Can't go home. Not today. Too far!"

"Well, let's get you back to Lipton's."

"Good idea. You're a smart guy," he said again to Henry.

"I think you're smart too," replied Henry again, this time taking him by the arm and helping him to his feet. "Lead the way, captain."

"Onward! To the Maverick!"

Henry smiled. *The Maverick.*

"You're staying at the Maverick?" Henry asked once they got out into the street.

"Yep. Welp, no. Guard the Maverick. Stay in a bunkhouse. Not nearly as nice as the Maverick, not by have." He made a face. "Half. No master suites in the bunkhouse. Just bunks."

"How do you get there from here?"

The lad laughed. "Walk. Sometimes horse."

"This way?" pointed Henry.

"Yep," said the soldier through a hiccup.

He walked with the young soldier, sometimes guiding him when he stumbled.

"What made you want to be a soldier?"

"Money. Travel. Respect."

"Those are good reasons. Got a girl you were trying to impress?"

"Oh...nah. She doesn't care about me. Who needs her? Fuck it. Never loved her anyways. Probably better she chose James."

"Well, there's plenty of fish in the sea."

"But I got no line! No hook!"

"But you're a soldier! The ladies love a soldier."

"Yeah?"

"Oh, of course. Just you wait and see."

"I'm Kurt," said the soldier, extending his hand to an invisible woman. "I'm Kurt and I'm a soldier and I think you're pretty!"

"That should work just fine."

"Nah. She said she loves James."

They reached a gate and two soldiers stopped them. Kurt turned and wretched like a dog.

"Goddamnit, Kurt," one of them said, stepping forward to help his comrade.

"I found him at a pub, looked like he could use a hand," said Henry. All three of the soldiers were young. Too young to die.

"Fuck. He's in rough shape," said one of them.

"I can get him to the bunkhouse if you tell me the way," Henry offered.

"Really?" asked one of the soldiers. "I'm not supposed to let anyone in."

"But you're probably not supposed to leave your post, either."

The two guards looked at each other and shrugged.

"It's just up the path and to the right. The hotel is on the left. Come right back and try to not let anyone see you. Just dump this poor bastard on the doorstep and come right back."

"You got it," said Henry in his most compliant tone.

Henry half led, half dragged Kurt to the bunkhouse. There were more men inside, and Henry glimpsed a card game through the window.

"Can you make it from here on your own?" he asked, leaning Kurt against the doorframe.

Kurt nodded, and Henry turned to leave.

"What's your name?" Kurt asked, wavering like a tree in a breeze.

"My name is Henry."

"Thanks, Henry," Kurt said and went inside.

"You're welcome, Kurt," said Henry, turning towards the Maverick.

Henry tuned all his senses to the main building. There were so many guards. He would need to be fast and silent. The second a shot rang out, no less than forty men would snap into action all at once. Henry would not be able to escape. He stepped off the lamplit path and made his way through the shadows. There were two soldiers at the front door, but they could not see him yet. He pulled out his flask and took a sip, letting it run down his chin, then he splashed a little more on his neck and then he stumbled into the lamplight and staggered to the front door, singing with feigned drunkenness, "Ain't got no place to call a home, only chains and broken bones, ain't got no place to call a home..."

"Stop right there," commanded one of the soldiers, but Henry kept stumbling and singing,

"The devil's gonna make me a free man, the devil's gonna set me free..."

The two guards stepped up to him, and one of them reached out to grab him. Henry grabbed the man's arm with his left hand, and with his right, he drove his Bowie knife up through the soldier's throat and into his brain, changed his grip, and ripping it out of the man's throat, smashed the pommel into the other soldier's temple and then the blade into the man's chest three times before the first soldier hit the ground.

He moved quickly, pulling them out of the lamplight and dropping them under some shrubs. There was still blood on the path where the bodies had been dragged, but there was nothing to be done about that. He moved up to the door and placed his hand on it, closing his eyes, and with the senses Rust taught him to use as a boy, spotted another pair of guards in the foyer. He knocked on the door and waited.

A bolt slid, then the lock clicked and the door started to open out toward Henry. He yanked it open the rest of the way, pulling the soldier off balance, and lunged into the man knife first. The blade moved quickly, and Henry ran at the second soldier in the foyer using the first soldier as a shield for as long as the man could stumble backwards. The second soldier had time to draw his sidearm and raise it, but Henry sidestepped, discarding the body of the first man, and in a single strike hacked the second man's hand off at the forearm. The gun clattered to the ground but did not fire, then a second slash nearly severed the man's head from his shoulders.

Henry turned to the stairs and bounded up them three at a time. He saw two more soldiers in front of him, but he heard a sound to his right. Two more guards came out of a door a few yards away and glanced over the railing at the two bodies in the foyer. They drew their weapons. Henry faced them and, picking his target, threw the Bowie knife with all of his strength. It flashed through the air and thudded fatally into one of the soldier's faces. But the other had his weapon raised.

The shot was deafening.

A bullet whizzed past Henrys head and buried itself in the wall behind him.

God. Fucking. Damnit.

Henry whipped out his revolver and sent three rounds through the chest of the man who was shooting at him. The two soldiers at the end of the hall began shooting. Henry lunged to the side, but one of the shots still grazed his shoulder. He shot one of the soldiers twice where his throat met his torso and sent his last round through the other man's right shoulder, leaving his shooting arm hanging limp at his side as the man's rifle crashed to the ground.

For half a second, they caught each other's eyes. Then the man went for his sidearm with his left hand as Henry began to reload. As fast as he was, the soldier managed to draw his sidearm and fire before Henry could slap the reloaded cylinder back into place. But the man was shooting with his left hand, and he was obviously right-handed. Henry leveled his pistol at the man's head and sent a round through it.

Even though his ears rang loud enough to split his head, he could hear alarm bells clanging from every direction. His arm was bleeding, and everyone on the grounds and in the house was on the move. The talents Rust taught him flared up, and for a moment, it was like he could see every beating heart on the grounds, and he drew a deep breath inward. It would take all his strength, and it might cost his own life, too. *Just this once, maybe I could break The Rule.* Then Henry thought of Kurt.

No.

With great effort, he broke his concentration on the hearts, and he was once again limited to five senses and the weapons he could hold in his hands.

The Maverick was three palatial stories, and he had no idea where Lipton was, but he knew he would most likely be upstairs. He thought of Bentley.

Bentley's a smart boy. He knows. Surely, he knows. Surely, he remembers the way.

Henry ran to his right, replacing the one spent round with a fresh one, and slipped his pistol back into its holster. He grabbed an unused rifle off the soldier who had alerted the Maverick initially with a shot from his sidearm. Just then, soldiers started flooding into the foyer. Henry braced the rifle on the railing and fired down on the soldiers. The rifle had ten rounds, and he released them all in quick succession. In the commotion, he managed to drop four more soldiers before a volley of shots sent him retreating up another staircase to the top floor. Bullets tore through railings and stairs and smashed into walls, showering Henry with splinters and chunks of plaster, but he managed to avoid getting shot again. The last staircase led him into the middle of the corridor at the front of the building. There were soldiers to the right and the left in the corridor, four or five on each side. They saw Henry, and knowing that they could not shoot at him without possibly hitting their comrades on the other side of him, they drew heavy clubs and charged.

Henry spent all six rounds of his revolver before they could reach him, but more were coming up the stairs from below. As strong, and fast, and skilled with his razor as he was, there were too many of them. He opened as many veins as he could in the melee, but in what seemed like an instant, a club found his head, and he remembered no more.

Chapter Twenty-Six

Henry woke up in pain. He was face down on a stone floor and it was dark. There were shackles on his wrists and ankles. There was a metal collar around his neck with a chain connecting him securely with the floor. Slowly he moved, every inch of his body pulsing with shooting, throbbing pain. He got to his knees and rested. A bolt clanged, and a door opened, letting some light into the basement.

I didn't come all this way to die on my knees.

With another great effort, he stood. Someone was coming down the stairs with a lantern. His eyes could scarcely focus between the pain and the dark, but he could see that there were two men coming down the stairs, the first also shackled. When they only had a few steps left, the man behind the lantern kicked the other shackled man the rest of the way. It was Kurt. He landed flat on his face with a gut-wrenching thud and moaned in pain.

"Shut up, ya fucking rat," said the unbound man as he took a chain bolted to the floor and attached it to the collar around Kurt's neck.

Kurt lifted himself to his hands and knees, but the man kicked him hard in the ribs and sent him sprawling again. Then he glared at Henry. "Thought you could get past us, eh? Thought you could crack a shot at Lipton?"

Henry said nothing.

Kurt began to lift himself off the floor again, but the man turned and kicked Kurt, this time in the face, and he went still.

The guard took a step towards Henry, "We found your inside man." He took another step. "Clever trick, I've got to hand it to you." One more step, and Henry could almost reach him. "We're going to kill you soon. And your little friend here. And anyone else that comes for you." The man took one last step.

In spite of his shackles, and his pain, Henry was still a Collector. He grabbed the man's face with both hands and twisted his head nearly halfway around. A sickening shriek erupted from the man, and Henry twisted his head a little more. There came a popping crack and the soldier fell limp to the ground. Henry checked him for keys, but the only thing he carried was the lantern, which had gone out. Henry sat down. He thought of Eli and Moraya and Clarke and hoped with all that was left within him that they would run. Run and hide and never let Lipton find them. Then he laid back on the cold stone floor and tried to keep his mind from racing.

There were no windows in the basement. No clocks or watches or hourglass. And even if there had been, there was no light. Henry sat in the pitch black, unable to see his hands in front of his face, and listened to Kurt's breath, faint and raspy. The lad had not woken up since the last kick in the head. *Maybe he never will.* Henry pushed the thought from his mind.

"Sometimes people wake up from comas," he whispered to the dark. "Sometimes they pull through."

Eventually, the door at the top of the stairs opened again, and several men entered the basement, hanging lanterns here and there, illuminating the blood-stained stone floor. Kurt stirred and opened his eyes, but Henry signaled to him to be quiet, so he closed his eyes again and by all appearances remained comatose.

The men said nothing as they dragged away the body of the man Henry had killed for kicking Kurt. They produced two chairs and a small table and placed them within the perimeter of Henry's tether. One of them went back up the stairs and a moment later returned. He carried a tray with a glass of water, a bottle of the finest brandy money could buy, and two glasses.

Then Lipton came down the stairs. He sat at one of the chairs and motioned for Henry to sit in the other. Henry complied. He sniffed the water and drank it. Lipton poured two glasses of brandy and held one out to Henry.

"This stuff is too fine to poison. Drink with me."

Henry took the glass.

"I've heard some very troubling reports, Henry," Lipton said as he leaned back in his chair and took a sip.

"Reports can be unreliable."

"I remember when a handshake meant something."

"I remember when having children Collected was frowned upon."

"Oh, please," Lipton spat. "Don't pretend to have a conscience. You kill people, Henry. You've been killing your entire life."

"It wears on a person, but then again, you must know all about that," said Henry.

"As a matter of fact, I don't. I'm a businessman, Henry.

I'm a baron. I have my own land back east that I was born with, and I have power out here. Before he died, Clarke's grandfather and I were quite close. I was his head advisor. I helped him oversee all his generals. All his stewards. Ours was a powerful partnership, and we stayed as far above the fray as possible."

"Forgive my ignorance, oh benevolent puppet master."

"That's what I like about you, Henry. Even when you're beaten, you still have a taste for humor."

"What do you want, Lipton?"

"Initially, I wanted to be to Clarke what I was to her grandfather, but eventually it became clear to Thorpe and thus to me that she, being young, had no interest in preserving order in her family's empire. She would let it all crumble away to nothing, all for the sake of misplaced compassion. Women can be so ignorant when they're young."

"Men can be so ignorant when we're old."

"Yes, but it's an effective ignorance. There's something to be gained from the ignorance of the wise." The anger grew in his voice as he spoke.

"Why are you here? Why not just let your men avenge their comrades and be done with it?"

"Oh, they will have their revenge. As will I."

"Oh, please. Your revenge? I refused to kill a little girl. It's a Collector's right to spare a life."

Lipton glared at Henry. "Yes, but you never do. Have you ever not followed through?"

"I had never been asked to kill someone who didn't deserve it."

"Deserve?" Lipton shouted. "And did my son deserve it? Do you even remember killing him? Do you remember his supposed crime?"

The world turned sideways. "What?"

"Did you weigh his sins against his youth when you snatched the life from him?"

"Your son?" asked Henry in a daze.

"Yes, my son, you fucking animal. He was seventeen."

"I killed your son," Henry spoke quietly as to himself.

"Do you even remember him? Do you?"

"You knew I killed your son, and you didn't even have the balls to try and have me killed. You're pathetic."

"Killed? Death is too kind a punishment for you. Or at least it was at the time. No. I wanted you to suffer first. And you have, Henry. Do you not agree that losing your family was worse than losing your life?"

"What do you know of my family?" Henry's voice was quiet and cold.

"I know they died painfully, wondering why you had not protected them."

"I killed the men who murdered my family. I killed them the next day."

"Yes. But you never killed their employer."

Henry said nothing.

"Did you think they were working on their own? Did you think that those idiots knew where you kept your gold? Or your wife? Your daughter?"

Henry sat silent. Letting the words sink in.

"You crossed me, Henry. I hurt you for it. I took from you what you took from me, and I thought I had destroyed you, but by not killing Clarke, you showed me that there was still some tiny part of you that had not been destroyed."

Henry stared at Lipton.

"As it turns out, there is still some part of you in there that retains a bit of humanity, which means you can still be hurt. So, what should I kill next? Your horse? Clarke? Your new friends at the Ranch? Tell you what. I'll just kill all of them.

Unfortunately, you won't be alive to see Clarke and everyone at the ranch die, but your horse...you can watch your horse die." He stood. "And your helper. Closed eyes and heavy breathing doesn't fool me."

"Wait," said Henry. "I don't understand."

"Shocking." Lipton spat the word out like it was poison.

Chapter Twenty-Seven

Eli woke slowly, as he did every morning. *Lord give me the strength, wisdom, and love I need to live this day.* He felt peace in every fiber of his being as he recalled one of his favorite Psalms: "Be still and know that I am God." *The day is only starting, and it is already won.*

He opened his eyes and looked about. Henry's bed was empty, but him being an early riser, Eli had expected that of him. So, he thought little of it as he got dressed and headed downstairs. Henry was not in the dining room, which Eli thought was strange, but he didn't trouble himself over it. He found a table and ordered a cup of coffee.

Clarke and Moraya joined him shortly after he sat down, and the three of them had breakfast together.

"Do you know where Henry's off to this morning?" Moraya asked him once they had pushed back their empty plates.

"I haven't seen him yet, but I'm sure he'll show up soon enough," said Eli.

Moraya looked worried. "I'm going to ask the waitress if she's seen him."

The plump girl came back to clear their plates, "Well, friends, I'm about to go home and sleep for a day. The usual morning waitress didn't show up today, so I had to work a double. Is there anything else I can do for you before you leave?"

"Yes, actually," said Moraya. "Our other companion we arrived with last night, did you see him leave this morning?"

"I saw him leave last night. He was asking about where he might find his cousin."

"His cousin?" asked Moraya.

"Well, yes, he said your cousin worked for Lipton and he had to deliver some bad news."

"Our cousin?" Moraya repeated.

The waitress gave her a quizzical look. "Yes, he said you were all cousins here to deliver bad news to another cousin working for Lipton."

Eli and Moraya shared a look of worry.

"I don't mean to be rude," the waitress continued, "but I've been working all night, and I'm very tired. You should check the western bank. It's—"

"I know where it is," Moraya interrupted.

"Best of luck," the waitress curtly as she took her leave.

"Goddamnit," said Moraya.

"Surely, he wouldn't have tried anything on his own," said Eli, trying to convince himself. It wasn't working.

"We need to find him," said Moraya. "We need to go now and find him." There was an air of desperation in her voice that Eli hadn't heard from her before.

Eli kept his tone level. "We'll find him, Moraya. Let's start moving towards that section of town. Clarke, I'm sorry, but we can't risk anyone seeing you. You'll need to stay in your room. And if we're not back by dark, you need to run. Get on a boat and never look back."

She started to protest, but Moraya laid a hand on her little forearm and gave it a squeeze. "I'm sure we'll be back. I need you to do this for me, Clarke. Keep your ears open. We'll be back for you as soon as we learn anything."

Clarke nodded and said, "Okay."

"And Clarke," said Moraya, "there's a spare pistol in my bag. If anyone comes through that door that's not me or Eli, shoot them."

Clarke flushed white, the gravity of the situation setting in. "Okay."

Eli noticed that Moraya's hands were shaking slightly as she saddled her horse. "He'll be fine. We'll find him." But he did not believe himself.

She said nothing but nodded and swung up into the saddle.

It was not far to the western bank, but they were hesitant to go straight there in case someone recognized Moraya. The city was busy, and Eli was suddenly very aware of how crowded the street was. He felt like all the people and the noise were squeezing the air out of his chest. He wanted to leave. His mind began to race, and he couldn't seem to get a handle on his thoughts. What if Lipton had already given the order to destroy the ranch when he received the message that Henry had not carried out the Ask? What if something had happened to Grace?

"Little brother?"

The voice jolted Eli out of his mind and back into his body.

"Little brother!"

Eli looked, and saw a surprised, grinning Dembe approaching him from the sidewalk. Moraya reached instinctively for her pistol, but Eli stayed her hand.

Eli's voice was laden with relief. "This is Dembe. He is my brother in every way but blood. Dembe, this is Moraya."

Dembe smiled at Moraya and shook her hand. She nodded and smiled politely.

"You have no idea how good it is to see you, big brother."

"Likewise, Minister," said Dembe, clapping him on the shoulder.

Eli shuddered at the name he had given himself. "Please, just Eli today."

Dembe gave him a sly smile.

"Did you bring help?" asked Eli.

"The Vault said they would not intervene. You've been gone too long, and they don't generally play favorites... The Althing Guard said the situation would compromise their neutrality and offered their regards, but no help. It was worth a try, but I'm not surprised at this outcome."

"Damn," said Eli, shaking his head

"What are you doing in Portland?" Dembe asked.

Eli looked at Moraya.

She languidly raised her hand, stopping his explanation before he started it. "Dembe," she said, "the plan went to complete shit."

Eli quickly explained everything from start to finish. At the end, Dembe gave a reassuring smile.

"Be at ease, little brother. On the road a couple hours ago, just south of Portland, I ran into one of Lipton's soldiers. I stopped him and asked him his purpose. He told me the same story from a different perspective. He was on his way to the ranch with a kill order. I scarcely believed it but, I figured I'd come back to the city to see if you actually were here. It's nothing short of a miracle that I actually found you."

Eli shook his head in disbelief. "He just told you?"

"I have my ways of persuading people to share," said Dembe, tapping the handle of his kukri.

"What did you do with him?" asked Eli.

Dembe hesitated for the briefest moment. "I cut his throat once I got the story out of him. It was a mercy, given the state he was in once he had finally told me everything."

"Good." Eli's voice was cold.

Dembe seemed surprised for a moment, but again he didn't raise a question.

"I'm afraid that won't be the only blood we spill today, brother," said Eli, looking deep into Dembe's eyes.

"I understand."

Eli ran his hands through his hair, visibly exasperated. "We need to stop wandering around on this side of the river and go retrieve Henry."

"The soldier said that Lipton would be at the Maverick," Dembe said.

"If Lipton is at the Maverick, then that's where we need to go. But the place will be crawling with his men," said Moraya.

Eli didn't realize that his hand drifted to the handle of his whip. "With three of us, we have a much better chance at getting him out alive if that's where he is. We'll have to improvise a plan as we go."

"I do not know this Henry personally, but if you say he's worth saving, then save him we shall," said Dembe.

"I know the way," said Moraya. "Follow me."

It wasn't much of a plan, but it was all they had. The matching coats Eli and Dembe wore concealed the weapons hanging on their belts, their hands were tied behind their backs, loose enough to slip at a moment's notice but tight enough to fool the casual observer. Moraya walked behind them, pistol in one hand and a lead line in the other with their horses in tow.

"State your business," said one of the two guards at the gate.

"My name is Moraya. I'm here to deliver these two rogues to the same fate as their Collector friend, Henry, who I believe is already captive here."

"Moraya," said the soldier, straightening instinctively. "Lipton left the compound this morning and won't be back until tonight. Thorpe is in charge until he returns. Would you like me to send for him?"

"No, I'd like to get these men secured with their compatriot, then I'll find Lipton myself and deliver the news."

"Of course," said the soldier. He waved to another soldier within the grounds, who jogged over and stood at attention.

"Escort Moraya and her captives to the basement. And don't get close to that animal down there. He killed Brad despite the chains."

Eli kept his head low, but he felt his heart pound at the mention of "that animal down there." *He's still alive.*

"Of course," said the escort, who nodded at Moraya and began leading them into the grounds of the Maverick.

"Keep the horses here for now. I'll be back to tell you if they'll need stabling, or if I'll keep them myself once I've spoken with Lipton," said Moraya, handing the lead line to one of the soldiers.

Eli tried to gauge how many soldiers there were, but it was impossible to tell. There were long tents set up to house some, and the hotel itself could sleep around a hundred. Eli dismissed it for the time being.

They made it through the front door into the foyer. There were men scrubbing the floors, which were mostly clean now, but Eli couldn't help but notice how red the water in the mop buckets was. They went through a door straight ahead of the main entrance and down a large hallway, then they stopped at a small door. The guard opened the door for them and stepped aside.

"Don't get near the man chained down there. You'll find plenty more shackles on the walls." He took a lantern off the wall, lit it and handed it to Moraya.

She took it and poked Eli with her pistol. "Move."

Eli could barely see the steps, but he made his way down to the bottom of them just the same. He heard the door close behind him, and it was dark until Moraya reached the bottom with the lantern. The first thing Eli noticed was a body laying still and broken on the ground, but before his heart fell, he saw another shape in the corner. Moraya cast the light over to it.

"What the hell are you doing here?" said Henry.

Eli slipped the ropes that tied his hands and embraced his friend. "We came to get you out."

Chapter Twenty-Eight

Henry could scarcely believe his eyes. Eli squeezed him tight enough to hurt, and his enormous companion undid the chains that bound him. He hugged Eli back once his hands were free, but his eyes were on Moraya. Her expression was tight and didn't betray her feelings. Henry took an apprehensive step towards her. She placed the lantern on a table and then pressed herself against him. He held her and forgot that he was in pain.

"You shouldn't have come here," he said once Moraya had taken a step back.

"You shouldn't have either. What were you thinking?" said Moraya.

"I made this mess we're in. I wanted to end it without putting anyone else in harm's way."

"We can talk about all this later," Eli said. His voice was steady. "Right now, we need to move. Once we're safe, we can make a plan."

Henry glanced at their new companion. He extended a hand. "I'm Henry."

"Dembe," said the man, shaking Henry's hand. Henry rarely felt small, but he did then.

All of Henry's gear was piled on a table in the basement. He knelt by Kurt's body before collecting his things. It was cold.

"Is Bentley with you?" asked Henry.

"They must have him here in the stables," said Moraya. "If we leave out the back door, we can grab him. Our horses are at the front gate. Let's move now. Quick and quiet."

Eli was the first one up the stairs, then Henry, then Moraya, with Dembe taking the rear.

The hallway was empty, but then a door opened, and a well-dressed man stepped into the hallway and faced them directly. He looked at Eli and his face went from surprise, to disbelief, to a vengeful, ugly expression.

"Thorpe," said Eli.

"Minister," said the man.

"Not today," Eli replied in a tone that sent a chill down Henry's spine.

Henry knew many Collectors had Talents. Some of them were tied to specific tools crafted at the Vault. Henry could feel heartbeats, Moraya had her fangs and their deadly venom. Eli's hand drifted to the handle of his whip.

As if time slowed, Henry saw everything that happened next. Thorpe began to draw in a breath to scream for help. But Eli was faster. The whip was off his belt and uncoiling towards Thorpe. Thin silver lines began to emerge from the tightly braided black leather of the whip, and from the tip of it, another thin silver line extended about five inches. The whip cracked at its full extension and then snapped back towards Eli, who grabbed it. All the thin silver lines had retracted back into the braided leather.

Thorpe had a shocked expression on his face. Then

Henry noticed the cut. Blood pulsed from a line across his neck, and he fell over backwards.

"I've never seen one of those in action," said Henry.

"The craftsmanship of the Vault is unparalleled," said Eli in a flat tone. "Let's move."

They stepped over Thorpe's body as they made their way down the hall towards the rear exit. There were two guards in the rear foyer. They saw the four Collectors, but before they could make a move, Eli's whip leapt towards them. In a single, fluid movement, the whip danced and both soldiers fell just as Thorpe had a moment before.

Dembe was first through the door this time. There was one unsuspecting soldier outside the door who met his fate at the edge of Dembe's kukri.

Henry pulled out his revolver, but Eli shook his head. "Blades," he commanded. "We need to keep it quiet as long as we can."

Henry nodded and slipped the handgun back into its holster, drawing his Bowie knife instead.

"Stables," said Moraya, indicating across the grounds to a large horse barn. It was on the other side of an expansive hedge garden. The hedges were meticulously trimmed and shaped, and paths ran throughout like a maze. They would provide excellent concealment.

They encountered six more soldiers in the hedges as they made their way to the stables. None of them had the chance to cry out. The first, Dembe took with his kukri. The next two met their end by Eli's whip. Henry took one with his Bowie knife. The last two felt the sting of Moraya's fangs and then felt nothing.

It was a straight shot from the maze's exit to the stable's doors. There were a lot of men between them in the open space.

"It's going to be hard to do this part quietly," Henry whispered.

Just then, an alarm bell rang from the hotel. Then from the front gate, and all around, bells rang, and men began to shout.

The four companions looked at each other, and at a nod from Eli, they drew their pistols. Eli took the first shot, and an officer fell where he stood, dead before he hit the ground. The rest of them released a volley of rounds, and the soldiers fell one after another.

Chaos broke out over the grounds of the Maverick. The company rushed from the maze towards the stables. The doors were closed, but Eli sprinted, then launched his shoulder against one of them. It blasted open, knocking a soldier to the ground. Henry was seven steps behind and sent a round through the man's head before he could stand. There were soldiers on the ground level and along the loft that circled the stable. They scrambled and began firing rifles and pistols, some charging at them, and what Henry witnessed next was unlike anything he had ever seen before.

Eli, whip in his right hand, the revolver of a fallen soldier in his left, struck Henry in the chest with such a force that he fell backward into Moraya, and both of them into Dembe. All three hit the ground, gasping for air. A bullet whizzed past Henry's ear on his way down, and if he had still been stand-ing, it would have surely killed him. Eli's arms seemed to work independently but in perfect symmetry, each a weapon of the dark figure. The whip arced into the air, cracking, jerking, and slicing enemies every which way it went. Eli lunged and leaped like a dancer on a stage to and fro, bullets pounding into the earth around him. The soldiers that were too far for the whip caught hot lead in their chests from Eli's revolver. Henry struggled to get up, but Eli kicked him down again, keeping the attention of the shooters on himself. They fell like wheat before a reaper, and after a few moments, the only man in the stable still on his feet was the dark figure standing motionless in the middle. Bodies lay torn and mangled all around him. Henry stared in awe. Eli dropped the revolver and turned to his friends, who shakily got to their feet.

Henry heard a whinny and looked to see Bentley jerk his tether free from a post and dance over to him. They had never removed his tack or groomed him—cruel but convenient. Eli stumbled, and Henry threw an arm around him for support. He looked at his friend, and his stomach turned.

"Eli, you're bleeding."

"We have to go. We have to get Clarke and go."

Dembe and Moraya jumped on mounts bareback, Henry mounted Bentley, and with great effort he pulled Eli up behind him. They quickly reloaded their weapons, except for Eli, and readied themselves to charge towards the partially open doors of the stable.

"Wait a moment," said Moraya. She pulled a cylindrical object from her coat that Henry recognized as an explosive and twisted the top hard before throwing it through the open doors. The sounds of soldiers turned to panic. A moment later, there came an earth-shattering explosion that blasted the stable doors nearly off their hinges, sending clouds of dust and debris into the air. Nearly all perceptible sound was reduced to a piercing ring in Henry's ears.

They charged out into the courtyard. Most of the remaining soldiers had been killed or wounded by Moraya's bomb. The remaining few were disoriented from the blast.

The group rode too fast to make good targets. Three of them managed to get a few well-placed shots off, but Eli just clung tightly to Henry, trying to keep his seat. As they approached the gate, Moraya stood on her horse and launched herself into the saddle of the mount she had left upon her entry. In a fluid motion, Dembe slipped from the back of his mount, took two bounding strides, and swung onto the saddle of his own great beast, snatching the reins of Eli's gelding. But Eli stayed with Henry.

A few of Lipton's soldiers tried to pursue them on horseback, but Dembe and Moraya shot them from their saddles before they made it across the bridge leading out of the western bank. Crowds parted before them as they rode as fast as their horses could bear. Soon they approached the hotel they had checked into when they'd arrived.

"I'll get her!" called Moraya as she dismounted and ran into the hotel. Henry could barely make out the words through the dull ringing in his ears. A few moments later, Clarke trotted around from the back on her horse, Moraya close behind, and then they were riding again furiously. Buildings swept by and then grew sparse. They were back on the ancient highway. They kept their pace as long as they could, but soon the horses began to lather dangerously, and they were forced to slow them gradually so as to not run them to death.

After a couple miles on the highway, Moraya pulled off the main road through the trees, up a little path, and into a small clearing by a stream. They quickly dismounted; Dembe took Eli in his arms and gently helped him down off Bentley. Henry's hearing had begun to return slightly, and the adrenaline began to wear off. He slid off Bentley and his legs gave out. Clarke rushed over and helped him up.

"You're safe," he said,

"You're alive," she replied, tears in her eyes, and not for the last time hugged him. "Your back is covered in blood."

He held her tight as his heart quickened and he looked around. Moraya was leaning against a tree, catching her breath. Dembe was kneeling on the ground next to Eli, who was sitting with his back to a huge, old maple.

Oh god. Eli.

Henry rushed over to his friend and knelt down. "Let's get your jacket off. We need to patch you up."

"Henry," said Eli.

"It'll be fine, Eli. You'll be fine. Just gotta get you patched up."

"Henry," said Eli, grabbing his friend's hand to keep it from fidgeting with his jacket buttons.

Henry tried to shake Eli's hands free. "Let's just get the jacket off. Let's see what we're working with."

"Protect them, Henry. Protect Grace."

"You'll protect them yourself, Eli. You just—"

"Dembe's already promised. Now you must promise me too."

"Goddamnit, Eli!" said Henry, banishing his tears.

"Promise me Henry," said Eli, his breathing increasing and rasping coming from his chest.

Henry stopped struggling and looked at his friend. His chest was tight and his eyes were burning. He couldn't breathe right. He couldn't feel his hands.

Henry pulled Eli to his chest and held him like a brother. "I'll protect the ranch, I'll keep your people safe. I'll see you again. I promise."

"Thank you," whispered Eli. "Thank you, Henry." Eli's breath began to falter. "Leave me here. Leave now. Hurry. There's not much time. Tell Grace...everything."

Henry leaned Eli back against the tree. He felt like his senses were expanding beyond his own body and mind.

"This isn't the end," said Eli, glancing to each of his friends and then up through the branches of the maple, through its blazing red leaves to something beyond. "I'll see you again. Beyond the edge of time. Past the brink of the cosmos, where all forgotten is remembered." His breathing was pained and tired. "I always knew I would leave in October." Then he closed his eyes, and took a long, deep, clear breath. He let it out long and soft as peace overtook him. Then he was gone.

They didn't have the time, but they took it anyway and buried him under the tree in a shallow grave dug with sticks and knives. Clarke found dried wildflower buds and planted them on the grave. Dembe found a small boulder and somehow, away from the rest of them, carved an inscription. Henry and Moraya sat side by side, each too full of wrath and shock to shed a tear.

Once the inscription was done, and the grave was covered with flowers that would bloom in the spring, they stood together and each of them spoke a few short words that were only ever shared with Grace. Then they rode.

There is not much to tell of their return journey except that it was grueling. They rode fast, occasionally dismounting and walking to let their horses rest on the move. Resting for only a few hours a night, the three Collectors slept in shifts so that they were never unprotected. It had taken them eleven days to reach Portland from the ranch. In the late afternoon on the ninth day of their return journey, Dembe announced that there was only an hour left to travel and that warm beds awaited them. Their only comfort was that armies traveled much slower than lone riders.

Chapter Twenty-Nine

Henry was exhausted. The wounds he had received when Lipton captured him still ached and throbbed, exacerbated by riding hard, very little food, and even less sleep for eight full days and the better part of a ninth. He looked at Clarke, who barely seemed awake, staring straight ahead, her eyes glazed over. Poor thing. She had managed the ride as well as anyone her age, or any age for that matter, could have. She had not complained; in fact, she had scarcely spoken at all.

He glanced at Moraya, and for a moment his mind wandered. Then he clicked his tongue to Bentley and covered the short distance between himself and Dembe. "How long do you suppose we have until Lipton's reinforcements arrive?"

Dembe shook his head. "Not long enough. Three, maybe four days at most. There are already fifty soldiers at the Ranch. They will be our first order of business."

"And here I was hoping to go to eat and sleep once we arrived."

"You shall. And tomorrow morning, so will they."

Henry looked at him questioningly.

"They say poison is a woman's weapon, but I've found it works quite well when outnumbered."

Henry shuddered as he remembered the terrified look in the eyes of the soldiers he had paralyzed and burned in Chico.

"Forget I said anything," said Dembe. "You need to rest tonight, my friend. Not far now."

Soon they rounded a hill and saw lights twinkling in the expanse before them. A few minutes later, Henry could see the main house. Jack stepped out of the shadows as they dismounted and approached Dembe.

"It's good to see you, Dembe. Where's the Minister?"

"Jack," said Dembe, embracing his friend and then shaking his head. "Would you take care of the horses for us? They've just had the hardest ride of their lives."

In the dark, Henry could hear Jack's breathing labor, then go shaky in his chest, then he nodded and led the horses away. The four travelers walked up the steps onto the porch and the front door swung open. Grace swept out and smiled, then she hugged Dembe and Henry.

"I can't tell you how good it is to see you both," she said warmly. "Who are your friends? And where's Eli?"

She looked from one to the other.

"Grace," said Henry.

Her smile faded. "Henry, where's Eli?"

"Grace, I'm so sorry."

She stepped back and dropped into a chair, pulling up her legs and hugging her knees, burying her face in them. Martha stepped out onto the porch and took in the situation. She needed no explanation. "You four go and sit down in the kitchen. I'll be right there."

They obeyed as Martha knelt in front of Grace, stroking her back lovingly.

Clarke slumped down on a bench at the table and leaned

forward onto it. Henry and Moraya sat down on either side of her, their backs to a wall. Moraya put an arm around Clarke. "You did so well," she said as she ran her fingers through Clarke's tangled hair and scratched her back. When Martha entered a few minutes later, Clarke was fast asleep.

"You must be famished," said Martha, disappearing for a bit, then returning with a large platter of cold biscuits, cured ham, and cheese. Henry went to wake Clarke, but Moraya stopped him.

"Let her sleep for now."

Henry nodded and turned his attention to the food.

Martha spoke as the three of them ate. "I'm so glad the rest of you are alright. It's a terrible thing, but you mustn't blame yourselves."

"You don't understand Martha. It was my fault. If I hadn't gotten captured—"

Martha snapped her fingers, cutting him off, and shook her head. "No, Henry, *you* don't understand. Eli knew what he was getting into. Of all the men on this earth, he knew that his choices were his own. 'What if' is a dangerous game, and there's already more than enough danger to go around."

She looked at them all until each had nodded their agreement.

"You all look exhausted, but there are plenty of spare rooms. Rest tonight. Tomorrow at breakfast, we can get the whole story."

"What of Grace?" asked Henry.

"Grace...Grace will be okay in time. That's not your concern. Right now, you need to rest."

"Lipton's soldiers that are here," said Dembe, "I think I should be the one to bring them breakfast tomorrow."

"No!" said Martha urgently. "No, Dembe you will not. Poor lost boys. None of them wear that man's insignia now.

Ten of them died protecting us from Fairchild men that came after you left. Seventeen of them left on the 15th. The rest of them are with us now."

"But how?" asked Moraya in disbelief.

"Most strong men will crumble in the face of love, my dear. A soldier's wages hold little weight in comparison to kindness and goodness. And my cooking." She said the last with a whisper of a smile showing through her damp eyes.

They said no more as they finished eating, save Martha telling them where to sleep. Moraya followed Henry as he carried Clarke to her room. She did not wake when he laid her in bed and barely stirred as Moraya tucked her in.

They stepped into the hallway, and Moraya looked at Henry. "I think I'm beginning to understand what Eli was fighting for."

It was too much for Henry. He was too tired to fight tears.

"Oh, okay," said Moraya, mostly hiding her surprise.

She held him as he hid in the space between her neck and shoulder, and she stroked the back of his head. He thought about his friend. The friend he never expected to make and never imagined losing. He had not known him long, but he knew him well. So Henry wept.

After a time, he regained his bearings and straightened up. "I'm sorry."

"You don't need to be," she said with a small smile that made Henry believe her.

"Goodnight," Henry said.

"Goodnight, Henry."

He stepped into his room, the same room he had stayed in his first night at the ranch, and he could feel sleep beginning to take him as he undressed. He laid down exhaling heavily, and he was asleep before he drew his next breath.

Chapter Thirty

Morning came sooner than Henry wished. Though he'd slept better than he had since the last time he had awoken in that bed, he was still road weary and healing from the battering he took in Portland. He sat up and repeated the vow he had made to Eli: *I'll protect the ranch, I'll keep your people safe. I'll see you again.*

He found Clarke and Martha in the kitchen. Clarke was sitting cross-legged on the counter drinking tea and smiling for the first time in over a week.

"Good morning, Henry dear," said Martha, coming over and hugging him. "There's coffee and a full breakfast just there. Let me cook some fresh eggs for you."

"You're an angel, Martha," said Henry, pouring himself a mug of coffee.

Martha chuckled and shuffled to the pantry.

"How're you feeling?" Henry asked Clarke.

"I slept well. Martha is so nice."

"She really is. Am I the last one up?"

"Dembe is out and about somewhere. I haven't seen Moraya yet."

"Speak of the devil," said Moraya, entering the kitchen.

Henry handed her his mug of coffee and went to the cupboard to retrieve another mug for himself.

"How do you like your eggs, dear?" asked Martha, bustling back into the kitchen.

"Over medium," said Henry and Moraya in unison.

"Good, good," said Martha. "Sit down, they'll be done in just a minute."

Henry and Moraya happily obeyed as Clarke slid off the counter to join them at the table.

The food was better than Henry had hoped, and there was more than he needed. No sooner had he finished than Dembe entered.

"Good, you're up. Can I steal you, Henry? We have much to plan, and I'd like to find Jack."

"I'm ready."

"Get your boots, then follow me."

Moraya stood as well.

"Moraya, dear," said Martha, "I was wondering if you wouldn't mind helping me clean up?"

Moraya hesitated.

Henry spoke up. "She interrogates everyone she feeds. It's a small price to pay for meals like hers."

"It's true," said Martha. "The boys will catch you up on everything they discuss, I'm sure."

Moraya squeezed Clarke's shoulder and smiled. "We would love to help you, Martha."

It was a pleasant enough day for a walk. Henry's body still hurt all over, but with a great effort and strength of mind, he managed to move unencumbered by the pain.

Jack lived in a small cabin nestled into a stand of trees in a quiet corner of the ranch. There was a one-horse stable attached to the back of it and smoke puffed up from the chimney. The place was tidy and suited to a solitary life. Jack sat on his porch, smoking a cigarette, drinking coffee, and petting his dog as if he had been waiting for them.

"Morning, boys," said Jack as they approached. "Coffee?"

"Please," replied Henry.

Jack nodded and went into the cabin, while his dog greeted Dembe warmly and sniffed cautiously at Henry. Dembe sat down the rocking chair next to Jack's, and a moment later, Jack brought out one more chair. "Coffee's almost ready."

Henry rolled a cigarette for himself; Dembe declined. Jack returned with a pot and two more mugs. Henry gladly accepted the coffee and offered Jack a cigarette.

"I have my own," Jack said.

The three men sat in silence for a long moment, taking sips of the black coffee and long drags of tobacco. Eventually Jack spoke up.

"I suppose you'd like me to ride out and see where the bastards are at. See how much time we've got to prepare."

"Actually," said Henry, "I was hoping you'd stay here and start training those who aren't already used to shooting."

"I know the area well," said Jack in a tone that was almost a challenge.

"So does Dembe. He'll join me when I ride out to find them."

Jacked inhaled through his nose and raised an eyebrow. "Do you have a plan, Collector?" he asked, looking at Henry.

"I have the beginnings of one."

"Fending off an army is quite different than cutting a single throat."

"I certainly do not think the situation is hopeless," said Dembe.

"Then you're lying to yourself, Dembe." Jack spoke with vitriol in every word. "Not hopeless? Fuck, man."

Henry stayed still and silent.

Jack lit another cigarette. "We'd be better off running. All of us. That little girl may be a Fairchild, but she's not in control of the army. Thorpe is."

"Eli killed Thorpe," said Dembe.

"He did?" said Jack, then shrugged off his own question. "It doesn't matter. Lipton probably bought their contracts. He's got an entire army. More guns, more men, more time, and we've got somewhere in the ballpark of four days to either dig in and get ready to die, or leave and find a boat headed for Australia."

"We promised Eli that we would protect this place," said Dembe in a calm tone.

"Well, good for you," Jack spat. "I didn't."

"Yes. You. Did," said Dembe, violence swirling just below the surface. He took a breath, held it, then continued. "Yes, you did, Jack," he said in a kinder tone. "We all did. And if you intend to abandon that promise, then get on the horse that Eli gave you and leave. Now."

Jack stood and paced. He glared at Henry and then looked at Dembe. He crushed out his cigarette and then sat back down in his chair, sighing deeply. "What do you need me to do?"

"How many are we?" asked Henry.

"Including the soldiers that stayed, we are thirty-seven."

"Does that include boys that can hold a rifle?" Henry asked. Dembe gave Henry a concerned look. "I'm not saying we put them in the vanguard, I'm just trying to get all the facts straight."

"There are ten boys between the ages of nine and twelve. There are eight between fourteen and sixteen," said Jack.

"Not including them, how many non-combatants are there? Women and children?"

"Those boys are children," said Jack.

"Those boys are men in the making," said Henry. "Not including them, how many?"

"Last I counted, forty-two," Jack said, refilling his coffee.

Henry nodded thoughtfully and looked across the grounds to the original building of the ranch, a stone church perched atop a rise. "Can you show me the chapel?"

Dembe nodded. Once they had drained their mugs, he led the way back across the grounds to the chapel. It was farther away than it looked and the three men did not speak as they walked.

"This will do," said Henry once they were at the chapel.

Henry could tell that it was a pre-Crash structure. The walls were more than two feet of solid-cut stone. Even the roof was made of thick stone shingles. The doors were stout wood, nearly petrified by ages of weather and careful tending, and bound with some kind of pre-Crash metal, a rustless steel of which the secrets of forging had been long lost. All the windows had shutters wrought in the same way as the heavy doors, doors that would laugh off bullets and think very little of flames.

"I'd like to see the bell tower," said Henry.

Dembe led him through the massive front door into the vaulted room, large enough to comfortably fit 120 people. They walked to the back of the sanctuary up onto the stage, and through another door into a small chamber. There was one staircase going up to the bell tower, and one going down into the cellar. They went up. The first landing had four small windows with shutters providing 360 degrees of firing capabilities. Another long staircase led them to the peak of the bell tower.

"Old priests must have built this place with battle in mind," said Henry with a smile once they had exited the building.

"They were Catholics before the Crash, and they would not have admitted it, but yes, they most certainly did," said Dembe.

"The eight older boys will man the four windows below, and the four sides up here. The younger boys will be their loaders, fully out of harm's way. Even the eight shooters will have more cover than they need and clear firing lanes in every direction to cut down the soldiers on their approach. The women and children will be locked in the sanctuary," said Henry. "They'll probably have us three to one, I admit. But we'll have the high ground at the chapel. And some of us can set up ambushes before they get within range of this old stone keep."

Dembe nodded, his face stern.

Jack was unconvinced. "I've already been teaching the boys how to shoot and load. They hunt for sport." He paused and looked at Henry with a pained expression. "But if we survive, you'll need to teach them how to live with it."

"Teach them to shoot," said Henry.

Jack nodded. "I guess that's a start."

"I'm ready to talk to the soldiers," Henry said to Dembe.

They turned to leave, but Jack cleared his throat and spoke again. "Were you with him when he died?"

"I was."

"He was a better man than you. Than all of us."

"He was."

Jack looked at Henry, his jaw clenched. "He wasn't supposed to die."

"I agree," said Henry. "But I made him a promise, and I intend to keep it."

Jack turned and closed the chapel doors behind them, his knuckles flushed white on the handles. "I'll round up the boys and start drilling them on rifles in the east pasture."

"Thank you," said Henry.

"You're welcome. But I'm not doing this for you," said Jack.

Dembe led Henry down the low sloping hill in the direction of the bunkhouses. "All the permanent custodians have their own or a shared residence scattered around the ranch like Jack, but we have a lot of passer-throughs, which is why we maintain adult bunkhouses. They've come in handy for taking in Lipton's deserters."

"I don't like deserters," said Henry. "I'm glad they chose the ranch over Lipton, but they've turned once. They may do it again."

"If they do, you and I will end them," said Dembe matter of factly.

"I think I'm beginning to see why Eli kept you at his right hand."

"I *was* his right hand."

"I wish it had been me," said Henry.

"And I wish it had been me," replied Dembe, "but it was not. And we must not spend energy on 'what if.' It's a dangerous game to play."

"Martha said the same thing," said Henry.

"Martha is a wise woman."

Dembe held open the door to the bunkhouse and Henry walked in. All twenty-three soldiers were in the bunkhouse. Some were eating, some were lounging, some were laughing and playing cards, but upon seeing Henry they all stopped what they were doing and snapped to attention in two lines facing each other.

"Who is your leader?" asked Henry.

There was no reply for a moment, then one soldier near Henry turned to him. It was the same soldier he and Eli had talked with before they had left. "You are, sir," the soldier said.

It was not the answer Henry expected, but he found it satisfactory.

"If there are any amongst you who are not willing to die protecting this ranch," Henry said, "then you may leave now with no consequence from me. Think hard on it and do not take the choice lightly. Either you leave now, or you fight and probably die with me. Very soon we will face your former employer, and if at that time I sense your allegiance switching back to him, I will send a bullet through your skull without a second thought. No one's requiring you to stay and fight. But, if you do stay, then you will fight."

No one moved. No one spoke.

Henry walked down the middle of them, looking each in the eye as he moved.

"No one? No one wants to leave with their life?"

"Sir," said the same soldier who spoke before, "if we leave, and Lipton prevails, our lives will be forfeit. You speak to dead men walking. Our lives will be returned to us when Lipton's is taken from him."

"All that agree, say aye," Henry commanded.

In immediate unison, every single soldier barked "Aye!" and stomped twice with their right foot.

"Attend to your weapons and await your orders," Henry ordered. Then, to the soldier who had spoken, he said, "You, come with me."

The soldier followed Henry and Dembe out of the bunkhouse, belting on his sidearm as he went.

"Remind me of your name?" Henry asked once they were outside.

"Dom, sir."

"Dom," Henry repeated. "I assume you are the captain of this band?"

"Yes, sir."

"Have you seen action, Dom?"

"I quelled three small uprisings against Lipton in New York. Before that, I was a bodyguard to a very unpopular man."

Henry nodded. "Take your men and your weapons. Jack will be in the east pasture teaching the younger ones how to shoot. He knows the ranch better than me. Do as he commands."

Dom placed his right fist over his heart and nodded.

Dembe led Henry away from the barracks. "I think there's someone you should go see."

"Lead on," said Henry.

Dembe and Henry walked back past Martha's house and past a number of barns, storehouses, and what appeared to be a sugar shack for the maple trees.

Stopping suddenly, Dembe placed an enormous hand on Henry's shoulder. "Eli knew what he was doing, Henry." Henry said nothing and found it difficult to hold Dembe's gaze. "I'm glad you did not die."

Henry swallowed hard and nodded.

"That's Grace and Harriet's cottage just there," Dembe said, pointing out a little white house a few hundred yards away. "You should go and see them. I'll ready the horses. Meet me at Martha's when you're ready."

Henry shook his head. "I think I'm the last person in the world Grace wants to see right now."

"I think you may be mistaken," Dembe said. "Go. Meet me when you're done." With a squeeze of the shoulder and an encouraging nod, he turned and left Henry standing alone.

A knot formed in Henry's stomach as he looked at the

little white house. *I wish Bentley was here*. He began walking up the path, his legs growing weaker with each step. When he was still twenty meters away, Grace stepped out from behind the house. She was planting flower bulbs, and very poorly at that. She was wearing riding clothes and an apron, and her hands were dirty as she knelt down and buried the bulbs too shallow to survive the winter. Henry approached and stood a few yards behind her, observing, considering turning away and leaving silently before she noticed him. But he could not bring himself to leave.

"You should bury them a little deeper," he said.

Grace turned to him. Though it was apparent she had been crying, she smiled at Henry, then came to him and embraced him.

Henry cautiously wrapped his arms around her and felt the tremble of tears move through her. He felt their warmth through the shirt on his chest where her face was pressed. He rested his cheek upon the top of her head and steadied her as grief took her mind and body.

Though it was but a few minutes, it felt much longer. He was riddled with guilt, loss, and rage, but some part of him knew that he was helping.

"I didn't know him long," he said, "but I knew him well enough to know he loved you. He loved you more than anything."

Grace could not speak through the tears.

"I wish," said Henry, "I wish it had been me. I wish I had never accepted this Ask. I wish I had taken Lipton the first night I met him." His voice grew weak, but he continued. "I wish Eli was here with you." He took a breath to steady himself, but to no avail. "I wish my family were still here. I wish all this were anything but what it is."

At this, Grace pulled her face free of his shirt and rested

her hand on his chest as she steadied her breath and slowed her tears. "Don't speak like that, Henry. Wishes are for the future, not the past."

"How can you say that?"

"Because it's what he would have said."

Henry felt his hands tremble.

Grace breathed away the last of her tears.

"How can you not hate me?" asked Henry as she lifted her face towards him.

"Because I don't." She held him by the forearms, and now it seemed she was steadying him. "You did the right thing. You saved that little girl. You were a friend to Eli. And you came back to protect us. You're a good man, Henry."

"No."

"You *are* a good man, Henry." She gave him a little shake as she spoke.

Henry stared at his feet and said nothing.

"Come and sit with me. Tell me how it happened."

She led him into the little house and sat him down. He told her everything that had happened since he and Eli had left the ranch twenty-two days earlier.

He told her of how he and Eli had overcome their differences, how they had killed Thorpe at the Maverick. He spoke of Moraya and Clarke and the happy moments here and there that they had shared. Then he spoke of how he snuck away from them to kill Lipton on his own and of his failure and capture. He told her how Eli had managed to steal into the Maverick and save him and how he had succumbed to the many wounds he had sustained in the process. He told her that she was the last thing Eli spoke of before he passed, and once she had stopped crying again, he spoke of their grueling journey home. It wasn't until he had told his whole story that he noticed Harriet sitting on the stairs that led up to the sleeping loft. He nearly jumped to his feet out of surprise.

"How long have you been there?"

"I was here when you entered."

I must be slipping.

She came over and hugged him. He couldn't help but think that Moraya was a better hugger than her, and he surprised himself at the thought.

"Now what will we do?" asked Harriet, taking a chair and directing Henry back to his seat on the couch.

"Dembe and I will ride out to see what we're dealing with. I'll need you two and Martha to get as many supplies as you can into the church. Enough water and food to last for as many days as you can. When the time comes, the women and children will hole up in there. The older boys...the young men...will be in the bell tower with a clear range of the surroundings. The other men and the soldiers will be around the property. With luck, none of Lipton's men will reach the church."

"Do you think we can win?" asked Harriet.

"I think we have to win," said Henry.

Grace spoke, all traces of tears gone from her. Her voice was clear and strong, and there was a look of steel resolve in her eyes. "We will."

Henry wished he believed her.

Grace and Harriet accompanied Henry back to Martha's house. Bentley was tethered outside next to Dembe's enormous draft horse, as pale as he was dark. Inside, Martha was packing travel food and making lists of everything with which they would need to stock the church. Clarke was helping to the best of her abilities. Martha greeted Henry when he entered and then whisked Grace and Harriet away to assist her. Moraya approached Henry and put a hand on his forearm.

"You're going to ride and find Lipton?" she asked.

"Yes. Dembe and me."

"I should stay here. Martha gave me a rundown on all the supplies they have. I think I have what I need to make bombs."

"You made those bombs?" Henry asked in surprise.

"I did," said Moraya with a sly smile. "It's tricky and takes some time, but I think I'm starting to see a plan. We'll need to control their path as they enter the ranch, but if I'm clever, I think I can come up with something."

"You're nothing if not clever," said Henry, noticing for the first time that her hazel eyes had little flecks of gold and green on the outer edge.

"We should get a move on," said Dembe.

"He's right," said Moraya.

"Work with Jack. He knows the lay of the land. We'll try to give you as much of a heads up as we can, but you need to make sure everyone here is ready for action as soon as possible," said Henry.

Moraya nodded.

"And...look after Clarke."

"I don't need looking after," said Clarke fervently from behind him.

He turned to face her in time for her to hug him with both arms around the middle. She squeezed so hard that his injuries cried out, and he squeezed her in return. "Stay sharp, you little devil," he said affectionately.

Then he turned back to Moraya, and after a moment's hesitation, he embraced her. She placed a hand on the back of his neck as she held him with both arms, her breath warm on his ear. He held her to himself for less than half as long as he wanted to, but he knew he had to go, so he pulled himself away.

He nodded to Dembe, then they left the house without another word, taking the supplies Martha had readied for them and stowed them in their saddle bags. He held Bentley's face in his hands before he mounted and touched his nose to Bentley's velvety snout. Then Dembe handed him his gun belt and he strapped it on before pulling himself into his saddle.

"You ready, old boy?" he said, patting Bentley on the shoulder.

Bentley snorted and stamped, and they turned to the north, leaving Martha's house behind them.

Chapter Thirty-One

The sun began to swing low to the horizon. It had been an easy day of riding, with plenty of water and easy access to more, as well as saddle bags full of provisions from Martha. It almost would have been enjoyable if it had not been for the larger circumstances. Even so, Henry and Dembe had managed to make the best of it. They spoke more than they had on the entire journey back to the ranch from Portland, and Henry listened gladly to the stories Dembe told of growing up on the west coast of Africa. He related closely when Dembe told him of the destruction of his village and of stowing away on a merchant ship, only to be attacked by pirates that by some act of God took mercy on him and welcomed him into their fold. He listened intently as Dembe told him how he met Eli many years after that at the Vault and how they trained to be Collectors there together, always Collecting together and splitting the reward between them. He had only seen Eli's ferocity once, and hearing about his cunning and skill as a young man only deepened Henry's respect for him.

An hour before sunset, they led the horses off the road

to drink from a nearby stream. They splashed water on their faces and stretched their legs. It was a lovely place to stop for a few hours of rest, but they knew they had to keep moving. Henry stood at the edge of the road, taking long drinks of water from his canteen, when he heard the faintest clopping of hooves in the distance, approaching from the north.

He scurried back to Dembe. "Someone's coming. Tether your horse."

Dembe nodded, and a moment later they made their way back to the road and waited to see what would come around the bend.

"There's more than one set of hooves," Dembe whispered.

Henry closed his eyes and placed his hand on the cement-like road, clearing his mind and focusing as Rust had taught him to do.

"There are five of them," he said after a moment.

"How can you be sure?" asked Dembe.

"I just can. My teacher, Rust, he called it channeling."

"I didn't know you were that sort of Collector. You're a rare breed."

"They're close now. If they are forward scouts of Lipton's, we should keep one alive long enough to question him. Let them pass. We'll take them from behind. Quietly."

Dembe nodded.

The riders came into view. They were hardened men, not like the young soldiers under Dom's command back at the ranch. They wore Lipton's emblem. Henry slowed his breathing.

"It'll be getting dark soon and I'm getting hungry," said the tail rider.

"We ride 'til dark, just like every other day," replied the lead rider.

"There's no one out here. Not even farmers, traders, or travelers."

"Shut your trap, you lazy bastard. We should reach the ranch tomorrow. We'll take a look, then head back to the baron."

"I hear a stream. We should at least stop to water the horses and stretch our legs."

"Fuck your horse. And your legs."

They were nearly past. Dembe handed two throwing knives to Henry. "Now. Quiet," said Henry.

The pair moved noiselessly onto the road just as the last horse passed. Dembe unsheathed his Kukri and the blade sung a high note as it left the scabbard. It was enough to catch the attention of the tail rider, and he turned just in time to see Dembe leaping at him like a great cat. With enormous power, Dembe swung at the top of his jump, easily freeing the man's head from his shoulders. The nervous acceleration of the horse was not enough to cover the sound of the man's severed head cracking on the pavement, and the other riders turned and saw what was happening.

Henry released his throwing knives in quick succession at his mark. The first sunk deep between his shoulder blades, but just the same the man still almost had his rifle from the saddle holster before the second knife buried itself just below his ear.

Dembe tore one of the riders from his saddle, slamming him hard on the road and rendering him unconscious. Dembe had smashed him into the ground with such a force that Henry hoped he had not killed him, but the other two riders had their rifles out, so there was no more time to take chances. He sent three rounds from his revolver into the lead rider before the man could get a shot off. The last remaining soldier fired at Henry, and if it hadn't been for the frantic jolting of his mount, he would have found his target. The bullet whizzed past Henry and buzzed off into the trees after ricocheting off the road. Before he could work the lever of his rifle, Dembe had dodged a kick from his horse and slashed him across the belly, spilling his guts out onto the terrified horse, which bolted away from the scene. The soldier dropped his rifle and made it about twenty yards before falling from his saddle. Henry glanced at the soldier Dembe had ripped from the saddle and saw the blood pooling around his skull on the road.

Dead.

He sprinted to the disemboweled man, who was still struggling to push his intestines back into himself. Henry stood over him and looked into his frenzied eyes.

"How many soldiers is Lipton bringing?"

"Kill me!" screamed the man in pain.

Henry shot the man in the shin, and he screamed in a way that made Henry's stomach turn. "How many?" he roared.

The man's breathing was beginning to change.

Henry pointed his revolver at the man's face. "Answer me and it will be over quick. Otherwise I'll leave you here. It'll be twenty minutes before you die. Maybe longer."

The man whimpered and shook his head.

Henry shot his other shin and the man began to sob like a child. "How many?"

"Three hundred!" screamed the man. "Three hundred, counting me! Please. Please."

"Two ninety-five," said Henry and shot the man in the face, ending his suffering. He sat down next to the body, his shoulders slumped, and his breath faltered in his chest. "I'm sorry. No one deserves to go like that."

They did not speak as they rounded up the spooked horses and removed their saddles and bridles. Henry dumped the spent brass from the cylinder of his revolver and reloaded, filling the empty bullet slots on his gun belt with rounds he picked off one of the bodies. They lined up all the corpses on the edge of the road, making sure their emblems were clean and visible as a warning to any of their comrades. It was nearly dark by the time they were done, but they both felt the unspoken urge to put some distance between themselves and the dead men.

An hour later, they stopped for the night, not bothering to light a fire, and laid in silence, each shuddering at what they had done and what they still had to do.

Henry awoke before Dembe. It was cold and dark still, but he felt rested enough, and the actions of the previous day were a little further from his mind. He gathered stones and made a small fire pit for brewing coffee. It was easy enough to find dried twigs and leaves and pine needles to start it, and he found a longer dried branch that could slowly be pushed into the blaze as one end burned. Once it was crackling steadily, he grabbed his coffee pot and headed towards the stream a ways off in the woods. He walked slowly through the trees, partially because it was dark, and partially because it was quiet and peaceful in the cool dark of the morning, and he did not want to disturb the forest's slumber. He knelt by the stream and bent to dip the pot into it, then suddenly noticed that his ears were ringing in a different tune than they usually did. He froze.

"You've still got it, Henry. I trained you well."

Henry turned and faced the speaker. "Rust," he said in an apprehensive greeting.

"Henry," said Rust, mirroring Henry's tone.

Rust was tall and broad, half an inch taller than Henry and stronger by an immeasurable margin. He had bright, pale blue eyes, a thick reddish-brown beard with specks of grey, and long, pushed-back hair that reached halfway down his neck. Rust approached and knelt beside Henry. They exchanged a glance before both looking out into the woods.

"You got old, Henry," said Rust.

"You look the same as ever."

"I am the same as ever."

"Why are you here?"

"It looks like you've gotten yourself in pretty deep this time, boy," said Rust. "I came to see if you require my services."

"Now?" Henry spat. "After all this time, and all the shit I've lived through? Why now, Rust?"

"Because I thought you might actually take me up on it this time around."

Henry chuckled. "You always were a student of human desperation. Is my fear that obvious?"

"I heard it singing in my ears before I could see you through the trees," said Rust.

"Are you offering or bartering?" asked Henry.

"Not bartering. It would be a trade," said Rust matter of factly.

"Ah, yes, a trade. How could I forget? You never barter."

"Very rarely. And never for long."

"A trade," Henry repeated in a tone somewhere between shock and amusement. "And what would the terms be?"

"I take care of your problems. All 295 of them, and afterwards you come with me."

"Calenthis?" Henry asked.

"Calenthis," Rust confirmed.

Henry looked down at the stream, and then out into the woods. He thought of the ranch and all the people there. He thought of Clarke. Then he thought of Moraya.

"Well?" asked Rust after the moment had carried beyond comfort.

Henry inhaled deeply through his nose. "I will live and die as a man. Here. Now. I'm grateful to you, but I am earthbound, and my heart was not made to be eternal." He remembered the words only as he spoke them, knowing he had said them once before.

Rust smiled at his protégé in a way that could almost be perceived as pride. "Then I'll find another." He stood and turned to leave but then looked back at Henry. "You never needed my help anyway. Born of blood and gun smoke, your fate was always your own."

"I appreciate all the help you lent me just the same," said Henry, standing and facing Rust.

Rust's eyes seemed to catch a reflection of light from some unknown source, and he smiled darkly. "Gratitude is always rewarded. There are ten more men on the road. Look out for them around sundown." And then he moved into the trees without a sound and vanished into the long shadows cast deep by the rising sun.

Henry knelt by the stream again as the ringing left his ears. He finished filling the coffee pot and then returned to the camp.

Dembe slept deeply and silently as Henry skewered large chunks of cured ham on makeshift spits and rested them above the heat of the flames until the fat began to drip and sizzle onto the hot stones and coals beneath. He cut two thick slices of dark bread Martha had packed for them and put thick slabs of soft cheese on them. He divided the food into two thin metal bowls and poured the coffee into thin metal cups. Only then did he decide to nudge Dembe into consciousness. He knelt beside the enormous figure asleep on the ground and placed a hand on his shoulder. Dembe had a knife to his throat before he even opened his eyes, but he quickly relaxed and lowered the blade as soon as he gained his bearings.

"I apologize. Old habits," said Dembe, sitting up and rubbing his face.

"Don't mention it. There's hot food and coffee. Let's not linger long," said Henry, picking up his own plate and handing one to Dembe.

The pair savored the food and coffee in silence and Henry rolled a cigarette, lighting it with a twig he pulled from the fire.

"After all these years of it, killing really doesn't bother me. Hurting, on the other hand..." he said after a few drags.

Dembe nodded thoughtfully as he stared into the flames. "Too often, I find my lot in life is to do the most gruesome things to protect others from sullying their own hands. It was an awful thing. But don't dwell on it."

"I don't think Eli would have approved," said Henry.

"Certainly not. But he would not have stopped you. And now we know what we're up against."

Henry said nothing as he finished his cigarette.

"We should get moving. It will be light soon," said Dembe.

Fifteen minutes later, they were on the road again.

Chapter Thirty-Two

They rode for the better part of the day without seeing anyone else, aside from a few locals taking goods from one farm to another. Even so, it had been hours since they had seen anyone at all.

Henry grew uneasy at how quiet it was. The memory of his encounter with Rust that morning was like the recollection of a half-forgotten dream. Rust was like that when he wanted to be. Sometimes he was just a man. Other times, he was more —unnaturally silent, ungodly strong. Despite the mind fog, he clearly remembered Rust's warning, and when the sun began to stretch far towards the horizon, Henry readied himself for violence.

"I have a feeling we aren't alone on the road," Henry said after double-checking his revolver.

"Something you learned from your teacher?" asked Dembe.

"Something like that."

"One day you'll have to tell me about him, if we get through this."

"He's a very private individual. I would feel ill at ease

telling you anything about him, aside from the fact that he still exists."

"Still exists?" Dembe remarked. "He must be very old."

Henry nodded and took a sharp breath of air through his nose. "Indeed." Then he pulled Bentley to a halt. "They're near. I can hear them. Feel them."

"I can hear them too," said Dembe. "Ever so faintly."

"Let's find cover in the trees. We should be able to take a few by surprise."

They quickly pulled their horses off the road and led them a little way into the thick trees, tethering them out of sight of the road, then crept back, each finding a solid tree to hide behind.

Within a few minutes, they heard hooves on the road. The sun was almost behind the hills, and the dying light would not last long. It bode well for the Collectors.

Once again, they waited for the men to pass. There were indeed ten of them, as Rust had warned. Dembe and Henry locked eyes and nodded to each other. They stepped out from behind the trees and threw two knives apiece. Two riders cried out and fell from their saddles, but before the others could react, the Collectors released a volley of fire, sending hot lead through four more of the riders. The remaining four soldiers returned fire with their rifles, forcing Henry and Dembe back into cover. The soldiers bolted for the trees on the opposite side of the road.

Henry slowed his breathing as he reloaded his revolver and moved up the road, always staying out of sight. Dembe moved in the opposite direction. The soldiers fired blindly at the spot they had seen the Collectors initially take cover in. There was a moment of silence as they reloaded their rifles. Henry could hear their voices but could not see them. Then he saw a head poke up from behind a rock, and he fired three quick rounds at it. He saw an explosion of dust and shrapnel as his bullets hammered into the boulder, and the head ducked back down. Then came the screaming.

"My eyes!" the soldier cried out. "Fuck! Fuck, my eyes!"

"Shut up!" another soldier commanded, then the screaming faded to a quiet whimper.

Henry peeked out from behind his tree and saw one of the soldiers with his rifle trained on Henry's position. The man released a barrage of gunfire. Bullets smashed into the tree, sending splinters into Henry's cheek and shoulder. He threw himself to the ground and heard the shot of a pistol, and the rifle fire ceased.

Thanks, Dembe.

He crawled to a different position, replacing his spent rounds as he moved and peeked up from the ditch. He saw no movement but fired six shots at a steady interval into the general area where he had seen the last soldier. Dembe took the opportunity to sprint across the road and slide into the ditch on the other side. Henry reloaded and fired again to hide any sound of Dembe's movement. After six shots, the soldier popped out from behind a tree, but before he could fire, the blade of Dembe's kukri protruded from his chest, and he fell, gasping. Henry trotted across the road towards the boulder where he knew the blinded soldier hid and reloaded his revolver.

"I can hear you, motherfucker!" screamed the terrified, wounded man, and he fired a round from his rifle blindly from behind the rock. It whizzed off in the wrong direction, and Henry crouched and crept very silently to the side until he had a view of the soldier. The man's face was mangled by shards of stone, and Henry quickly sent a bullet through his head, ending his suffering.

Then he stood and took a deep breath, noting for the first time his new wounds.

"Hold still," said Dembe when he saw them. "I'll get you fixed up."

Henry sat down on a rock and Dembe knelt beside him, removing the large splinters, then he produced a small jar from his saddle bag. "It's a pumice of honey and herbs," he explained as he carefully covered Henry's wounds with the paste. It tingled and numbed the pain into a manageable level of discomfort.

"Thank you. That stuff is remarkable."

"It's an old recipe," said Dembe. "Something I learned from my mother long ago and far from here." He then rubbed his hands with dust until they were free of the stuff.

It took them a while to round up the spooked horses of the fallen soldiers and remove their tack, setting them free to roam until someone else captured them. Then they scavenged the bodies for ammunition before laying them out on the side of the road like they had those from the previous day. It was heavy, unpleasant work, and more than a little barbaric, but fear was a weapon they were willing to use against their enemies.

"We can't be far now from the main force," said Dembe once they had finished.

"I imagine we'll find them tomorrow," Henry replied. "We'll have to stay concealed, but if we're lucky, we might be able to thin the herd a little bit more than we already have. Either way, we should head back to the ranch tomorrow night."

Dembe voiced his agreement, and the pair returned to their horses. They rode well into the night, and once they stopped, they fell asleep on the cold ground with no fire. Sleep did not come easy to Henry as he worked over plans and strategies for the coming days, but eventually he did sleep, deep and dreamless, until a droplet of rain awoke him in the dark. Morning was coming, and he had work to do.

The two Collectors ate quickly, not taking the time to brew coffee. Instead, they crunched on beans as they rode, and eventually the drug seeped into their veins, bringing a buzzing awareness to their minds. The clouds were thick, and the smell of rain drifted on the air. Fog rolled heavily off the hills and mountains, and visibility was very low. This boded well.

"Can I ask you about that kukri?" Henry said after a long spell of silence.

"Of course," said Dembe, seeming to welcome the conversation.

"I've only seen a few of them over the years. The design isn't from this continent, is it?"

"No, far from here. I received this as a gift from my old captain after some time we spent in the Himalayas."

"I thought pirates were seafaring?"

"By and large, yes. We spent a few years picking off ships in the Bay of Bengal. There were strange and wonderful goods coming from the Himalayas. So, one day, the captain commandeered a boat that had come down the Ganges River. He took a small group of us with him, leaving his larger vessel in the command of his first mate. They made an agreement that once a year, every year on the summer solstice, the first mate would bring the vessel back to the mouth of the Ganges and wait for seven days for the captain.

"So, the captain, myself, and five others took the small boat all the way up the Ganges until it turned into the Ganga. We followed the Ganga to the Gandaki River and followed it to its source in Nepal. I saw many strange things in Nepal.

There were a few people there who knew a sort of magic. The same sort of magic I think you know a little of."

"I don't know any magic. It's nothing to do with spirits," said Henry. "It's just sound. Just learning to feel the frequencies in which everything sings."

Dembe laughed. "Whatever it is, it seemed like magic to me."

"Did you find much treasure in the mountains?"

"I found many things. Some treasure. Some knowledge. Much pain. The captain and I were the only two of our party that made it back down the Ganges. All told, it took us nearly three years. We brought many of the goods all the way to the California coast, where I took my leave of the crew and the life of piracy. Soon after, I met Eli."

"Do you ever miss the life?" asked Henry.

"I do not. There was even less honor in it than Collecting."

Henry nodded his understanding.

"Can I ask you about your razor?" asked Dembe.

"It was a gift as well. From my wife. Lily."

"Lily. It is a beautiful name."

"She was...everything," said Henry. "But she's been gone for a long time. I never thought the pain would fade, but somehow and slowly, the memory of her comforts more than hurts like it used to."

Dembe looked as though he was about to say something, then pulled his horse to an abrupt stop. "Do you hear that?"

Henry closed his eyes and listened. "They're upon us."

Chapter Thirty-Three

Henry turned Bentley around to head south again. "We need to stay ahead of them until they make camp tonight."

Dembe nodded and followed Henry.

They rode quickly, always making sure to stay out of Lipton's army's hearing range. They spoke very little, only exchanging glances when they passed the ten bodies they had laid out on the road the day before. Every hour or so, Henry would pull Bentley to a halt and dismount, laying his palms on the road and listening to see how close behind the enemy was. The fog held all day, and an hour before sunset, it began to rain.

They passed a large open pasture, one of the only ones in that area. "They will probably make camp here tonight," said Dembe.

"I think you're right," said Henry. "Let's ride up a ways, tether the horses, and double back through the trees."

"If they don't stop, that could put us in a precarious spot," Dembe warned.

"I'm willing to risk it if you are," said Henry.

Dembe pondered for a moment, then nodded his agreement.

By the time they had tied up their mounts and returned to the tree line at the edge of the pasture, Lipton's army had flooded the place. They were erecting tents, tending to horses, and bustling about. The sight of them was overwhelming. Nearly three hundred men and horses spread out over the valley. There were sentries everywhere, and the whole place was alert.

"Maybe we should have hidden the bodies," said Dembe.

"They're alert, but they're afraid," said Henry.

The rain picked up, as did the wind, and soon Henry was wet to the bone. He ached with cold, but he pushed the discomfort far from his mind. The rain was good. It covered sound and made seeing more than a few yards nearly impossible in the darkness.

"You should stay hidden," Henry whispered to Dembe.

"I don't like it."

"Yes, but someone needs to be able to make it back to the ranch. I'll be silent, but if you hear shots, do not wait for me."

After a moment, Dembe nodded his agreement.

Henry began to move away when Dembe placed a hand on his arm. "Do not be reckless."

"I'll be back soon. If I don't meet you here within the hour, wait for me at the horses, and if I'm not there after another hour, ride like hell."

Henry crouched low and crept through the tall wind-blown grass of the pasture until Dembe and the tree line were out of sight through the rain and fog and night. Then he crawled.

After a few minutes, he saw a sentry. The man wore a heavy poncho that would stop a throwing knife, so Henry moved very slow and even quieter through the grass. He felt like the serpent tattooed on his arm. The sentry was walking towards him, and Henry flattened himself against the soggy ground as best he could. The sentry nearly stepped on him but stopped just short of where Henry lay hidden in the long grass. Though it was only a few heartbeats of time, it felt like a lifetime before the sentry turned around to walk back in the other direction. Henry rose from the ground and drew his Bowie knife. He rammed it into the side of the man's neck and quickly slashed forward through the man's throat, cutting off any sound before it could leave his mouth. He pushed the man to the ground and quickly stripped him of his poncho, putting it on himself. Then he stood and began walking the sentry's perimeter.

He could see the glow of fires under open-sided tents and the movement of men around them, but he was far enough from the glow that he would not be visible to those in the main part of the camp. So, he walked until he saw the next sentry. He waved to the man, and the sentry began to approach. Henry dipped his head, concealing his face under the brim of his hat, and clenched his knife, hidden in a fold of the poncho. When the man was a few feet away, Henry lunged at him, driving the knife into his throat and slashing out the side, nearly severing the head from the body. The rain washed off the blood as he continued along the perimeter.

He made his way in a circle all the way around the camp in under thirty minutes. He killed seven sentries in total and was nearly back to the tree line where he had left Dembe when he heard an alarm go up through the camp. First shouts, then bells and bugles. He broke into a run and nearly tripped over Dembe, who caught him by the shoulder and slammed him against a tree with his kukri at the ready.

"It's me!" he hissed in a whisper.

Dembe relaxed in time. "I did not recognize the poncho."

"We need to move now."

The pair of Collectors ran as fast as they could through the trees back to where they had tethered the horses. They mounted and made their way back to the road, riding south at a full gallop towards the ranch.

Once they had put a few miles between themselves and the camp, Henry slowed Bentley to a trot, and his hands began to shake slightly as the adrenaline wore off. Only 278 soldiers remained. They had thinned the herd by twenty-two.

They rode all night and most of the morning, not stopping until they reached the ranch. The storm raged until an hour before sunrise.

They rode up to Martha's house and dismounted. Their horses were nearly spent, and Henry ached with pain and hunger. A young man named Todd took their horses to the stable.

Moraya burst out of the house, and Henry nearly collapsed into her arms.

"You're alive," she said, supporting him as she led him up the steps.

"They can't be far behind," said Henry, holding her tightly around the waist. He could not help but smell lavender and elderflower emanating gently from her skin and hair. "Maybe tonight. Tomorrow morning at the latest."

"You have time for a little rest, at least." She guided him through the front door. "The house is empty. Everyone is in the chapel or at their post."

"Where is Jack?" asked Dembe.

"Near the chapel," said Moraya.

Dembe nodded. "Get some rest, Henry. I'll relay what we've learned to Jack, and then I plan to sleep for as long as I can before we must fight."

Henry nodded and sat on a chair in the entryway, stooping to take off his boots.

"You're wet to the bone," said Moraya as she peeled off his jacket. "There's hot water for a bath upstairs. I'll bring you some food."

Henry smiled at her and made his way up the stairs. It was a chore to get his wet clothes off himself, but the water in the tub was divine, and he sank down to his chin. A shudder ran through his body as it adjusted to the warmth, then he finally began to relax after what had been the longest nonstop ride of his life. He hoped Bentley would forgive him for pushing so hard.

The water smelled like lavender and elderflower, and it was milky with soap. He smiled and closed his eyes, laying his head back on a thick towel draped over the edge of the tub. He almost fell asleep but opened his eyes when Moraya entered the room.

She smiled at him and set a plate with a sandwich on a stand next to the tub.

"Thank you," he said.

"I'll leave you to it," she replied softly.

"Please," Henry said, then hesitated. "Could you stay?"

She nodded and pulled a stool up behind the tub sitting down. Henry found himself short of breath, then he felt her hands on his shoulders, messaging his neck and arms and the top of his chest.

"We've done all that we can do to prepare," she said. "There's nothing now but to wait, and to rest and ready ourselves for what's to come." She spoke slowly and quietly. It was comforting and sent a chill down Henry's spine.

"I won't argue with you."

"That's a first." Henry could hear the smile in her voice. He found himself drifting into sleep. When he awoke, the water had lost almost all its heat, so he dried himself off and went into his bedroom down the hall. Moraya was nowhere to be seen, and he fell asleep again immediately when he laid down in the bed.

It was still dark when he woke, but he could feel the sunrise was near. He went to the window and saw the sun paint red light across the horizon. It was October thirty-first. He relished the stunning canvas of deep red, orange, and purple that the sun painted across the landscape with its rising, and he prayed for the first time in years that he would live to see it set that evening.

Chapter Thirty-Four

Things were quiet on the ranch. All the animals that would normally be grazing in pastures were barned or corralled. All the young children who would have normally been playing or learning with teachers were huddled in the stone chapel. All the young boys who would normally be hunting in the woods and fields sat staring through slots in the stone, rifles in hand. Today was a hunt of a different kind. Their younger companions perched on stools behind them, a replacement rifle in hand and piles of unboxed ammunition ready to be loaded. The women watched over the young children, mothers all of them in body or spirit. All except for one. Moraya had left Clarke in the charge of Grace with stern orders for the girl to listen to every word Grace told her. Then Moraya walked quickly from one place to the next, examining traps, checking in with the small groups of soldiers under the command of Dom, and taking in a few slow breaths of crisp autumn air.

Henry and Bentley waited at the edge of the ranch, with a long, clear view of the road leading in from the ancient highway on which Lipton's army approached. At the first sign of movement, he would ride back and set the alarm—any hour, any minute, any second. He crunched on coffee beans and steadied his nerves. He had never been in a battle.

He heard Moraya coming long before he saw her. She was on foot, and she spoke to Bentley once she approached, taking his velvety snout in her hands and whispering something Henry could not hear.

"Everyone's in place," she said to Henry.

"Good. It's nearly noon. They'll be here any time now."

She nodded, then they were quiet together.

"How's Clarke?" asked Henry after a minute.

"It's hard to say. She can be so regal at times. She appears to be the least frightened person on the ranch, but I imagine she's terrified. Like everyone else."

"And you?" asked Henry, looking deep into Moraya's eyes.

"I'm prepared to die today, Henry." She looked away from him, out to the road. "But I don't want to."

"I know the feeling. For so long after I lost my family, I wandered aimlessly, leaving nothing in my wake but blood. It's easy enough to kill for money. I never thought I'd find something to live for. This month has been full of unexpected discoveries."

"Good things can be planned for, but the best things are always unexpected."

Just then, movement down the road caught Henry's eye. He strained his vision and sure enough, a line of horsemen began to move over the crest of a high ridge a mile or so away. The time had come.

"They're here," He said to Moraya and extended a hand to her.

She took it, and he pulled her up into the saddle behind

him and turned Bentley towards the camp. But before he spurred him on to warn the others, he let his hand drop and rest on Moraya's calf.

"Moraya."

"Henry," she said, gripping her arms around his waist to keep herself steady.

"If I live to see this night, I intend to spend it with you."

"Yes."

The words were fire to his heart, and he clicked his tongue to Bentley, speeding away back to the chapel.

They reached the chapel a few minutes later, and Henry signaled to a boy in the bell tower, who shouted to someone below. A moment later, the enormous bell began to swing, clang, and sing its warning across the entire ranch.

Moraya slipped out of the saddle as a few of Jack's men appeared from behind barriers. They carried extra rifles and ammo satchels and wordlessly offered them to Henry and Moraya. Henry accepted the weapon and hooked the ammo satchel into his saddle. Moraya shook her head. The men took their places again, checking and rechecking their weapons, each face expressionless.

Henry stood tall in the saddle and looked across the ranch towards the road. Moraya and Jack had planned the defense well. The ground had many trees here and there, and there were many buildings in the open places on either side of the lane leading to the chapel. The natural cover was a blessing and a curse. Henry could see groups of men here and there strategically placed, waiting for the enemy to come into range. He looked up at the chapel. The boys were well hidden behind the heavy stone walls of the bell tower, but he could see their rifles bristling through the windows and out of the top.

God, let them live. Let me live.

Moraya was gone, vanished to her post, waiting.

The next thirty minutes were the longest of Henry's life. The only sound was wind rushing through trees and buildings. Even the birds ceased their singing. Then Henry saw smoke. First a single line of it, then more and more. *The bastards are torching every building they pass.*

Henry leaned down to Bentley. "Let's get to their flank, old boy." He spurred the beast toward a storehouse off to the side of the battlegrounds.

Then the first of them came. A group of riders advanced towards the chapel. They were riding hard up the gravel lane. When they were fifty yards from the first group of defenders, Henry heard a shot. Then the lane erupted into a massive explosion, sending gravel soaring into the air and blasting horses and riders to the ground—Moraya's first trap. The air was filled with dust and black smoke, and it seemed to be raining dirt and pebbles. Even a hundred yards away, the sound rocked him to his core. Bentley's ears were pinned flat against his skull. Henry inhaled sharply and raised his rifle. At the same time, the air was filled with the sharp cracks of gunfire.

The riders that survived had dismounted and found what cover they could. More of Lipton's soldiers poured into view, moving steadily from cover to cover advancing towards the chapel. Henry found his mark, a soldier leaning against a tree, unaware of the danger to his side. The man was a little over 100 yards away. Henry trained his rifle on the man's chest and pulled the trigger, adding the soldier to the carnage. The shot drew attention to Henry's position, and a moment later there were bullets whizzing in his direction, smashing into the storehouse he had taken cover behind and buzzing close.

He quickly swung Bentley around into full cover as he

dismounted. He took Bentley's bridle and pulled the horse's big snout close to his face. "You at least will survive today, old boy." He unbuckled the bridle and slipped it off, then he undid the saddle and pulled it to the ground. "Run, old boy. I'll find you if I can." Then he slapped Bentley's rump. But Bentley did not run. He stooped and pulled up a mouthful of grass. "Or just stay here, you stubborn bastard."

He picked up the rifle and the ammo bag and dashed to another building, drawing fire away from Bentley's position. A few bullets whizzed by him as he ran. He was lucky none of them found their mark. He stayed in cover long enough for the fire to stop coming in his direction, then he leaned out. Lipton's men had advanced past where the first group of defenders had been stationed. There were bodies everywhere, and he vaguely noticed muzzle flashes coming from the bell tower of the chapel. All the soldiers had abandoned their mounts, knowing that it only made them easier targets. He had a clear shot at more enemies than he could count in a glance and raised his rifle on a group huddled close behind a stone watering trough. He unleashed a fury of bullets on them, firing until the chamber was empty, then he ran again, farther away from the chapel, carrying the rifle and ammo bag.

He rounded the corner of a building and ran into a soldier. They were both caught off guard, and there was a moment of confusion as they looked at each other. Still, Henry was faster and stronger than the soldier, and in a flash he had a hand on the soldier's face and another on the back of his head. The sound of his neck snapping was enough to nauseate Henry.

Before he had time for regret, another soldier plowed into him shoulder first, taking him to the ground, slashing his knife down towards Henry. With his left hand, Henry kept it from plunging entirely into his chest. However, it did gash deep into him, but his right hand was on his revolver, and he sent three bullets through the soldier before he could strike again. Another soldier rounded the corner before he could push the dying man off him, and Henry emptied his revolver into the soldier's chest.

Henry stood but there was no time to reload. Two more soldiers rounded the corner, apparently trying to flank the defenses in front of the church. Henry snatched up a rifle by the barrel and swung it as hard as he could at the first soldier. It smashed his skull into an unnatural shape, but his companion was quick, getting a shot off before Henry could swing again. The bullet took a bite out of his arm but found no bone. Henry leaped at the soldier, crushing him against the wall of the building. There was a quick struggle. Henry grabbed the soldier's long knife out of his belt before he could get to it and rammed it into the soldier's rib cage three quick times before drawing back and plunging it through the man's throat, pinning him to the wall. Henry fell to the ground and reloaded his pistol.

From everywhere came the incessant buzz of battle and screaming like flies on a hot day, interrupted only by deafening gunfire that made Henry's ears ring and his head spin. He ripped a length of cloth from one of the soldier's uniforms and tied it as tight as he could just above the wound on his arm. It was time to move again. He needed to get behind the enemy force, knowing that Lipton would be there. The soldiers had advanced past where the second group of defenders had been stationed and were well within the range of all the young sharpshooters in the church.

Please, God, don't let the boys die.

He sprinted like a madman along the flank until he was

behind the remaining soldiers. Then he began making his way toward them. They didn't seem to notice him as he approached their rear. He looked out from behind an enormous tree and saw a group of soldiers charge towards the church. He stepped out and was about to raise his rifle when a white-hot pain seared through his lower shoulder and he was flung to the ground with the force of it.

Blood, more than he knew he held, was streaming out of a wound and he was gasping for air.

Sharpshooter.

He almost lost consciousness, the world was spinning, and he did not know if he could move. The battle raged on, but he could barely see as tears filled his eyes and the smell of his own blood flooded his nose. There was another shot. Louder and closer than most of the other gunfire.

Sharpshooter.

He struggled to his knees, staying low and trying scramble to hide behind a tree. He glanced back towards the church. The soldiers were gaining ground. Another crack from the sharpshooter's rifle broke, and one of Dom's soldiers fell dead several hundred yards away. But Henry had glimpsed the muzzle flash. He cut off a piece of his shirt sleeve, and with a stifled scream he shoved it into the hole the bullet had left in his upper chest. It had gone clean through, missing everything important, from what Henry could tell. Even so, he only had a few minutes before he lost too much blood to stay on his feet. He had to move. He half crawled, half dragged himself across the ground, trying to stay out of sight.

The rifle cracked again, and he hoped it wasn't Moraya that fell that time. He was almost to where the sharpshooter was posted up, obscured behind a supply wagon which blocked the sightline to Henry, scrambling on his belly through the long grass. He had a clear shot at the man's shins and raised his pistol, but there was movement and another soldier who Henry hadn't seen stepped out from behind the wagon, seeing Henry on the ground. The soldier let out a warning cry before Henry killed him, and the sharpshooter swung out around the side of the wagon and leveled his rifle at Henry. He knew then that it was over, but he thought of Moraya's yes and in his final moment, Henry exhaled a silent prayer that he would live to see the night.

Click.

By some act of God or man, Henry never really knew for certain, the round in the sharpshooter's chamber was a blank. The man's face said it all, and he frantically worked the bolt of the custom rifle, but it was too late. Henry emptied his revolver into the man's chest.

He dragged himself to his feet and began stumbling back towards the chapel. He was headed straight towards the rest of the soldiers behind their line, and his head was starting to get light. He had already lost a lot of blood.

He looked at the fray. A wave of soldiers were charging the chapel, and it looked like they were going to break the defense. Then came an earth-shattering explosion as the ground erupted, blasting all twenty or so soldiers to tiny bits and sending shrapnel into the lines of fighters behind them. Moraya's second trap. It was like the changing of the tide. The remaining soldiers faltered, shocked, realizing all at once their numbers were almost depleted. First one, then two, then in droves, he saw them turn and run. Run like mad. Run like rats from a flood.

Then Henry saw him.

Lipton was crouching behind a boulder, screaming orders in vain as his men deserted him. Henry saw him raise his pistol and start shooting his own men in their backs as they tried to get out of range of the boys in the church. The defenders weren't firing anymore, and Henry caught his breath. He had not the heart to kill any of the young men who streamed past him, unarmed and unhinged. Lipton's army had been broken, and Henry was still alive.

Lipton was standing now, firing ineffectively at the last of his men who were far out of his feeble range. His revolver clicked empty.

Henry stood and faced him.

Fifty yards away.

Lipton saw Henry and flushed with fear. He began to fumble with the reload, his hands too unsteady to get a round in the cylinder.

Thirty yards away.

Henry slid his revolver into its holster. Lipton stumbled backwards into the boulder he had been hiding behind.

Ten yards away.

Henry had his straight razor out.

"Wait! WAIT!" Lipton stammered. "I can pay you, I can! I'll double it, I'll—"

The razor flashed in the sunlight. A line of blood appeared across Lipton's throat. Then it poured out. He dropped back onto his haunches, gurgling and choking. His eyes bulged with shock, and rage, and fear. Then he leaned back against the rock and was still.

There was silence. Henry took a deep breath into his belly, dropped the razor into the dust, and then let it go.

He walked through the bodies towards the church. Some of them he recognized, but most of them he did not. Something nuzzled at his ear, and he turned and held Bentley's big velvety snout up to his face. "You were supposed to run, old boy. But I'm glad you didn't."

He saw Jack and Dembe pull open the doors of the church, and he saw Clarke step out and then quickly look

away from the carnage, burying her face in Grace's belly. He
saw Dom sitting on the edge of a well, fumbling to light a
cigarette.

Then he saw Moraya, and his breath shook and faltered in
his chest, and he felt himself smile.

Chapter Thirty-Five

Henry sat on the porch of his little house in the glade, breathing sweet, warm spring air and listening to the stream gurgle along its path. The sun was low in the sky, casting its first rays of light over the ranch. Everything looked new and alive; fresh paint on new buildings with only one winter to harden, and new leaves still stretching out young and pale green on the branches. It had taken months, but his wounds had finally faded into scars.

The door opened, and Moraya stepped out, handing Henry a cup of coffee and sliding comfortably onto his lap. She kissed him like it was the first time. Henry placed a hand on the roundness of her belly, feeling gently for kicks.

"He didn't want to let me sleep in this morning," said Moraya.

"It's too nice a morning for sleep anyways," said Henry, leaning towards her and kissing her neck.

"Gross," said Clarke as she stepped out the door, plopping down in a chair next to them. "And how do you know it's a he?"

Moraya placed a hand on her belly. "I just do."

Clarke shrugged and smiled. "Think you're right." She opened a book and found her place. It was the copy of the *Odyssey* that Just Blake had given to Henry on the first of October the previous year. Then she looked up at Henry and Moraya.

"If it is a boy, what will we call him?"

Henry and Moraya looked at each other. Henry cleared his throat and took a breath. Moraya smiled at him knowingly, lovingly, and he felt the knot in his chest loosen before he spoke.

"I've always loved the name Eli."

The Beginning

Acknowledgments

Special thanks to my editors, Amber and Dave, and to all of my friends and family. Your encouragement has kept me going.

And to Miriam, thank you most of all.

From The Author

If you enjoyed this story and would like to contribute to my dream of being a full-time author, there are a few things you can do that are incredibly impactful:

1. Leave a review on Amazon.
2. Subscribe to my email list at nateburbury.com (there's a QR below).
3. Tell people about the book. Word of mouth is the best way for this thing to gain momentum.

Becoming a full-time author is a long road. With your help, I just might be able to pull it off. Thanks for reading.

Fair winds and following seas,

Nathaniel Nielsen Burbury

www.ingramcontent.com/pod-product-compliance
Lightning Source LLC
Chambersburg PA
CBHW011515240626
47154CB00010B/3034